From Arctic S

Book 6 in the
British Ace Series
By
Griff Hosker

Published by Sword Books Ltd 2017
Copyright © Griff Hosker First Edition

Cover by Design for Writers

Prologue

1918

I had thought my war was over. I was wrong. On my return from France I had been told that I was to take over a new squadron in March. However, as I enjoyed my new son and family life, a hundred miles from London I was sent a message from the Air Ministry. A motor cycle despatch rider arrived mid-morning with a sealed envelope for me. I was ordered to report to speak with one of the civil servants. I had no idea why. Bates, my servant from the war, was still serving with me and he lived in our home.

"John, better pack an overnight bag for us. We are off to London."

He frowned, "But, sir, it is almost Christmas. You do not take up your new post until March. This is a bit much, sir. Even for the Royal Flying Corps; sorry sir, the Royal Air Force."

"Bates, you know the way the service works. I am still a serving officer. I have to go."

"Very well, sir."

He was not happy but he was a good soldier and he obeyed orders. Beattie, having served as a nurse, understood what orders meant. She was optimistic. "Perhaps this just means you will be taking up your post a little earlier. It would be nice to live in something which wasn't rented. As a squadron leader, you should be entitled to a larger house." Since having our son, Tom, she had become more of a nest builder. But she was right. The house was too small.

"Perhaps, but it is winter and the last thing you need with young Thomas here is for you to be setting up a new home on a new station. Perhaps I can persuade them to delay it. Surely I must have a little bit of clout left."

She laughed, "You know that is not in your nature. You will salute and say, *'yes sir, three bags full sir'*!"

She was right. That was in my nature. Obeying orders. My son was asleep in her arms. I stroked the soft downy hair on his head. "But I begrudge even one night away from Thomas here. Perhaps we can get back tonight. I might not need to stay over, eh?"

"That is possible but the roads are atrocious at this time of year. You know what the A1 is like! Stay over. I will sleep easier that way."

I kissed her, "I don't deserve you."

"Of course, you don't! Now drive carefully. Bates is not as fond of speed as you, Ted and Gordy."

It was my turn to laugh. "They are now out of the service and speed is the last thing on their mind."

"I will put Tom in his cot. Don't make a noise while you are getting ready. I don't want him waking."

"I will go and check out the old bus." I had a pre-war Sunbeam 25/30. She was a beautiful car. His lordship would have loved her. Gordy and Ted had helped me to bring her back to her best and this would be the longest drive I had taken in her. She was big and she was fast. I was not certain that she was a family car but she suited me. I did a complete check before I was satisfied and I headed back into the house.

I washed up and put on my driving coat and hat. I looked at my watch. Time was wasting. A short while later Bates came from my bedroom. "I have packed your weapons from the war, sir."

"What on earth for!"

He shrugged, "Force of habit. Should I unpack them?"

Shaking my head, I said, "We haven't got time for that. Put the bags in the boot. We will stay at the Army and Navy club."

"Yes sir."

I hugged Beattie and kissed Thomas on the top of his sleeping head. She looked carefully at me, "Make sure you and Bates have a decent meal tonight."

"I will. Now that the war is over the food will be better at the Army and Navy."

As I pushed down on the accelerator I felt the power from one of the biggest cars Sunbeam had made. Beattie and I had planned for more than one child. This car would be big enough for now. We were soon on the A1. Parts of it dated back to the Romans and it was both long and straight. It was relatively quiet and I put my foot down. The Sunbeam could motor. I was aware, after twenty minutes, that Bates was being very quiet. Normally he chattered like a house sparrow. "Have you a problem, old chap?"

He coughed. That was a sure sign that he was uncomfortable. "Well sir, I am wondering what this journey means. Do you think you will be in action again?"

I burst out laughing. "There is no one left to fight. I can't see it being that. Probably a change of orders. Is that what is worrying you?"

"Well sir not really, it is just." He sighed, "Can I be brutally honest with you, sir?"

"John there are no secrets between us. You know that. Whatever you have to say then out with it. I promise that it will not upset me."

Well, sir, I am happy to continue to be your servant. You are a gentleman and I enjoy serving a gentleman."

"There is a but coming."

He smiled, "Always a bright and perceptive gentleman! It is just that I am not certain you need me anymore. Not with Mrs. Harsker and your son. I feel as though I am intruding."

"Well you aren't."

"Hear me out, sir. I beg of you. When I said that I would stay on I had not thought things through. I had purpose at the front. I was no soldier but I could be there for you young men. Now I am redundant. If I am to be really honest sir I am not happy with the situation. I know it is one I chose. None of this is your fault in any shape or form."

"I appreciate your honesty. Yet I am not certain what it is you wish to do."

He sighed again, "There is something serendipitous about this journey, sir. I was already going to ask if I could have a few days in London."

I nodded. "And I would have approved, you know that."

"The thing is I have been offered a position."

I jerked my head around, "As a servant?"

"Good grief, sir, no. I will not be another man's servant. There is a small hotel in London, my cousin, a widow, owns it. She has asked me to help her to run it. She wants someone who can deal with the clients and to organize the staff. She thought with my experience in the military it might suit. I was going to ask if I could visit with her."

"But of course, and if you wish to take her up on the offer then you have my full support. Although I shall hate to lose you."

"You shall never lose me, sir. We have served together. We both know that there is an invisible bond which ties us and the other gentlemen together. I feel as close to you as any member of my family. Closer perhaps. No, sir, I will wait until you have had your meeting. We can chat during dinner."

"That would be splendid, John."

"Thank you, sir. I had been worried about this conversation. You have, as always, made it much easier for me."

After that he was the same chatty Bates who had helped my war be as civilised as it was. The rain had stopped by the time we drove down Pall Mall and we reached the club. It was just after noon and we had made excellent time. They had a room for me and one for Bates. Leaving him to see to the bags I decided to walk to Whitehall. It was only half a mile and I could go through St. James' Park. I had often met Beattie there when we had been courting. That seemed a lifetime ago.

I was wearing my flying coat and, when I approached the building, the sentry recognised my cap. He smartly saluted. I stepped inside and took off the coat. I had the letter which had been delivered. It gave little away. It said I was to present myself and ask for a Mr. Balfour. That seemed strange. On the way down I had wondered at that. I had met Trenchard who had been the driving force behind the Corps and now the Royal Air Force but it was not him I was to meet. I had expected this to be a military meeting.

Mr. Balfour was a small and neat man with a permanent smile. He reminded me of a bird. "Squadron Leader or do you prefer Major?"

I shrugged. The new rank was just that, new. I would grow used to it. He took that to mean he could use the new title and nodded. "Whichever you are more comfortable with."

His voice was a cheerful little voice. His sentences went up at the end. He sounded like a happy man. I wondered if he had spent his war safely ensconced in some building in Whitehall. He seemed like a clerk who might pore over the figures of dead and wounded. "If you would like to follow me, I will take you to Mr. Churchill."

"The First Sea Lord?"

He laughed as he led me up the stairs. "Oh, you are behind the times, sir. He was the Minister of Munitions. He is about to relinquish that title but I expect he will tell you that. He is a very energetic man, I can tell you. Always the first in his office. He will soon sort this place out I expect. He will sweep through these dusty halls like a new broom."

He led me through an office with four female clerks busy typing. Before the war, this would have been done by men. Things were changing. Mr. Balfour swept me through and into the office of Winston Churchill. I had heard of the man who had ordered the failed attack on Gallipoli. He was the exciting young aristocrat who had fought at Omdurman and escaped the Boers. He had a huge cigar and the room was filled with smoke.

He cocked an eye, "This is the chap then, Balfour?"

"Yes sir, Squadron Leader Harsker."

"Right, well off you trot! I shan't need you again for an hour or so! Make yourself useful eh? But stay close!"

Mr. Balfour seemed disappointed but he nodded and closed the door behind him. Mr. Churchill stood and poured two large brandies. He handed one to me and then sat down again. "I read your file. You are most unusual. Rose from the ranks to become the most successful ace who is still alive. V.C., M.M., M.C. You have it all. Trenchard says you are a good man and he rarely has a good word to say about anybody." I nodded. I did not know what to say. "Drink up. You aren't teetotal, are you?"

"Er, no sir. Sorry." I drank some of the brandy. It was a good brandy.

"Smoke if you like."

"Thank you, sir." I took out my pipe and filled it. It was more to keep me occupied than anything.

"Now I am about to become Minster of the Air. It is both a new title and a new ministry. Officially I don't start until January but I was keen and so I am here. Now your file shows that, in addition to shooting down the Hun you know how to fight ground troops. I like that. I see aeroplanes as aerial artillery. That was the trouble in the war; both sides knew when a barrage was coming and would take shelter. You chaps just appear out of the air. You have bombs and you have machine guns. One squadron is more effective than a battalion of infantry supported by a couple of batteries of artillery. Between you and I, young man, there are some around here who would like to see the Royal Air Force dead and buried. I don't believe that. I see it as the future. I have great plans for it and for you."

My pipe was going well and I sipped my brandy, nodding to show him that I was listening.

He stood and went to the wall. I saw that he had a map pinned to it. It was northern Russia. "There is a war going on here. These Bolsheviks are fighting the legitimate rulers of the country. We have men helping them there." He pointed to the north. "There are some men here and," he tapped a point just south of the Baltic, "and some here." He puffed on his cigar and drank more of his brandy. "I am sending you here." He pointed to the Arctic. "You will command the aeroplanes which are there."

"But sir, it is winter and they have snow and ice there. We don't fly in that kind of winter!"

He nodded, "I know. Hear me out. I have it on good authority that the Bolsheviks have managed to get their hands on some German aeroplanes. I think someone in Germany was keen to make some money before they are punished for the war. Anyway, the Bolsheviks have begun training pilots and by the time spring comes then they will have a putative air force. We can't have that. We also know that they intend using them to attack White Russian troops on the ground. That would be disastrous and you will stop them. All we have at the moment is a flight of three Sopwith $1^{1/2}$ Strutters flying for the Royal Navy. I want you to lead them. We want you, on the ground, so to speak. Your job is to stop the threat of Bolshevik air force threatening our flotilla."

"A tall order, sir."

He smiled. "I have not finished. You are temporary. I have a new commander training pilots to take over but it takes time to train new pilots. When he arrives then your work is done; there at least. We have more aeroplanes, Camels this time, down here on the Dnieper. When you have shown these Royal Navy fliers how to fight then you will head down there and lead those fellows too." He leaned back in his chair, "I am using you, Squadron Leader to show the generals that this is the future. You will prove my theories for me. After the Baltic I intend to send you to the Middle East but that is for the future."

"Do I have a choice, sir?"

"Of course, you have a choice. You can stay in the Royal Air Force or hand in your resignation. All men have choices."

This was an ultimatum. I had heard that the former First Sea Lord was ruthless and now I had seen it for myself. "How long do I have to think it over then, sir?"

9

"Until you have finished the brandy. I want the answer before you leave this office. I have no time for shilly shallying!"

I picked up the brandy. I was tempted to down it in one and resign. It would be a magnificent gesture but it was not me. I wanted to stay in the air force. I knew ambitious officers but I was not one of them. I had become a Squadron Leader by accident. I liked flying and I liked the men who were in the Royal Air Force. This was a job I enjoyed. I would stay. I downed the brandy and said, "Well sir as I want to stay in the service I will accept your ultimatum!"

He laughed, "That's what I like, spirit. You aren't letting me bully you! Good show! It's for the best. Now one thing to remember, Harsker, I don't want this a full-blown war. We are there to help the Russians, not to fight their battles for them. You and your aeroplanes will destroy their aeroplanes and that will protect the flotilla up there. If you can support the Russians without risking your aeroplanes, then so much the better. I want as few casualties as possible. This country has just paid a high price in brave young men. I would not add to that number."

"I understand sir. You want us to kill the enemy without getting killed ourselves. I think we would all agree with that sentiment, sir."

"You have wit as well as intelligence! That bodes swell. Now there is a ship waiting for you at the Surrey Docks. She will be leaving on the early morning tide and you will be on it. Your aeroplane is already on board as well as two fitters. They will be attached to you. I will send other chaps to help you out but that will be in the New Year. I need you there first. The Squadron Commander, Major Donald, is busy training new men. But I want you aboard tonight."

"Tonight sir?"

"Of course. Everything you need is on board."

"But what if I had refused?"

"I didn't think that you would but I had another officer on standby. Not as good as you but he would have done at a pinch."

I was going to ask who it was and then realised that I didn't want to know. The information might colour my opinion of the officer and I might serve with him in the future. "Do you mind me asking how long the posting will be? I have a wife and a young son."

"A fair question. We will say six months or until Major Donald arrives. Then you may return to the bosom of your family. How's that? When you return, we will chat. I want weekly reports. You will address them to Mr. Balfour. He will give you all the information that you might need. The White Russians will keep you supplied with fuel, ammunition and that sort of thing."

"Sir, this information about the German aeroplanes, is it accurate?"

He leaned forward, "I can say with all certainty that it is true. You need not worry about how I know but trust me that I have complete faith in the information. I can tell you how much was paid for each aeroplane and which official has pocketed the money. I chose you, Squadron Leader, because you are a thinker. You are not a glory hunter. You are a leader of men who has a brain. I need those qualities. Like you I have been stranded behind enemy lines and, like you, I was resourceful enough to get home. That is what I am looking for. I do not want a mindless killer. I want someone with a brain who can weigh people and situations up and make the right decisions. Rear Admiral Alexander-Sinclair is a good fellow but all he worries about are his ships. You will have to decide on the best strategy. The result I want is the putative Bolshevik air force destroying Is that clear?"

"Yes sir."

He stood. "A pleasure speaking with you. I am certain that we will speak again. Good luck, oh and Merry Christmas too!"

I shook his hand, picked up my coat and hat and left. When I closed the door behind me I just stood still. I had so many things to do and yet the only thing on my mind was telling Beattie. I knew that I would not be able to do so; not directly at any rate. I forced myself to breath slowly. This was like a dogfight. Don't think of the end think of the next thing you are going to do. I would speak with Mr. Balfour.

He was waiting, "I take it you agreed, Squadron Leader?"

"I did."

He had a leather satchel. He opened it. "In here is all the information that you will need including the authorisation you will require." He snapped it shut. "Come along to my office and I will take you through it."

An hour later my head was buzzing. Mr. Balfour was an organized man. He had meticulously prepared everything that I would need. I knew who my Russian liaison was as well as the Naval Attaché I would be dealing with. I had maps of the area as well as the numbers and types of German aeroplanes. I would be flying a Sopwith Camel. I was happy about that and the two fitters were also experienced armourers and riggers. Both had served on the Western front.

He handed me two Sam Browne's. They were fitted with Webleys. "These are for your men; the fitters. This part of the world is dangerous. You need to protect yourselves. I know you have a pistol but your air crew don't. Be on your guard." There was something in his eyes which told me that Mr. Balfour had a past. His voice was cheery but his eyes were cold. Mr. Balfour had been more than a clerk. "Now, Squadron Leader, I think we should go to the Surrey Dock for that is where the freighter is waiting."

"No, Mr. Balfour. First, we go to the Army and Navy Club. My luggage is there."

"But everything you could possibly need is on the freighter."

"We go to the club. I have to send a message to my wife and my servant is waiting for me there. There will be no argument, Mr. Balfour. The tide will not turn until later this evening. We have time. You have a car?" He nodded. "Then there will not be a problem as it is still eight hours to high tide."

I glared at him and he subsided, "Very well sir but…"

"No buts. Let's go."

I had walked from the club in about the same time as the car took for the roads were busy. When we arrived, I said, "Make yourself comfortable, Mr. Balfour. I intend to have dinner before I leave. Wait here, driver."

The driver was an Royal Air Force Corporal and he recognised the tone, "Righto sir. I'll have a smoke if that is all the same to you."

I reached into my pocket and took out a shilling, "There is a café around the corner, get yourself a bite and a brew eh, Corporal?"

He grinned, "Thanks sir, you are a gentleman!"

Bates was waiting for me in the foyer. He frowned when he saw my face, "A problem sir?"

"Just a little one. Let's go and eat now. I have news."

The club was quiet and we were given a quiet table. I ordered drinks and then told Bates most of my news. I omitted the Intelligence I had been given. When the drinks arrived I quickly ordered dinner. Bates knocked the whisky back in one. I smiled, "I have never see you do that before."

"Well, sir, you have taken me aback. Fighting again and in Russia." His hand went to his mouth, "Mrs. Harsker and the baby!"

"I need you to drive the car home for me and tell my wife what I have told you. After I leave here I have to take a ship. I shall write to her but you will have to tell her first." He nodded. "And John?"

"Yes sir?"

"I am guessing this has made your mind up about the hotel."

He smiled, "Actually sir, I had made it up already. I visited Edith earlier. It is a lovely hotel and would suit me. I was trying to think how to tell you. You made it easy sir. I don't want to see young men die anymore."

I knocked back my drink. "Nor do I but I fear that will be my lot in life. Let us enjoy this meal. It might be the last decent one I have for some time."

Part One
Arkhangelsk
Chapter 1

The S.S. Castletown was a relatively new ship. Her captain, however, had been a sailor for thirty years. He knew the waters of the Baltic and the White Sea as well as any man. My two men, one a Sergeant Mechanic and the other an Air Mechanic First Class, and I were the only passengers. The ship was laden with cargo. There was not only my Sopwith Camel and spares, there was also a great quantity of munitions for the allied troops based in the Baltic. I had arrived at the ship in plenty of time and he took me into his cabin to enjoy a companionable pipe.

"Just so's you know, Squadron Leader, we are not going to Murmansk. I know it is closer to the front but the waters are dangerous at this time of year. My orders are to deliver this cargo and you to the closest port to the British forces. Between you and me I think the whole idea is daft!"

I learned, over the next days, that Captain Hesketh was both bluff and honest. I liked both of those traits. "And let us say I am in agreement but it is orders and we both have to obey them. So where will you be landing us?"

"The White Russians hold Memel. It is not far from the front and the British Flotilla is there keeping an eye on Kronstadt. That is where the carrier, H.M.S. Vindictive is based. The flotilla is in Finland at Terijoki. I am not risking that. The German battleships at Kronstadt would blow us out of the water."

"You seem to know an awful lot for a merchant seaman, Captain?" I took my pipe out and filled it. The captain was smoking his and I could see that he had more to say.

He laughed, "I have been around a bit. I did convoys during the war and I know about submarines and commerce raiders. The Navy are the ones who know what they are doing. They are happy for me to offload at Memel. Take some advice, Squadron Leader, be careful around these White Russians. I am not saying the Bolsheviks are saints but the White Russians are as bad. This is a

nasty war. Anyhow it will take us ten days or so to steam there."
He pointed the stem of his pipe at the satchel. "You will have lots
of time to study the papers you are hanging on to. What I will say
is I hope this aeroplane of yours can cope with the cold because
believe me, we will be chipping ice off the ship before we reach
Russia! You and your lads all have your own cabin and there is a
steward to look after you. You will eat with the officers in my
mess. If you want to eat alone then you can. No skin off my nose."

"No, Captain, we will be quite happy to eat with your men. Can
you tell me which hold the Camel is in?"

He laughed, "It isn't. It is wrapped in canvas on the main deck. It
will be as safe as anywhere. We double wrapped it. Your lads saw
to it. They looked after it like it was a baby!"

I shook his hand, "Well I had better go and meet them."

"You seem a nice bloke sir. I can see from the medals on your
chest that you are no coward but this is not a war we should be
getting in to. I will do my best to get you there safely but I don't
envy you your job." He reached into a drawer and brought out a tin
of tobacco. "Here you are Squadron leader. As you smoke a pipe
you might like this. I did the Caribbean run a couple of times and
picked up some nice baccy. This one is from Cuba. They soak it in
rum. Very nice too."

"Thank you, Captain. That is kind."

He pointed the stem of his pipe at my medals. "You have the
Victoria Cross there, Squadron Leader. That tells me that you are a
bloke I can respect and trust. I'll get you there safely and I'll tell
you who you can trust but after that sir, you'll be on your own."

"Thanks."

"We sail at midnight so we will eat at seven. We don't dress."

As I left the captain's cabin I pondered his words. This would not
be like the Western front where the enemies spoke German and
you could trust everyone else. This was a vicious civil war. I did
not think how we could possibly benefit from it but I was under
orders. I consoled myself with the fact that it would only be for six
months.

My two men were standing at the gangway watching London.
This would be their last sight of England for some time. Throwing
their cigarettes over the side they stood to attention and saluted. I
smiled, "You can smoke if you like. I will be."

The Sergeant nodded, "Thanks sir. Some officers are funny about that sort of thing." He was about thirty years old and had the oily fingers and bitten down fingernails of a true mechanic.

I nodded, "But not me. I am Squadron Leader Harsker. I only found out about this little mission this afternoon. I am guessing that you two had more warning?"

"Yes sir. We found out last month. We were just waiting for you, sir."

That told me they had probably offered the operation to someone who had refused. "So, let's get the introductions over and done with."

"Sergeant Mechanic Bert Hepplewhite from Bolton sir."

"Bolton eh? I come from Burscough. That's not far from you."

"No, sir, but it is a bit cleaner. Some nice pubs out Burscough way."

"There are indeed. And you?"

"Air Mechanic First Class George Baker sir, from Stoke on Trent."

I recognised the accent. He was younger. I guessed he was in his early twenties. Well, Bert, George, that is what I shall call you. We will save Sergeant and Air Mechanic for special occasions; how is that?"

They both smiled, "I heard that you were a decent officer sir. I know some of the lads who were with you in France." He pointed to my medals. "Where you got the V.C."

"Well I don't think there will be any medals coming out of this little expedition. I have to warn you that it will be pretty cold. I fear that you will have a harder job maintaining the aeroplane than I will flying it."

"They are a nice little bus, sir."

"I know. I have flown them before. It may well be March before we get to fly though."

"It could be worse sir. We could be back on the Western Front!"

"We will have to be very careful in Russia. I do not speak Russian and I have little diplomatic training. I will rely on you two keeping your mouths shut and your ears open."

George flicked his cigarette butt over the side, "What do you mean, sir?"

16

"There are Americans, French, Czechs, Serbians and goodness knows who else in this army we are joining not to mention the Russians, Lithuanians, Estonians, Finns and Galicians. You two will have to nurse and guard the Camel like it was your baby. We are getting more personnel but it won't be until the New Year. For the next month we are going to be it. You two will be the Camel's babysitters."

Bert laughed, "Then it will be a lot more interesting than working in the stores at Wolverhampton."

"Stores at Wolverhampton?"

"We had a choice sir, we could leave the service, have a job in the stores, or come on this jaunt. We both jumped at it. It should be interesting and when we found out we had a genuine ace as our pilot... well sir there was no thinking twice about it was there?"

I liked them both, they reminded me of every mechanic and fitter with whom I had served. Lumpy would have got on well with them both. "One more thing. There are side arms for you. When we get to White Russia then wear them at all times. Have you used a Webley before?"

"Only in training sir."

"Well I shall give you a couple of refresher lessons. Right then show me to my cabin. Apparently, we eat with the officers so let's get washed up. Dinner is at seven."

There were just eight officers on the freighter. The meal would be unusual in that all of them would be present. As the captain told us after we had said Grace, as soon as we set sail then at least a third would be on duty at all times. They were keen to question us about the war. They had seen it from the sea. It had been the newspapers who had given them their version of the war and they wanted to know the reality. As I had served in the cavalry first I was able to give them a unique insight. Bert and George also had stories which brought looks of sadness to the sailor's faces.

In return the sailors told us of submarines and ships lost in the icy waters of the Arctic and Atlantic. "Aye, Squadron Leader, when a man falls into the Arctic he measures his life in seconds, not minutes. That's why the lads don't bother with lifejackets."

I saw George and Bert exchange a worried look.

The Captain laughed, "Don't worry lads there are no U-Boats where we are going and I promise I shall get you to dry land." He turned to the steward. He was a West Indian called Desmond. "Steward, I think we will end this meal with a rum and a toast."

"Yes sir."

He poured us all a generous measure. Captain Walter Hesketh stood, "Here's a toast; to the sailors who never came home and the soldiers who died for their country. Let's never forget them. To the dead!"

"To the dead!"

It was both sombre and apposite. The rum was Navy strength and I saw George's eyes begin to water. The Captain just licked his lips. "Right lads. Let's get this boat ready for sea."

I had started to write a letter to Beattie in the car coming from the club. After dinner, I hurriedly finished it. I knew that the customs officer would be coming aboard before we sailed and I intended to ask him to post it. In it I tried to explain to Beattie why I had taken the posting. I hoped she would understand. Who knew when I would be able to write to her again?

The customs officer, who would be my postman, had a limp and a scarred face. He was an ex-soldier; a lieutenant who had served in the Middlesex Regiment. Wounded on the Somme he had still found a way to serve his country. He was more than delighted to post my letter for me. He took in my medals. "How long were you at the front sir?"

"From Mons until the end."

He shook his head, "I was in for just six months, sir. If I had been there any longer I think I would have gone mad at the insanity of it."

"I know what you mean but I was luckier. I was a flier. There was death in the skies but it was a slightly old-fashioned war. It was not as heroic as the newspapers made out, death in a burning aeroplane is never pleasant, but you had slightly more control over your own destiny."

He nodded to the canvas covered shape on the deck. "And you are still serving sir. Will you be fighting?"

"I would like to say no but that would be a lie. Yes, my war is not over yet."

He saluted, "Well mine is over and I thank God for that. Good luck, sir."

I stood by the rail as the ship was made ready for sea. The engines were started and the umbilical cords which held us to the shore were severed. We were off. I watched a darkened River Thames and England slip by. The last time I had left by boat had been in 1914. Then it had been a troopship packed with the Yeomanry. Now there were just three of us. I headed for my cabin to read the intelligence which the efficient Mr. Balfour had provided.

My cabin was cosy. Next to a small sink there was a bed with storage underneath, a bedside cabinet attached firmly to the bulkhead, and a wardrobe. I hung my flying coat and battle dress in the wardrobe and then examined what Mr. Balfour had provided. He had been a resourceful fellow. Apart from the satchel, filled with papers and maps, he had provided winter clothes. There was an oil skin sweater amongst the clothes. I could see that being useful. The sou'wester would be less useful. I did not envisage myself having to brave the decks in a force 8 but it showed how thoughtful the man was. There was a tin of tea, biscuits, a fruit cake and a bottle of brandy. I saw Mr. Churchill's hand in that. Finally, there was a bag with toiletries. I had my own but after a few months I would run out. It was a good kit.

I packed everything away; it was the way of the soldier to be neat and tidy. Then I laid out the papers. I was not tired. My mind was too full of the mission. I began with my superior officer. Rear Admiral Alexander-Sinclair commanded the small flotilla which watched the Bolshevik fleet. It was not a large number of ships. The two seaplane carriers and converted carrier were the largest vessels he possessed. It was hard to see what he would do if the Bolsheviks chose to bring him to battle. The Bolshevik ships had twelve inch guns. His largest vessel mounted six inch guns. I saw now why they wanted aeroplanes. The seaplanes could do little for him. They were worse than useless in aerial combat. Even the oldest German aeroplane could outfly an aeroplane which had two huge floats.

I filled my pipe with some of the Captain's tobacco. As I puffed the sweet leaves I wondered at the wisdom of sending a Camel. There were other aeroplanes which could carry torpedoes and bombs. They would be more use against a fleet. It was then I realised I was not there for the fleet. I was there to shoot down

German aeroplanes. I took out the intelligence papers for the enemy aeroplanes. I smiled, ruefully. It was a catalogue of every aeroplane I had fought since the days of the Gunbus. All of them had been terrors in their time from the Fokker Eindecker through to the Red Baron's Triplane. None of them, however, were new. None was as fast or as manoeuvrable as the Camel. Even the little Sopwith Pup had the firepower to defeat them. The Strutter was an upgraded version of the Pup.

I put the list to one side. There might be thirty aeroplanes but they were not the worry. I looked at my resources. I ruled out the seaplanes. The Sopwith Baby was as slow as the Germans and, with their huge floats, sitting ducks for the Bolsheviks. It was the Sopwith 1½ Strutters I would be leading. There were three of them and all had been RNAS. They were flown by three lieutenants. From their service records, they all appeared to be young. They were in Finland with the flotilla. That was a problem. I was being landed on the other side of the Baltic. My pipe had gone out and I took that as a sign that I should sleep. I looked at the brandy bottle. I would keep that for the cold of Russia.

I awoke to a grey day heading, slowly, up the east coast of England. The breakfast was a hearty one and like all old soldiers I took advantage. Who knew when the next decent meal might arrive? The air crew and myself had been on short rations many times. The three of us took a stroll around the deck. It was partly exercise and partly to check on the condition of the Camel. The aeroplane was in three sections: fuselage, wings and undercarriage. Everything else was below decks.

"You have plenty of spares?"

"Yes sir. Two of everything and three of the parts we are likely to need more often."

I nodded, "The oil, fuel and the ammunition we will be getting from the Navy. They are flying Sopwiths too. Without wishing them ill if anything happens to them we can cannibalise them for spares. I have a feeling that, until the rest of the flight get here, we will be well worked."

"We were told, March, sir."

"That is more than I was told but I will believe that when it happens. Anyway, I need to go and do more homework about our allies and the terrain."

The wind was blowing too hard for me to read on the deck and so I went to the officer's mess where I could lay all the paper out. In terms of numbers there were not a huge number of British soldiers: 236th Infantry Brigade, 548th (Dundee) Army Troops Company, Royal Engineers, 2/10th Royal Scots, some Royal Dublin Fusiliers, 52 Battalion Manchester Regt. These were all based around Arkhangelsk. The Americans, Estonians and Italians had far more men. In addition, a Major Bruce commanded a number of tanks further south. We had the only aeroplanes and the only ships. That was useful information.

I then looked at the men alongside whom I would be operating. The commanding officer was a count. Count Yuri Fydorervich. I learned little from the notes that Mr. Balfour had provided save that he was young and had fought against the Germans. He was based at Memel.

I looked at the airfield we would be using. There were no photographs but, from the description, it had not been used very much and appeared to have been abandoned in October 1917 when the Revolution took place. From the map, it appeared to be close to the coast and I could only hope that it might be snow free. The maps of the front were crude and, from Mr. Balfour's notes, unreliable. What I did know was that the range of the German aeroplanes the Bolsheviks would be using was considerably less than the Sopwith. I had a three-hundred-mile range whereas the Fokker Triplane could only manage one hundred and eight five miles. That gave me a distinct advantage. In the hands of Richthofen the triplane was deadly but, as the Germans had found to their cost, in the hands of a lesser pilot its superior climb, speed and ceiling could cause unexpected crashes. I just had to use my range and my speed to defeat them.

I leaned back and lit my pipe. It helped me to think. The base at Memel was no good for a number of reasons. It was over four hundred miles from the British Flotilla. More than that, it was over two hundred miles to the front line. I needed to be based closer to both. According to Mr. Balfour the Estonians had just driven the Bolsheviks from most of Estonia and General Yudenich had asked for British support. It struck me that Reval might be a better base. We would be only a hundred miles from the British Flotilla and the same from the front. We would have safety and the ability to strike at the enemy. I went up on deck for some air.

Captain Hesketh waved down to me from the bridge. "Settled in, Squadron Leader?"

"Aye, aye captain. Are we on schedule?"

"The wind is a little against us but we should be there in a week or so. Enjoy the voyage."

"A little grey, isn't it?"

"Make the most of the grey. Soon it will be white!"

He was right. As we ploughed north the weather became increasingly windy and stormy. We had flecks of snow which became a blizzard on the third night out of London. You needed a strong stomach to hold down your food.

I spent the time studying maps and intelligence gathered by Mr. Balfour. I learned that, like our present voyage, it would not all be plain sailing. There were factions in the White Russian army and there were traitors and rebels all around. There had been an attempt at sabotage on the engines of a British warship in port. That was worrying. According to Mr. Balfour they didn't know if it was Bolsheviks or sympathisers on the ship itself. I remembered when we had had German saboteurs trying to attack our airfield. We had managed to control that easily. How would we do it in a land where we did not speak the language? I saw now that Mr. Churchill had given me a poisoned chalice.

I also had information about the old Russian air force and, after reading it, discovered why they had bought from the Germans. The best aeroplane the Russians had had was the Nieuport 17. Ensign Vasili Yanchenko had sixteen victories in the fighter before he was shot by Bolsheviks. The rest of their aeroplanes had been Spad A4s or Lebed X11. Their top speed was just 87 mph. Their pilots had either defected or they had been executed. Either way the Bolsheviks were starting from scratch.

By the time, we entered the Baltic I was familiar with the material. I took to walking the deck more rather than being closeted below decks. I was anxious to see the land. The sea was calmer as we headed east but there was a sheen of ice on the sea. I did not see how we could operate while the winter gripped the land. Although the land we were passing was at peace, as in

England, the people were still suffering shortages and trying to repair the most devastating war the planet had ever suffered.

My two crew wandered over. They had gradually become used to my addressing them by their first names. George looked at Bert who nodded and spoke. "Sir, we are just two ordinary blokes. We are not certain about this war we are getting into. I mean the other war, the Great War, that was easy to understand. The Kaiser invaded Belgium. We went to help them but this is a civil war. Isn't it just blokes like us who rose up to throw off the shackles of the oppressor?"

I laughed, "That doesn't sound like you Bert. Where did you get that from?"

He took out a pamphlet from his tunic. "Some ex- soldiers were giving them out at the docks. We hadn't read it until last night and we got bored."

I shook my head, "This is what they call propaganda. The revolution in 1917 did get rid of their Emperor but what they have put in place is just as bad. These Bolsheviks are killing anyone who disagrees with them. That isn't the British way is it lads?"

George threw his cigarette butt over the side. "I don't know, sir. How is it right that some folk have all the money and others don't?"

I saw this was more serious than I had first thought. "Let's be honest, George. You think that because I am an officer I am a toff and I have money."

He looked shocked, "Well no, sir. Look I am not being insubordinate sir I..."

"My mum and dad worked on the estate of a lord. They owned nothing. My brothers also thought that money should be shared around too so I understand what you are saying but I am an example of what you can achieve in England. I began life as a trooper who was shovelling horse muck. Bert, you could be an officer."

"I am just a sergeant, sir."

"And so was I. You live in England and that means you can be whatever you want to be. But you don't want someone telling you what to think do you?"

"Of course not, sir. A man has the right to his opinions."

I played my trump card, "Not in Bolshevik Russia they don't and that is why we are fighting so that the Russian working man can say what he wants without his leaders disagreeing and having him shot." I was aware that I had simplified it but, in essence, what I had said was the truth. "Just think about it, eh lads? And remember, you can talk to me."

Bert nodded, "I know sir. I know." He nodded to George, "I told you the Squadron Leader would explain it." Turning back to me he said, "What do we do about speaking the language sir? I mean in France we picked up the odd word or two but this is Russian!"

"We will just have to muddle through together. One thing, I intend to have us moved a little closer to the front. Don't bother to put the Camel together. Keep it all packed up. Captain Hesketh can't take us but I am certain we can move it closer to the front."

"What about the other Sopwiths, sir?"

"That's the thing, George. They aren't even at Memel. They are in Finland! The weather there is even colder than in Estonia and Petrograd. I intend to move us all to Reval as soon as possible."

"Can you do that, sir?"

I smiled, "The orders I was given, Sergeant, was to take charge of the air war against the Bolsheviks. I think that puts me in charge but if they are unhappy back in Whitehall, they can always recall me." My words were full of bravado but I knew that if they had had another option they would have used it. I had no doubt that I was a stop gap until the men who ran the Royal Air Force could find someone who would do their bidding. I took some comfort from the fact that the new Secretary of State had appointed me. Speaking with Mr. Churchill I gathered the impression that he knew his own mind and would do things his way.

Memel was not a large port but it was a busy one. There were no warships but many freighters and coastal vessels. The papers in the satchel told me that the Military Attaché here was a man called Mervyn Rees and he would be my first point of contact.

As we were guided in by a pilot I stood next to the captain. We had had many chats during the voyage. I liked him. He took me to the lee of the bridge. "A word of advice, Bill, the folks hereabouts rarely know who their master is. Sometimes it is the Germans, sometimes the Poles and sometimes the Russians. The Lithuanians used to have their own country. I have drunk with some of their captains. They are a proud people. They do not want to be used. It wouldn't surprise me if they didn't try to be independent again. Now I am telling you this because they like the English. We are among the few people who haven't tried to rule them." He laughed, "God knows we have done that in enough other countries. So, if things go wrong or you need help then go to a Lithuanian."

I stared at him, "What about the White Russians?"

"They are Russians and I wouldn't trust them as far as I could spit. But I am biased. You will have to make your own mind up. This is just an opinion." He tapped his pipe out. "Anyway, I do this voyage once a month. I hope I shall see you again."

I had written a long letter to Beattie. "Could you post this for me when you get back? It is for my wife."

"Of course. Glad to. I'll have the stewards sort your bags out for you. I daresay you will be busy with your aeroplane and finding your Mr. Rees." He shook my hand. "Good luck."

He went back to the pilot and I left the bridge to get a closer look at this new country. It was covered in snow but the buildings looked to be medieval. I was surprised at how many were made of wood. It surprised me. As we neared the dock I saw a couple of lorries and a man who had to be Mr. Rees. He just looked dapper. He had a Homburg hat and a tailored overcoat. He wore white kid gloves which I took to be an affectation for the others around him had thick coats and mittens. He also used a smart walking stick. The head was that of a dog and it looked to be silver. He looked to be an official who spent his life in foreign postings such as this. The Empire had been run by them. It was a good sign that he was waiting for us. He had his finger on the pulse and he was efficient. That was a start.

The port was busy and it took us some time to finally dock. As the gangway was lowered I descended leaving my two air crew to stay with the Camel. It was Mr. Rees who was waiting for me. He strode up to me and held out his hand. "Mervyn Reece, Military Attaché to the Russian Government in Memel."

The fact he said Russian Government so loudly told me that he was speaking for the benefit of those around him as well as me.

"Squadron Leader Bill Harsker, commander of the Air Task Force supporting the Russian Government." I saw his eyes crinkle into the hint of a smile. I had done the right thing.

"Now I have a couple of lorries to take your aeroplane to the airfield. It is a three-hour drive from here."

I leaned in and spoke quietly, "Mr. Rees would it be possible just to load them on the lorries? I would like to chat to you about that."

He nodded, "There is a café over there. They serve a nice cup of tea. I will have a word with these fellows. I should have your air crew supervise them while your camel is being loaded."

"They don't speak the language."

He waved over a youth. He looked to be no more than eighteen. "Vladimir, would you accompany these two gentlemen?" Hepplewhite and Baker had arrived. "Help them to give instructions to the workers."

"Of course, Mr. Rees." He managed to give Rees an extra couple of syllables but he looked keen enough.

"You two chaps see to the loading of the Camel. The steward will bring our bags over." I looked at the attaché. "Do we put them in the car?"

"Of course, but I would suggest your men travel with the Camel. It is a valuable piece of equipment."

"You heard the gentleman. We will be over shortly."

As we strolled towards the café he said, "Vladimir is a bright young chap. His family were killed in 1917. How he got here I have no idea but I found him starving and close to death. He had had all of his belongings stolen. I felt sorry for him and took him on. That was a year ago. He has more than repaid me. His family were close to the Royal Family and he can speak six languages. I don't know what I would do without him. He has just begun to recover what was lost; both his dignity and his possessions."

We sat in the café and Mr. Rees imperiously waved over a waiter. He rattled something off in the local language and then turned to face me. "Now then Squadron Leader. What is wrong with our airfield?"

"Quite simply it is too far from the front. In addition, the other aeroplanes are in Finland!"

"There are plans for them to be brought over on the Vindictive when the weather improves."

"Good but that still means that we are too far away from where we are needed." I lowered my voice. "You know about the German aeroplanes?"

He smiled, "It was I who sent the message to London."

I was impressed, "I am amazed that you found out that information."

"Oh no, you misunderstand me. Captain Crombie was the naval attaché in Petrograd. He had a network of spies there. He got the information to me before he was killed. A shame, he was a fine chap. Yes, I know about them and it is all accurate."

"Then you know where they will be based."

"Of course. Just south of Petrograd a place called Peterhof. The Bolsheviks have their fleet at Kronstadt and the aeroplanes can attack our ships if they get too close. You will destroy them."

"Then we will have to be closer. How about Reval?"

"Politically that is a little sensitive. The Estonians are allies of the White Russians and they have almost recovered the whole of their land but they want independence."

"How about the British base then? Terijoki?"

Our tea had arrived and he paid for it and sipped it, "Acceptable. Actually, Squadron Leader, that is not a bad idea except that you would have to fly over the sea and I understand you pilots are not keen on that."

"We prefer land. It is easier to navigate. They don't call them landmarks for nothing. However it is the shortest route and so we would live with that."

He chuckled, "Very droll, Squadron Leader. I would have to ask the Count but if he agrees then that would be possible. Of course you would still have the problem of getting there."

I pointed out of the window with my cup. "There are plenty of ships here."

He pointed further east, "And there is a Russian fleet there. Still we might be able to get you a ship from Reval. The only problem is that the Bolsheviks invaded two weeks ago, and are quite close to Reval." He drained his cup. "I will tell you what, I will go back to the consulate. We have a radio there. I will get in touch with the Rear Admiral and speak to your Mr. Balfour."

"And what do I do?"

"Well I would suggest you keep an eye on your aeroplane, Squadron Leader. We wouldn't want it stolen before it could be used eh? I will leave Vladimir with you. I should only be gone a couple of hours. Stretch your legs eh?"

He strode away. Although older than I was he was spritely and I had to stretch my legs to keep up with him. He reached the car and waved Vladimir over, "Keep the Squadron Leader company eh, there's a good fellow. I shan't be long."

With that he was gone. I had only been in the country for half an hour and already things were going awry. This did not bode well. Vladimir smiled up at me. "You have many medals. Have you killed many Bolsheviks?"

He sounded so earnest that I looked at him again. He had almost a girl's face. I had expected Russians to have heavy beards but the young man appeared to have delicate features. His words belied his face. "I have yet to fight the Bolsheviks. It was the Germans I fought."

"General von der Goltz is an ally of ours. He leads a German army. They fight and kill Bolsheviks." I nodded. "You fly an aeroplane?" He gestured to the lorries.

"Yes, a Sopwith Camel."

"It has guns?"

"Two machine guns."

"If the Bolsheviks had not killed my family then I would have done as my father did and joined the cavalry."

"I was in the cavalry but the day of the horse on the battlefield is over. Our horses were slaughtered by machine guns."

"Even the Bolsheviks use horses but I would not like to see horses killed in that way."

We had reached my men. "Well sir, what's goin' on then?"

"Mr. Rees is speaking with London. We may not be staying here. If we travel I want you two in the lorries."

"Aye sir, a wise move." He looked at Vladimir.

I said, "You can trust this gentleman, Sergeant."

He sniffed. It was a sign he did not agree but he would defer to me. "A couple of these fellows have shifty eyes, sir."

"Listen, we have to watch out for everybody, shifty eyed or not." I pointed to their tunics. "You haven't got your side arms. Go and get them and from now on wear them at all times. If you have to then sleep with them!"

The saluted and scurried off. Vladimir said, "Mr. Rees will not let me have a pistol. He said it would invite trouble."

"He might be right but in my experience a loaded gun is always a nice piece of insurance."

The snow was falling, again, and so we hurried to the cafe and sat in its cosy warmth. We had more tea. They knew how to make tea in this part of the world but they did not serve it with milk. I smiled. My old comrades, Ted and Gordy would not have been happy about that. They liked lots of milk and heaped sugars.

"So, Vladimir, what do you plan for yourself?"

"Plan, sir? I do not understand."

"What do you want to do with your life. You are young and you have many years ahead of you."

His face became grim and he clenched his fists. "Fight the Bolsheviks. I have asked the Count if I can join his staff. When he says I can then I will join him. He will give me a gun and I will fight the people who murdered my Tsar and my family."

I had nothing I could say to him. I had not lost my family and my country but it seemed a rather bleak future for the young man. I could see now why Mr. Rees had not given him a gun. "Tell me about the Count. What is he like?"

His demeanour changed immediately. His face became animated and his voice almost sang. "Count Yuri Fydorervich is my hero. He has fought the Bolsheviks since his family was killed. I knew him as a boy although he was older. His family had estates which bordered those of my own. I would have joined him at the start but he was away organizing armies and I was having to make my way through the Bolshevik lines."

"Away?"

"He was in the army and was fighting the Germans. Mr. Rees found me first and nursed me back to health. I owe Mr. Rees my life."

"And so you are paying Mr. Rees back before you serve your friend."

He smiled, "You understand. Yes, it is a duty I owe him. I must give him back a life before I can begin mine. I still practise with a sword and pistol when I can. I do not want to become rusty."

"I fear the days of using a sword are long gone."

The afternoon drifted into evening and the snow stopped. The clear skies predicted a wickedly cold night. We left the café and headed towards the lorries. When we reached them I saw that the lorry drivers had a fire going and my men were warming themselves around it. A bottle was surreptitiously hidden as we approached and I smelled raw alcohol. I frowned, "Sergeant…"

His head lowered in shame the Sergeant murmured, "Sorry sir. They handed us the bottle and we drank before we knew."

I was going to say something when Vladimir suddenly rounded on the lorry drivers. He gave them what I would have termed a sergeant major tongue lashing had I been in Britain. The men actually cowered as though he might hit them.

Vladimir turned to me, "I am sorry Squadron Leader but these men are peasants. They do not know better. I have told them I will have them whipped if they do this again."

"Whipped?"

"Of course, it is the only way you keep such men in their place. They are simple and need to be taught how to behave. The Bolsheviks are peasants who are beyond teaching. The only thing they understand is a bullet."

At that point I heard the sound of vehicles and turned around to see Mr. Rees returning followed by a Rolls Royce Silver Ghost, a Rolls Royce armoured car and four lorries.

"It is the Count! Mr. Rees has brought the Count!"

A figure with a tailored uniform festooned with braid and medals stepped from the car. That was the first time I saw Count Yuri Fydorervich. He was an imposing figure. The first thing I noticed was that he had four of the biggest soldiers surrounding him and they had bandoliers of ammunition draped about their shoulders. They had pistols, swords, knives and a rifle. They were body guards although they looked like brigands. It told me much about the Count. The Count himself was in his mid-twenties. I should have expected it because of what Vladimir had said but I had expected a general in the White Army to be older. Then I remembered that he had served in the war. He had a cigarette holder in his mouth. I had never seen a man with a cigarette holder and it surprised me. I saw that everything about him was intended to impress. His uniform was loaded with braid and his chest with medals. He wore a sword and had a pair of pistols at his waist. I saw that they were American Colt .45s. This was a man trying to get noticed.

He smiled when he saw me, "You must be the British ace we have heard so much about. I am so glad that your Government listened to my request. Now we have an Air Force! Now you can begin to reclaim my country! We can drive these Bolsheviks back into their holes. "

My heart sank. I now saw that I was not the stop gap. It was me they wanted. I was not here to protect the fleet. I was here to take the war to the Bolsheviks and I had one Camel and three relics to do it. What had seemed a difficult task now looked to be an impossible one. The snow which began to fall again mirrored my feelings about the task. There was no end to it.

Chapter 2

"I have but four aeroplanes, sir and only one of them here." I saw him frown and I did not know why.

Mr. Rees said, quietly, "You should address the Count as Count or General, Squadron Leader."

"I am sorry Count, I did not know."

"It is no matter." His English was excellent. I learned, as we travelled east, that he had attended English public school. His look told me that it did matter. "The important thing is that your arrival is perfect. Our allies in Estonia are about to defeat the Bolsheviks there. General Yudenich has sent a message to me, only today, asking for my support. I have asked your Government for ships and they are on their way. Now we have aeroplanes! We can crush the Bolsheviks in Estonia and move on to Petrograd."

"I have one Camel!"

He waved a hand, "Mr. Rees has arranged for the other three to be sent from Finland. Within a week, they will be with you."

"But the snow? How do we fly?"

He shrugged, "You are the flier you will find a way! Come we are wasting time." Ducking back into his car he waved the column forward. One of his men shouted something to the lorry drivers and they started their engines.

Mr. Rees said, "Come along the two of you. Get inside and I will explain."

I sat in the front with Mr. Rees. "Surely he cannot be serious?"

"I am afraid he is but to be fair to the Count he is right. General Yudenich has won a great victory. Rear Admiral Alexander-Sinclair is on his way to Reval to bring in supplies. He is bringing Vindictive with your three other aeroplanes."

Mr. Rees overtook the lorries so that we were behind the Rolls Royce which was following the armoured car. In the back Vladimir said, "So I get to fight?"

"No, you do not." He lit a cigarette. With the slippery road beneath our tyres it was skilfully done. "Listen Squadron Leader this helps you. You will have your air force all together as well as support from the navy. You will be closer to the front too. That is what you asked for is it not? You can take off and land on the Vindictive. That means you can be in action sooner."

I had never yet taken off nor landed from a carrier. I had no doubt that I would be able to manage it but it was still another worry.

"And will there be enemies between us and Reval?"

"Probably. That is why the Count has the armoured car." He stubbed out his cigarette, "About the Count; he likes to have his rank used when you speak to him. A little deference would help."

"Mr. Rees, I served with a lord and he expected no deference. I will treat the Count as a superior officer but that is as far as it goes. I will not bow and scrape to the man."

"Then he will not be happy."

"The Count's state of mind is of no consequence to me. I am here to do a job and then I can go home. And is there any more information about the German aeroplanes?"

"We have the actual numbers now. We also know that they are based at Peterhof. There are loyal Russians and other agents who send us information. I should tell you that they have had pilots training to use them."

"I am not concerned with the pilots. It is the buses they will be using that is important."

"Buses?"

"It is what we called aeroplanes."

"Ah, well they have six of the Fokker E.1. There are seven Fokker D 1. There are four Fokker Triplanes and three Albatros D.1."

I was quiet. That meant the majority of the aeroplanes were Camel fodder. The Triplanes would be death traps but the three Albatros would take some handling. They were more than a match for the Sopwith 1½ Strutter. However, it was better than I hoped.

"And how far is it from Reval to Peterhof?"

"A hundred and eighty miles."

"Then we have to be closer. We need your Rear Admiral to take us to within fifty miles." The attaché was silent. "Is that a problem?"

"It puts the flotilla a little close to Kronstadt and the Bolshevik fleet. Their guns could shell them if they came too close."

"Then you have a problem. The maximum range is a hundred miles or so. That gives us time to get to the target, engage the enemy and get back. Aeroplanes need fuel and there is a limit to what we can carry."

"Very well. I shall try to persuade the Rear Admiral."

As we drove I took out my service revolver and made sure that it was loaded. The rest of my guns were with my luggage but if we were travelling through recently liberated land then I would need a weapon close to hand. As we drove, even though it was night time, I found it hard to reconcile the countryside of Belgium and France which had been torn up by war. Here, there was little sign of it.

"Mr. Rees, what is the size of the Bolshevik Army?"

"We have intelligence which tells us of the money they spend on their weapons but the soldiers? It is just an estimate. They had millions under arms when they fought the Germans. Now they fight from Vladivostok in the east to the borders of Poland in the west. What is certain is that they are struggling to make weapons. That is the advantage that the Count and his men have. The leaders of the Russian Army joined the Whites. They are the ones who understand weaponry. The fliers they had were aristocrats. There were perilously few of those anyway. The ones they are preparing to be pilots now are being trained by Germans."

"That is not as big a problem as it might have been. By the end of the war their better pilots had all been shot down. If we had a squadron of S.E 5s then we could defeat every aeroplane they sent against us and most of their armies too."

"Really?"

"Yes Vladimir?"

"Then why has your Government not sent them? Why have they only sent one aeroplane?"

I shrugged, closed my eyes and laid back in the seat, "You would have to ask Mr. Rees that question."

I fell asleep as Mr. Rees tried to whitewash the young Russian. Vladimir was a bright boy and he worried at the diplomat like a dog with a bone.

When I woke, we had stopped. We were almost in the middle of nowhere. There was a single petrol pump and what looked like some sort of inn. Mr. Rees was smoking and Vladimir was not in the car. "Where are we?"

"The Rolls Royce and the armoured car needed fuel. Your men have eaten. Are you hungry?"

I looked at my watch. It was three a.m. "How long until we arrive?"

"We should be there by seven. The roads are quiet and there does not appear to be the trouble the Count anticipated."

"Then I will wait until we arrive. When will the flotilla be arriving?"

"It will take two days for them to reach us. They will sail west first to avoid the Bolshevik's fleet."

"And what do we do until then?"

"The Count will ensure that we have accommodation. He has a great deal of influence in these parts."

Vladimir came back to the car with two loaves. They appeared to be filled with a variety of meats and cheeses. "Here you are gentlemen. Freshly made."

I did not really wish to eat but Vladimir had obviously gone to such great lengths to feed us that I accepted. I had no idea what the meat was and it also had far too many pickles in it for my taste but it was filling. By the time I had finished the sandwich we were approaching civilisation.

"I spoke with the Count. He is confident that General Yudenich will have captured Riga by the middle of the month. That means we have another port."

"Isn't Riga on the way to Reval?"

He nodded, "We passed it while you were asleep. That is how he knows. He spoke with the officers there. The people of the town have no food and with your Royal Navy blockading they cannot be supplied."

I dozed off and awoke again just as we were entering the port. I was bone weary. The car had been comfortable enough but I had been in the car for almost twelve hours. When I got out I looked for the lorries but they were not there. "Where is the Camel?"

Vladimir said, casually, "When we stopped the Count told the drivers that he would not wait for them. He told them that if they were not here by ten then they would be punished."

Bearing in mind that the flotilla would not be here for a couple of days, I thought it excessive. I went to the boot to take out my bags.

Vladimir said, "Wait for the Count to send one of his men over for them, Squadron Leader."

"That is not a problem, Vladimir. Besides my weapons are in here. I am keen to keep a close eye on them."

"As you wish sir." He pointed to a large house, "We are staying there. I will wait for our bags to be brought over."

Like me Mr. Rees was carrying his own bag. He travelled light. He was similar to Mr. Balfour. I suspected there was more to Mr. Rees than met the eye. I think the dapper act was just that, an act to make enemies think he was ineffectual.

He had seen my look at Vladimir's questioning comment. "The Russian mentality takes some getting used to, Squadron Leader." He lowered his voice. "I don't think that our people back home would endure the same treatment that they dish out to those who are at the bottom end of the social ladder. Still we are allies and we must do what we can eh?" He pointed with his stick. "The port is just on the other side of this house. We won't have far to travel when the flotilla arrives."

When we entered the house, the Count was berating a rather well fed man who cowered before the aristocrat. I later learned that he was the owner of the house. "I must apologise, Mr. Rees. This fool has failed to follow my orders and the rooms will not be ready for an hour or so. We will retire to the dining room and I will read these reports." He proffered a sheaf of documents. "At least the fool got that right!"

He swept into the dining room. It was a large one. Burscough Hall had a magnificent dining room but it would have fitted into this one four times! Servants raced to the three of us with bowls of lemon scented water and warm cloths. I was bemused. The count took off his gloves. The servant used a flannel to wash his hands and then dry them. Then he wrapped the warm towel around his face. I had never seen the like. Mr. Rees said, sotto voce, "Just go along with it, eh Squadron Leader? When in Rome and all that."

I did so but I was going to have to be very tolerant. I wondered what my two air crew would make of all this. While the Count read his papers, we were served coffee and freshly baked croissants. Vladimir arrived and sat down between Mr. Rees and the Count. The Count pushed the papers to one side and snapped his fingers. More food was brought in. I recognised some but not all. I had learned, over the years, to save experimentation for those rare times of leisure. I had just arrived in the country and the last thing I needed was an upset stomach. I ate the bread, eggs, cheese and ham followed by fruit. It filled me.

The Count put away a far greater quantity of food than any of the rest of us. He leaned back and lit a long thin cigar. "Things are going well, Squadron Leader; even better than we anticipated. There is however, as you English might say, a fly in the ointment. "Those German aeroplanes have been seen over Narva."

I looked to Mr. Rees who said, "On the border."

"Have they attacked yet?"

"Not yet. The peasants there had never seen an aeroplane before and they became frightened. Superstitious fools. So, you will need to take your aeroplane up as soon as possible."

"They were probably just training with them, sir. It takes many hours in the air to get used to an aeroplane. Besides we can't do anything until the carrier gets here, sir."

He frowned, "Why not?"

"We need a runway. The carrier has one. Even then it is not perfect but as there is no airfield here then we cannot take off until there is a runway. I am sorry, sir."

"I was led to believe that this weapon was unbeatable. You are saying it is not so?"

"I am saying, sir, that once in the air, the four aeroplanes we have can knock out any enemy aeroplane that the Bolsheviks have."

"Good!"

"However, they can be shot down, sir. If the guards at the border had opened fire and if the aeroplanes had been low enough then they might have caused some damage. But, as you say, they had never seen an aeroplane and panicked."

"I see. Well your ships will be here some time tomorrow." He yawned. "I will go to bed." Leaning forward he said, "I would stay close to the house if I were you. There may be some Bolsheviks unaccounted for in the town. General Yudenich has had most of them shot but one never knows."

"Where will my men sleep when they arrive?"

He looked surprised at the question. Shrugging he said, "With their vehicles? Surely, they will have to guard your aeroplane! I would not wish anything to happen to it."

With that he turned and left. I looked at Mr. Rees, "I cannot believe that man."

"Ssh, Squadron Leader. Keep your voice down. The walls have ears." He looked pointedly at Vladimir who was still eating.

"My men will be exhausted. They cannot sleep in the vehicles. I would not ask it of them."

He nodded, "But the Count is right. Your aeroplane is the most powerful one for a thousand miles. It must be protected."

"And it will be. I will share my room with my men. We will each stand a duty and guard the aeroplane."

Vladimir showed that he had been listening, "But you are an officer!"

"And a good officer never asks his men to do something that he is not willing to do. If the Count is right, then I will have to keep watch on the camel too."

The lorries arrived an hour after the Count had retired. Poor Bert and George looked like death after they climbed down from the two lorries. "I wouldn't want to do that again in a hurry, sir. The seats were rock hard and there was no suspension at all. I am ready for a bite to eat and then get my head down."

I waved the sergeant and George closer. I explained the situation. Bert nodded philosophically but George said, "Sir, that's not right!"

"Baker we are all in the service and we are British. Now you volunteered for this. We will make the best of it. Vladimir will take you to my room. You can sleep there. Sergeant, you will relieve me in six hours. Baker you will relieve the Sergeant six hours after that. Six hours on and twelve hours off. It is just until the flotilla gets here tomorrow. Then I will get us accommodation on the Vindictive."

They nodded and saluted. Baker said, "Sorry sir, I was out of order. I have a big mouth and I need to learn to think before I speak."

"You do indeed, Baker, and you are not on a charge as I put it down to tiredness but don't let it happen again."

"No sir."

I wandered over to the lorries as Vladimir took them into the house. Mr. Rees had been watching me. "You are a tolerant officer,

Squadron Leader. Are you certain that you have no Bolshevik tendencies?"

"I came through the ranks, sir. I understand what they are feeling. Don't worry, if I need to become heavy handed then I will be. Horses for courses. These two lads will be keeping me in the air. I need them on my side."

He yawned, "Very well. I shall get some sleep too. When I wake, I will keep you company. Until then Vladimir will fill in for me."

"He doesn't need to. I am happy to do it alone."

"You don't speak the language. Humour me, Squadron Leader. This is all moving slightly faster than Mr. Balfour and Mr. Churchill intended. We all need to sing from the same hymn sheet."

By the time Vladimir returned I had checked the canvas and nothing had either come loose or been lost. "Mr. Rees says I am to wait with you, Squadron Leader."

"Then let us make it productive. I want to learn some Russian."

Surprisingly he looked pleased, "Really?"

"Of course. This is your country and I should make the effort. Besides it will stop us becoming bored."

It proved to be quite enjoyable. I made sure that the words and phrases he taught me were pertinent to my role. I did not need to know how to ask for a cup of tea! I appeared to have an ear for languages. I had no idea how that came about but it meant I made rapid progress and young Vladimir was impressed. When Mr. Rees returned a few hours later I said, as he approached, "Let's keep the lessons our secret. I would like to surprise Mr. Rees and the Count."

"Of course."

I felt slightly deceitful for I intended to use my new-found knowledge to listen to the Count as he spoke to his inferiors.

"Not tired yet, Squadron Leader?"

"No sir. Young Vladimir was delightful company."

"He is desperate to serve alongside the Count."

"I know and I have been keeping him safe with me."

"Safe?"

"The Count's confederates and aides have a habit of getting themselves killed. The Bolsheviks have a price on his head. Those four bodyguards are just the latest. Last month the other four he had threw themselves in front of him to save themselves from a grenade."

"They are loyal."

"Their loyalty comes at a price. If he is hurt, he will have their families imprisoned. All of them work on his estates. He can be quite ruthless but he brings many soldiers to fight against the Bolsheviks. London wishes him safe."

"I see. Well at least I shall be out of his sight when I am on Vindictive."

"Perhaps. Rear Admiral Alexander-Sinclair has also had run ins with him. You heard about the sabotage on the carrier?" I nodded. "The Count was convinced it was members of the crew. He advised the Rear Admiral have them flogged until he found out who they were. That did not go down well."

"Did the Admiral find out who it was?"

"He did. It was Bolshevik dockyard workers in Memel. That is why he relocated to Finland. He felt it was safer. I agree with him. Your Camel will be safer on board the Vindictive."

"There is nowhere else we could have her, sir. There is neither airfield not hangar!"

"I think, Squadron Leader, that you are a victim of your own success. The exploits of the Royal Flying Corps, taking off and landing from little more than farm fields made Mr. Balfour assume that you could land anywhere. That and the escapes you had in France gave you a certain reputation." He nodded, "I have read your record. It is impressive. You have a long career ahead of you."

I shook my head, "I am not sure about that."

Sergeant Hepplewhite woke me as soon as the flotilla arrived. "Sir, sir, the fleet is here! The carrier is tying up."

"Right, get our gear from the room and take it to the lorries. I will get Vladimir and Mr. Rees. We will get the Camel, and us, aboard, as soon as possible."

He grinned, "And not before time either sir. It has been hard sneaking around this house, like!"

"Sorry about that, Sergeant, but the Count has his rules."

"And those bodyguards of his, they make my skin crawl. Steer clear of them, sir. They are nasty pieces of work. I heard them with the servant girls… it wasn't right sir."

I had to agree with the sergeant. Alexei, Igor, Ivan and Boris were thoroughly unpleasant. They were not soldiers, they were thugs. I had never seen their like in the British Army. They were a new phenomenon for me.

I woke Vladimir. "Get the lorry drivers and have them drive the aeroplane around to the quay. The carrier is here."

He was up in a flash, "Really, Squadron Leader? And will I be allowed on board?"

"As Mr. Rees and I will be aboard then so shall you!"

There was an infectiously happy mood amongst us all. I had been on tenterhooks the whole time I was with the Count. I was afraid of upsetting him. I was not worried about me but I was aware that I represented Britain. I would not be the one to break the accord. I know now that I should have told the Count that the flotilla had arrived but he was asleep and I did not relish getting by his guards. Nor did I wake Mr. Rees. He had spent more hours awake than even I had. The Count was very demanding.

I clung to the running board of the lorry as the drivers drove around to the quay. The flotilla was made up of C- Class cruisers and W- Class destroyers. Vindictive had been a C-Class cruiser before she had been converted. However, the flight deck made her look completely different.

"Sergeant get the ropes off the Camel. I will go and see about getting her aboard."

I almost ran to the side of the carrier. The gangplank was just being lowered. Two marine sentries stood there with rifles at the ready. A young sub-lieutenant came down the gangplank, "Squadron Leader Harsker?"

"Yes."

"Sub Lieutenant Nash. If you would like to come aboard, the Captain wishes to speak with you before the others arrive."

"I have an aeroplane needs bringing aboard."

"Yes sir, Chief Petty Officer Ashcroft will go ashore and help your men. They are just rigging the crane up."

I followed him up the steps. At the top the two marine sentries there saluted as well. "Are you expecting trouble, Lieutenant?"

"Since the sabotage the Captain is ultra-cautious sir. You only have two men, is that right?"

"Yes, a sergeant and a mechanic."

"Good, Captain Parr does not like too many new faces."

There was palpable tension on the carrier as I was taken to the Captain's cabin. There was a marine sentry on duty at the door to his cabin. His eyes flickered to my uniform for a moment and then returned to stare at a spot on the wall.

The Sub Lieutenant knocked, "Come."

As we entered the young officer said, "Squadron Leader Harsker sir."

"Thank you, Nash. Have my steward bring us some tea eh?"

When the door closed, he said, "Take off your coat Squadron Leader." I did so. The cabin was warm. "Rum do this."

I was aware that the Navy had been, in effect, told what to do by the Count and the Navy never enjoyed that. "Sorry about this, sir. The Count is a strong-minded man."

"I know. Still it will give my young pilots something to keep them occupied. They are desperate for action."

The Steward arrived with the tea. "Put it down there, Barker." The Captain poured the tea. I could see he enjoyed his from the smile on his face. "Ah that's better. Helps a man to think, what? So, the problem is the Bolshevik fleet. The Rear Admiral is a little worried about their guns." He leaned forward. "Between you and me he intends to wait to speak with the Count on board the flagship. That is why I am having a talk with you now."

"Thank you, sir. At the moment, we can do nothing anyway. My riggers have to assemble the aeroplane. The Count does not seem to understand that. He appears to be a man who thinks that simply because he wishes it then it will happen."

"You will find many White Russians are like that. Our other problem is sabotage. I am afraid that we have a great deal of security. As soon as your Camel is on board and we have taken on coal then we shall moor out in the bay. It is a tricky little port. There is a reef out there to catch the unwary. If the Count, or anyone, wishes to speak with us they will come out on the tender."

I smiled. The Count would hate that. "And I will need to be able to practise take offs and landing."

"Of course. You were land based."

I nodded, "How many aeroplanes do you carry sir?"

"We can carry up to twelve although that would make us a little overcrowded but we just have three at the moment. Yours makes four. The rest will be coming in Spring. The new commanding officer for the squadron will be taking over. Major Donald. He is in England at the moment training the new pilots." I nodded. "He is a little old fashioned. He does not like the new titles. A good chap though."

"I'm sure." I put the cup down. "The thing is, sir, the Count is anxious to attack these German aeroplanes as soon as possible. The reason I had been foisted upon you is for that purpose; to destroy the enemy air force before it can hurt you."

"Aeroplanes would find it hard to attack a fleet, Squadron Leader."

I nodded, "I am not familiar with ships sir but I believe that these cruisers have their armour on the waterline and at the sides and turrets." He nodded. "So, a bomb dropped on the deck would only have, what, an inch or so of armour?"

"Actually, we have a wooden deck but the main deck has an inch of armour."

"The three aeroplanes you have on board can carry a total of three hundred and ninety pounds of bombs. They could destroy one of your ships easily. I believe that your main armament and secondary armament is designed to stop ships. The aeroplane has not yet been used to attack ships but one day…"

"I see. Most illuminating. So, it would appear that we need you to destroy the enemy aeroplanes. When I see the Rear Admiral, I will present your most persuasive arguments to him."

"I take it he is not keen on the idea?"

"He and the Count have had words. The Rear Admiral is no diplomat. They parted on bad terms." He finished his tea. "Well you will want to meet your men and get your aeroplane aboard, I take it?"

"Aeroplane first and then I shall meet the officers and crew."

He went to a voice pipe on the wall. "Sub-Lieutenant Nash to the Captain."

The officer must have been waiting nearby for he was there within a couple of seconds. "Mr. Nash will offer any help and advice you may need. He is the coordinating officer for the aeroplanes. Mr. Nash when the Squadron Leader's gear comes aboard show him where he will be billeted."

"Sir."

As he led me through the labyrinth of corridors to the main deck he said, "I saw the V.C. on your chest sir. Did you meet the King?"

"I have met him twice."

"Gosh, sir, what an honour." He looked wistfully at my medals as he stood aside to allow me to go up the ladders first, "I don't think they will give many medals out for this little action sir."

"Why not, Mr. Nash?"

"If this was important then we would have a battleship with us, the Warspite or one of her sisters. The Bolshevik ships would be blown out of the water by her guns."

"Mr. Churchill does not wish this to be a full-blown war. If it is any consolation to you, Mr. Nash, I never tried to win a medal. They just came because I was doing my duty. Do your duty, that is all that may be asked of any officer."

"Sir."

We had reached the flight deck. I realised that I would have to learn the route myself. I could not be reliant on the young officer all the time. I looked for my Camel and I could not see her.

"Where is the Camel?"

He pointed to the stern and two derricks. "There is a hangar below the decks, sir. They will be there. This is the fastest way to get to the hangar. The alternative is to go through the ship and that means negotiating crowded corridors. Unless we are launching or retrieving aeroplanes this is the quickest way. Of course, if we are in the North Sea and there is a gale blowing then this is the most dangerous place to be." He pointed. "No guard rails."

By the time we reached the hanger I saw that my two fitters were unpacking the Camel. There were some R.N.A.S standing and watching. They saw me and saluted. I said, "Sergeant, do you need any help?"

My two fitters were both tired and would not normally ask for help. However, Sergeant Hepplewhite nodded, "A little would not go amiss, sir."

I pointed to the other fitters, "If you chaps would give my men a hand."

They looked at Sub Lieutenant Nash. I walked over to them. "I am sorry that was not a request. Until Major Donald arrives I am in charge of the aerial element of this carrier. I am your commanding officer and when I shout jump you say 'how high?' Clear!" I used the voice I had used when a sergeant. I saw a wry smile on Sergeant Hepplewhite's face.

The fitters all roared, "Sir, yes sir!"

One said, "What can we do Sarge?"

I turned to Sub Lieutenant Nash, "I think we can go to my cabin now and then I shall meet my officers and sergeants." I pointed to one of the fitters who was standing with his hands on his hips watching events. "You, pick up my luggage and bring it along!"

"Sir!"

I had not asked for this command but if I had been given the duty then I would do just that; command!

Chapter 3

I did not bother to unpack. I had too much to do. I dumped my greatcoat on top of the luggage and felt my cheeks. I really needed a shave but it was more important to meet the men I would be leading. "Now, Lieutenant, if you would take me to meet my men eh? Then you can toddle off and catch up with your other duties. I have taken up too much of your time as it is."

"Oh no, sir. I am attached to you for the duration of your stay. The captain is keen for me to work with you."

"What do you normally do, Mr. Nash?"

"I am operations officer for the squadron, sir."

"Have you flown?"

"Not yet sir but I hope to."

My heart sank. They had given me an officer with no flight experience to organize and support our operations. He might be keen as mustard but someone who understood aeroplanes would have helped. This was not a good start. "Right, then lead on MacDuff."

He spoke as he walked. "We have an operations room, sir. Well, we call it that. It is a room with a blackboard and I thought we might use it for briefings and that sort of thing. We haven't used it yet. The crews are waiting there."

It was a cosy operations room. The six men who were already in there almost filled it. I had no idea how they would cope with twelve aeroplanes and their crews. They jumped to attention as I entered. "At ease, smoke if you wish."

As they took out cigarettes and pipes I saw that they were all very young. I would say most had enlisted in the last years of the war straight from school. I sat on the edge of the desk and realised, as I look into their eyes, that they were in awe of me. When did I change? It did not seem five minutes since I had been a young air gunner looking up to Lord John and the other pilots. Now I was the one they saw as someone to emulate. The war had changed me. There was no going back.

"You know who I am, Squadron Leader Harsker. I am not your permanent commanding officer; that is Major Donald. I will not try to change you into Royal Air Force pilots. What I will do, is teach you how to fight German aeroplanes flown by Bolsheviks and I will try to keep you alive. Now that you have your smokes going I will light my own pipe and you can introduce yourselves."

I used the pipe to give me time to observe them unobtrusively. I would learn much in the next pipeful of Captain Hesketh's rum soaked tobacco. Flight Lieutenant Greaves spoke first and that told me that he was the most confident. His voice raced along like a German machine gun. He even introduced his air observer too. I saw a wry smile from Andy Hood, his observer. He knew his pilot. That told me they were a good team.

Peter Rogers was a confident pilot. He waited until his comrade had spoken and then introduced himself. He had a measured and calm voice. I noticed that he smoked a pipe. He was composed while Greaves was excitable. He allowed his air observer and gunner, John Charlton, to introduce himself. He reminded me of Lumpy. Rotund and northern. His flat vowels made him sound, somehow reliable.

Lieutenant Robert Newton was the most nervous of the three and, I could clearly see, the youngest. He had an almost shy look to him. He reminded me of a skittish deer on Lady Mary's estate. His observer, Ralph Hunt was the one I took an instant dislike to. He had a sneer on his face as his pilot spoke and when he introduced himself he did so arrogantly. He bordered on the impertinent. I put that to the back of my mind. I would deal with relationships later on.

"Thank you for that. What you need to know is that I was an observer and gunner before I became a pilot. I flew the Gunbus. So, I know the problems that both pilots and gunners will have. What I have little experience of is using bombs. I have used them but not enough to be confident about them. Nor have I any experience in landing or taking off from a ship. I will need advice from the three of you for that."

Harry Greaves asked, "When will we be operating in the air then sir? We have just been sat around since we arrived in the Baltic."

"As soon as possible. One advantage we have of using a carrier is that we might be able to take off and land while the Bolsheviks are grounded. So long as the sea is calm and the deck clear of ice then we can take off. I intend to use every advantage we have. My

Camel is the only one which is superior to the kites the Bolsheviks are using. However, as my bus is still being built and rigged, that is a moot point. Speaking of which, who is in charge of the fitters and riggers?"

Air Observer Hunt said, lazily, "We call them Air Mechanics sir."

I smiled but it was a cold smile intended to worry the arrogant young man. "And I call them whatever I choose. I have been flying for four years now." I allowed a silence to fall and waited until his head dropped. "Lieutenant Nash, who is in charge of the fitters and riggers?"

"That would be Chief Petty Officer Banks sir. He is in sick bay at the moment."

"Oh, and why is that? Is he ill?"

"No sir, he was injured when the ship was sabotaged. He has a broken arm."

I saw now why there was such heightened security. "I shall visit him then. He is vital. We need well maintained aeroplanes. The Baltic appears to be a very inhospitable place as it is." My pipe had gone out and so I laid it down. "What I intend for the next hour or so is to take you through the German aeroplanes and their abilities. After we have had some lunch we will go through tactics. When we do begin operations, we will all be of one mind."

With the exception of Hunt, they were all attentive and interested. I would have to speak with him before the afternoon session. I went through the aeroplanes that we would be fighting. I knew all of their characteristics. While on the freighter, I had had time to make notes on them to refresh my memory. I spoke of how we might defeat them in the air using the Sopwiths' strengths. Once again, five of them were attentive and scribbling notes while Air Observer Hunt appeared to be doodling. I even saw Sub-Lieutenant Nash frowning. As the time for lunch drew closer I wound up my talk.

"Well done chaps. That was a good session. Of course, it was only theory and the real thing will be just that, real. You will have to make instant decisions in the air. That is why you need this knowledge in your heads. I must cram into them what it has taken me four years to learn. We shall head for lunch." They all rose. "Air Observer Hunt, I would like a word, if you please." Sub-

Lieutenant Nash and Lieutenant Newton both hesitated. "No, gentlemen, go with the others. I am certain that Air Observer Hunt will escort me safely to the mess."

When they had gone, he faced me, truculently, "I haven't done anything wrong sir!"

"I haven't said, yet, that you have. However, I do not like your tone for a start. I am a senior officer and you will to speak to me as such. If you do not then I will have you on charges. I think I need to explain a few facts of life to you. How long is it since you joined up?"

"Six months sir."

"You worked before you joined?"

He shook his head, "I was at University sir. I left."

"Do you mind me asking you why?"

"My business, sir."

"Of course." I would not let that lie and I intended to return to it later. "You wanted to be a gunner and observer?"

He shook his head, "I wanted to be a pilot."

"But..." I allowed an uncomfortable silence to fill the room. I watched him squirm.

"But I was not good enough. I failed the entrance and they put me in the course for observers."

"Which you resent. Well let me tell you, young man, that there is nothing wrong with being a gunner. It is how I started out. But I think there is more to it than that. I think you left University because it didn't suit. It was not what you expected. You look to me like the kind of young man who sailed through school without having to stretch yourself and you were found out when you were expected to do some real work. I am guessing that they asked you to leave. You probably made up some story for your parents and they felt sorry for you." He coloured and I knew that my bullets had gone home. "You are an only child and your mother was quite old when she had you." I said it as a statement and not a question.

He suddenly looked at me accusingly, "How did you know sir?"

"Simple, you are spoiled. You are used to getting your own way. When you don't then the toys come out of the pram. Now, all things being equal I would have you sent back to England with a report to have you dismissed from the service." He looked shocked. "But I can't as that would leave us one aeroplane short and I need every aeroplane I can get. So, starting now, you change your attitude. You will be attentive and you will make as many notes as the others. You will speak to officers with respect. Is that clear?"

"Yes sir."

"And one more thing; you will show Mr. Newton, in particular, more respect. If you do not, then I will have you on a charge! Believe me, Hunt, I am your worst nightmare. I know every wrinkle and dodge in the book. I served with some of the finest soldiers in the British Empire but I have met enough of your type to know how to deal with them. Now let's get to lunch and you had better hope that you have not spoiled my appetite!"

Lunch was pleasant. I recognised the food. Hunt was subdued but the others were full of questions about my time on the Western Front. I realised that these must have all been in training in the last year of the war. The end, when it had come, had been quicker than people had thought. The Germans seemed to collapse. These boys would have expected to fight in France and, instead, they had been sent to this frozen wilderness at the edge of the world.

I called in at the hangar to see how the work was going. They had done well. Sergeant Hepplewhite seemed quite happy with the progress and with his new colleagues. He was actually smiling. "Had a nice bit of lunch sir. Proper stuff. Not like the muck they have been serving us!"

"Sergeant, the food was adequate."

"Perhaps." He did not seem convinced. "The young Russian gentleman stayed for a while sir but the sentries wouldn't let him aboard and so he left to find Mr. Rees."

"That was my fault, Sergeant, I should have made arrangements myself. You have quarters?"

"Yes sir. There is a whole mess for air mechanics. With just four aeroplanes we are rattling around in it but what will happen when the other aeroplanes get here is anyone's guess."

"Well let me know when she is ready to fly. Oh, and we shall be setting sail as soon as we have taken on coal."

"I reckon we got our sea legs on the freighter sir. We'll be alright."

The air crew were waiting for me in the operations room. I sat on the edge of the table once more. I would need the blackboard to illustrate my points. "I will need to assess each pilot and discover what their strongest qualities are. We do not have the luxury of large numbers. Until I have seen you all in combat we will have to use a set plan and keep to it. I intend to use a four finger flight."

"Four fingers sir?"

"Yes, Mr. Greaves," I held up my hand. "You see how the fingers are. One sticks up more than the rest and one is tucked at the back. That is our system. I will be the longest finger. Mr. Greaves will fly to my right. Mr. Newton to my left and Mr. Rogers will be behind Mr. Newton to the left, the shortest finger. This means that when we attack we will bring five guns to bear. More importantly we will have the rear protected by three Lewis guns."

"But how will we maintain that formation in combat, sir?"

"Not easy, Mr. Rogers, in fact, downright impossible. Unless we manage to shoot them all down in our first pass then we will have to turn. In such a situation, I will bank right with Mr. Greaves watching my back and Mr. Newton will turn left with Mr. Rogers protecting his back. Your aeroplanes can turn inside the enemy. The one which can turn inside you is the Fokker Triplane. It is small and it is nippy."

"The Red Baron flew one."

"He did."

Lieutenant Rogers said, quietly, "You shot him down once, didn't you sir?"

I nodded, "Yes but that was some months before he was killed. How did you know?"

"I am a great reader, sir, and my great uncle is Colonel Pemberton-Smythe."

"My old commander!"

"Yes sir. He told me all about you. If I am honest I wanted to be like you. The war ended too soon for that."

"There are thousands of soldiers who would disagree with you on that!"

"Quite sir, I apologise that was a glib and thoughtless comment."

"Let's get back to the matter at hand. Air combat. The secret of winning is to use short bursts and at the closest range possible. The Vickers is the most reliable machine gun I have ever used. You might think that two hundred and fifty rounds are ample. They are not. The Lewis gun has less ammunition. You gunners need to be even more sparing." I tapped my service revolver. "I have used this in the air before now as well as a Lee Enfield. I have flown with Mills Bombs which I have dropped on aeroplanes as well as on the ground. As I recall I have managed to destroy an enemy in the air with one." They all laughed. "The point is you never have enough weaponry and when you are heading towards each other at a combined speed of over two hundred miles an hour then life and death are measured in seconds and inches."

The rest of the afternoon was spent in the minutiae of flying combat. Even Air Observer Hunt paid attention and made notes. Perhaps my words had got through to him. I hoped so. The ship began to move away from the quay as I was finishing my talk.

"Well gentlemen, I think I will end there. I am fairly tired and I think I have filled you with enough information to start with. As soon as my aeroplane has been assembled and checked I intend to practise some take off and landings. Once I have mastered that then we begin to practise manoeuvres. Study the notes I gave you. If you fail this test, then I fear that the result might be more serious than failing a test at school. This one could cost you your life. Air combat is unforgiving!"

After they had gone out Sub-Lieutenant Nash said, "You shot down the Red Baron?"

"I forced him to land yes. And I met him!"

"Really sir. Do tell me more."

"Can we save that for after dinner one night? I was not joking about being tired."

"Of course, sir. I forgot about your journey here. Oh, and before I forget, to welcome you tonight, it is number 1s that we will be wearing."

"Thank you for that Subbie! I owe you one."

I went to my cabin first and unpacked. This was where I missed Bates. He would have done this for me. My Number 1 uniform would have been sponged and pressed. Then I took my shaving gear and, grabbing a towel, I headed down for the showers. Number 1s meant I had to be dressed and groomed as an officer and a gentleman. At the squadron, we had just reserved our best for the King's birthday and special occasions. I did not think that my arrival merited such attention.

Before I left for the mess I scribbled a few lines to Beattie. She and Tom would have had Christmas without me. I wondered if she had gone to Burscough? Lady Mary and my family would have welcomed her. On the other hand, she was very close to Alice, my little sister. London might be an attractive prospect. As I put the letter away I knew with total certainty what Beattie would have done. She would have gone with Alice and Tom to Burscough. Christmas was for families. She would have taken Tom to see his grandparents and they would have loved it. For some reason that made me happy. I might have missed Christmas but they would have had a wonderful one and I knew that they would have all spoken of me and my omission. It was as I entered the mess that I realised the date. It was New Year's Eve. I had been guilty of arrogance. The Number 1s were nothing to do with me. It was to celebrate the New Year. That too made me feel better and I entered the mess feeling hopeful for the first time in many days.

The next morning, I had a relatively clear head. My pilots and Lieutenant Nash would be suffering. They had over indulged. It would do no harm. We would not be flying for a day or so. I allowed them time to recover with a coffee in the briefing room and I went to visit the Chief Petty Officer in the sick bay. Petty Officer George Banks was in his forties. He had one arm in plaster but the other hand, I could see, had the tell-tale oil and grime that marked a true mechanic.

He tried to stand and salute, "Petty Officer, as you were. This is just a courtesy visit. I have taken over the squadron temporarily and I want to introduce myself. Squadron Leader Harsker."

"It is a privilege, sir. I have heard of you. I was in the Corps before I transferred. I never thought I would get to meet you." He held up his broken wing. "I am sorry about this."

"Can't be helped. Sabotage wasn't it?"

"Yes sir. They wanted the aeroplanes disabled. I was checking over the hangar and I tripped one of their booby traps. It could have been worse. I just broke my arm. If it had been the next day we might have lost a bus sir. As we had no aeroplanes flying that wasn't a problem. Then you arrived, sir and I was stuck here."

"I have two good fitters and riggers with me, Petty Officer. I would rather you got well."

"Can you have a word with the M.O. sir? I might not be able to work but I can keep an eye on those who like to slope off for a tab when they can."

It was like listening to Flight Sergeant Lowery. "Of course. Now you know that we will have to fly soon?"

"Yes sir. Don't worry. We have anti-freeze and oil which operates at low temperatures. The problem might be the Vickers."

"The water freezing, you mean?" The Vickers was water cooled.

"Yes sir."

"I have thought about that. We need to rig blankets over them. Even if we have to discard them once we start firing it will be worth it."

His face beamed, "Good idea, sir!"

"I began my life as a mechanic and gunner. I think about these things."

"Well sir, the young gentlemen are all fine fliers but they are gentlemen. They have not got the first clue what keeps them in the air. And they do not like to get their hands dirty."

"I will go and see the M.O. now but promise me you will not overdo things."

"I will, sir. If I stay here much longer sir I shall need a padded cell!"

"Right."

The Medical Officer was quite happy to oblige and I had a spring in my step as I went to the hangar. The Camel was taking shape. Sergeant Hepplewhite grinned, "Tomorrow sir, we will fill her up with go-go juice and turn her over."

"Then I will take her up in the afternoon, Sergeant."

His face fell, "But suppose she isn't ready, sir?"

"Then it will be the morning after, Sergeant, but, one way or another, I will have to take her up and fly her."

"Sir." He turned to his men. "Right you horrible shower. I want to see you working like Trojans! Get to it!" The sergeant had a colourful turn of phrase but I saw them nod and grin. He had their measure.

When the air crew finally made the operations room, I was ready to begin going through what we had learned. We were interrupted by a messenger from the Captain. "The Captain would like to see you sir, now."

"Righto. If you chaps would like to talk about what we have learned. Tomorrow I fly and the day after we all fly. Test time!" I used those words deliberately for they had all recently been at school and knew the value of a test.

The Captain smiled when I entered, "I hear you have shaken the fliers up a little."

"Sir?"

"Lieutenant Nash was impressed with your approach and told me of your methods. I approve. Now this evening we are off to the flagship. The Rear Admiral wishes to meet you. Count Fydorervich has also requested the meeting. He and Mr. Rees will be in attendance." My face must have shown my feelings. "Is there a problem, old chap?"

"It is the Count. I fear he will make demands on the Rear Admiral. He seems to think that this will be easy; send over our aeroplanes, destroy the enemy and then he takes Petrograd."

"But the Bolshevik Fleet?"

"Exactly sir. Still it does not affect what I have to do. I intend to fly from the ship tomorrow. Will that be possible, sir?"

"Should be. We are coaled and all we need to do is to turn into the wind. What time?"

"Better make it early afternoon."

"I will check with the navigator and see what the weather will be like. My launch will take us over at 1800 hours. Number 1s again I am afraid."

"No problem sir, although we will all be overshadowed by the Count. His tailor must work for Gilbert and Sullivan."

"As bad as that?"

"Worse sir. If he has earned all the medals he has worn then we are talking about Hercules reborn and he has more gold braid than… let us just leave it at that eh sir?"

"I am looking forward to meeting this man. You and the Rear Admiral appear to share a common opinion of him."

The flagship, H.M.S. Cardiff, was the same class of cruiser, the Hawkins C class, as the Vindictive. It meant I would be familiar with the layout. The difference was the lack of 7.5 inch guns. The Captain and I were the first to arrive. Captain Parr was anxious that we speak with the Rear Admiral before the others arrived. His Flag Lieutenant ushered us into the ward room.

The Rear Admiral had led the cruisers which had first encountered the Germans at Jutland. He had also led the surrendered German fleet into Scapa Flow in 1918. He was no-one's fool. He shook my hand. "I have heard a great deal about you. You had a good war."

"As did you, sir, but there are many men I served with who might disagree about the good part."

His face crinkled into a smile, "Quite. You have successfully put me in my place."

"Sorry sir I…"

He waved a hand as the steward came over with some pink gins. "No, you are right. Apart from the battle of Jutland, we saw little action. That was not our choice, of course, and Jutland meant you either survived as I did, or went to the bottom like the poor chaps in Queen Mary and Indefatigable."

"Yes sir, the Squadron Leader has some interesting views on how strong our ships might or might not be."

"Really Captain Parr? Go on."

"The Squadron Leader thinks that our ships might be vulnerable to air attack."

"Explain Squadron Leader."

"Simple really sir. The armour on ships is mainly at the side. Ships fight broadside to broadside. You rarely get plunging shot. Perhaps that was what sank the battle cruisers but I know that I could drop a bomb vertically. Imagine one down a funnel sir."

Raising his glass the Rear Admiral said, "Cheers." We raised our glasses. "You may have something there, you know. I often wondered why our ships just blew up. This could be an interesting dinner. Now before this Count arrives I would like it from the horse's mouth, so to speak. In your opinion, what do you think we need to do, Squadron Leader? And I would appreciate honesty. Do not be afraid of upsetting me eh? I don't bite." He grinned, "Although I do bare my teeth now and again."

"Realistically sir, we need do nothing. At least not yet. The German aeroplanes the Bolsheviks have acquired are not very good. Major Donald will bring the rest of the squadron over in Spring and they should be able to easily deal with them. Even if they do train their pilots the ones they have do not carry enough bombs to damage the flotilla. The ones that could carry a bomb only carry one or two. Like you, sir, I am reluctant to risk young pilots on a hazardous and, in my view, unnecessary attack." He nodded. "However, the Count wishes me to attack the Bolshevik aeroplanes and I am under orders from Mr. Churchill to support him and to destroy the aeroplanes."

The Rear Admiral waved over the steward and more pink gins appeared, "I see your dilemma. Your Mr. Rees wants me to sail east so that you can attack them."

"I have studied the maps, sir. You need not get within range of the Bolshevik fleet. If the carrier can launch us when we are fifty miles from Peterhof we have enough fuel to get to our target, shoot up the aeroplanes and return to the ships. The flotilla would not be in danger."

He gave me a shrewd look. "But you and your fliers would be. You would be flying over the Baltic in less than ideal circumstances and then have to find the carrier."

"Yes sir, I am well aware that, unlike an airfield, a carrier does not stay in one place and we are closer to the North Pole which means our compasses might not be as accurate. As I said, Admiral, I am not keen on this operation but I have a plan to carry it out and do so successfully, I hope."

The Rear Admiral tapped my chest, "I can see that you have deserved the medals you have been awarded. You would risk your life but are reluctant to risk the lives of those you lead. Thank you for bringing the Squadron Leader over early, Captain Parr. I now have a much clearer picture." He swallowed off another pink gin. "This Count appears to think that we are his own personal navy. He is in for a rude shock."

The other captains from the squadron arrived and they bombarded me with questions. I was the outsider. This was like Nelson's band of brothers. They had served with the Admiral in the war and had many such dinners. They were easy and familiar with each other. The rough edges had been knocked off so that they melded into one harmonious unit. I answered all their questions as well as I could. I made a point of mentioning those with whom I had served; Archie, Gordy, Ted, Lumpy, Randolph and all the others. As a pilot, awarded medals and honours, it was too easy to be seen as the only one who did anything. However, it was a pleasant gathering. I slowed down my drinking and put my hand over my glass more often than I allowed it to be refilled.

When the Count, Mr. Rees and Vladimir arrived the atmosphere changed. I saw Captain Parr cover his mouth to hide his smile and nod at me when he viewed the Count in his finery. I had not seen him in his own version of Number 1s. He was preceded by a cloud of smoke from his cigar.

I hovered in the background next to Captain Parr. The Count and Mr. Rees made straight for the Rear Admiral. The Admiral was no actor. His face could not disguise his feelings for the Count. His Flag Lieutenant marshalled us to the table. Once there we toasted the King. The Count then insisted that we toast the Tsar. It seemed a little bizarre as he was dead but we did so, out of courtesy more than anything.

The happy buzz of conversation which had pervaded the room was now replaced by the mechanical sound of knives and forks. The only conversation we would hear was from the head of the table.

"So, Rear Admiral, now that you have your British Ace to command your pilots you can sail close to the enemy and destroy their air force."

The Rear Admiral chewed and swallowed before wiping his mouth with his napkin. "I think the Squadron Leader will need time to train and work with his pilots. Besides the weather is inclement."

"Inclement? Or is it that you fear to face the Bolsheviks? When I was at school in England they told me how your navy ruled the world. Perhaps that was a different navy."

The words were ill chosen and the Rear Admiral had had a larger number of pink gins than was wise. "Sir, do not impugn the honour of the navy nor of myself. Take it back."

Mr. Rees showed his diplomatic skills, "I am certain the Count meant nothing Rear Admiral."

The Rear Admiral leaned over and glared at the Count. "I command here, Count. I decide when my carrier will close with the enemy. I have decided that will be when Major Donald arrives with the rest of the squadron and the weather is a little better."

The Count had a strangely superior look on his face. He leaned back and looked pointedly at Mr. Rees. "I think, Count, that can wait for later."

"No, Mr. Rees, I insist. Now is the time." His face had the look of a wolf about to devour a sheep.

"Very well." He took a brown envelope from his inside pocket and handed it to the Rear Admiral. "As a reward for having captured those destroyers and handing them over to the Finns and Estonians you are relieved of the duty of protecting the land of Estonia. Rear Admiral Cowan and the 1st Light Cruiser Squadron are already steaming here. When they arrive, you will be able to leave. H.M.S. Vindictive will be attached to the1st Light Cruiser Squadron for the foreseeable future."

Rear Admiral Alexander-Sinclair nodded, "A reward eh? Count Fydorervich you are an unpleasant and loathsome creature. You have ruined the pleasant atmosphere aboard my flagship. Mr. Rees would you escort your friend from my vessel please. He fouls the air."

The Count stood and his hands went to his waist. His face was livid. He had been insulted. He had no guns but had he had weapons then I fear he would have used them. Mr. Rees said, "Rear Admiral your language is hardly diplomatic."

The Admiral smiled, "Then thank God I am not a diplomat. I can sleep easy at night knowing I did not jump into bed with every jumped up little warlord!"

The Count and Vladimir hurried out. Mr. Rees, shaking his head, followed them. We all looked at the admiral as he spread his hands, "I am sorry, gentlemen, but one has to draw a line in the sand. I am just saddened that Captain Parr and the Squadron Leader will have to stay here when we are gone. Still Tich Cowan is a good chap. He will stand up to the Count too."

I shook my head, "I fear not, Admiral. He will have direct orders from Mr. Churchill. If the squadron was already on its way, then nothing that you said or did would have made a difference."

Realising the truth of my words he slumped in his chair.

Chapter 4

The next few days were busy and I was able to put the acrimonious dinner from my mind. The Camel was made ready and Captain Parr left the flotilla and headed out into open water. The clouds had blown away and left us with a bitterly cold wind. On land, it would have been ideal conditions to fly. At sea, it was not so good. Sub-Lieutenant Nash made the decision that it was not the best conditions to try an untested carrier pilot. There was an irony here that someone who had never flown was advising the most experienced flier. However, I took his advice. My pilots concurred and we had to wait another day before I could fly. That did me no good at all. I was keen to get the first take-off and landing out of the way.

Petty Officer Banks had supervised my sergeant and they were both happy with the aeroplane. The two of them got on and that was a relief. My life, whilst in the air, was in their hands. When I had flown in France I had always had the option of crash landing. Captain Hesketh's words still rang in my ears. A dousing in these seas meant instant death.

Flight Lieutenant Rogers had given me advice. "The take-off is not as bad as the landing. If you time the take off right, then you use the rising bow to give you a little extra lift. The landing, however is a little trickier. That is where the air mechanics come into their own. One of them will have two paddles and he will let you know if you are misaligned. You adjust to his movements. If he waves you off then obey him, sir."

"Of course."

"If the worst comes to the worst there is the rope crash barrier, the lads call it the gallows, at the end of the flight deck."

"I am guessing that makes a mess of an aeroplane?"

"Yes sir. Flight Lieutenant Newton found that to his cost. He hit it on his first landing. Mind you he has been perfect since then."

That explained much. "Right, well as I have never flown this bus before I will go up fully armed and with a full load of fuel."

"All or nothing eh sir?"

"That's about it. Well there is no point in delaying the inevitable. Off into the wild grey yonder eh?"

As I climbed up into the Camel I was grateful that it was not a Strutter. They were bigger, heavier and slower. I had a much better rate of climb. The Camel was as forgiving and perfect an aeroplane as Sopwith had ever made. I saw a look of relief on Sergeant Hepplewhite's face when the engine kicked in on the first turn. The deck seemed to move up and down alarmingly although I had been told that the conditions were almost perfect. I got the thumbs up from Sub Lieutenant Nash.

I would have to use full power while keeping the bus straight on what seemed like a very narrow deck. I was used to a wide-open field! I waited until the bow dipped a little. That meant it would soon rise and I headed down the deck. I wondered if I had gone too early and then saw the bows begin to rise. As the bows came up I soared into the air and I gave a small whoop of pleasure. Once in the air I was in my element. I took her into a steep climb to 18,000 feet. As I had expected it was freezing cold and I saw ice begin to form on the wings and the guns. We had not fitted the blanket yet. I began a dive and, while my guns were unfrozen, I tried a burst with each gun. They were fine. That was always a difficult moment when you fire synchronized guns for the first time. Even a slight problem could tear away your propeller.

Satisfied that the guns worked I then began to do loops and sideslips. I was a little rusty. It had been months since I had flown and longer since I had been involved in any sort of air combat. I wanted to be as one with my new kite. Eventually I headed down to the carrier. I had kept flying loops with the carrier in the corner of my eye. She looked a very small target. I had been told that once they saw I was ready to land they would turn the carrier to facilitate landing. I made a slow shallow approach to give them all the warning they would need. Then I could put it off no longer. I had to land.

I slowed down the engine as much as I could. The stall speed was 50 mph and I kept it at 55. I saw the mechanic. He looked like a bird with his paddles held out. He held them down. I was too low. I raised the nose a little and increased the speed slightly. His arms were level. I kept it at 60 and, when I saw the deck less than a hundred yards away dropped it to 55 again. It was all a case of timing. I had to watch the mechanic, the stern and the bows. More by good luck than good management I hit the deck when it was as flat as it was going to be. I stopped half way along the deck. I saw George and Bert slapping each other on the back.

I climbed out of the cockpit as the mechanics began to push her back to the hangar. I turned to the Petty Officer. "Are the Strutters ready to fly?"

"No sir. They have all been working on the Camel. Sorry sir. They will take the rest of the day to be readied."

I nodded, "Not your fault. Tomorrow it is."

He stroked the Camel as it was wheeled past. "Lovely little bus this is. I wish we had a squadron of them."

"They are my favourite single seater that is for sure. I will go and see the skipper."

Captain Parr was more than happy to sail again the following day. "You and the Strutters are our priority, Squadron Leader. You landed as though you had been doing it all your life."

I shook my head, "Pure luck."

The next morning I gathered my pilots and air crew, along with Sub-Lieutenant Nash, in the operations room. "We will practise my formations today. The navigator tells me we will have this weather until tomorrow and then a storm is forecast. I want us to fly as many sorties as we can. I will take off first. It will give me a chance to see you all take off and I will land last." In the absence of radios, we had worked out hand signals. "You will be fully armed. I want you to practise firing. You all know that signal. I will keep my speed to below your maximum speed. Questions?"

There were none but I could see they were nervous. I was the teacher and this was the first part of their test. I was more confident about the take-off this time and I circled the carrier to watch them take off. Flight Lieutenant Harry Greaves rose steeply into the air after he had taken off. He was eager to join me. Flight Lieutenant Rogers was much more economical. He rose steadily into the air and took longer to reach me. Flight Lieutenant Newton almost pancaked into the sea. He barely got the nose up in time.

I waited for them to join me. Once they were in position I gave them the sign to bank to port. It was a little ragged especially Flight Lieutenant Newton but I was pleased. We banked to starboard and we climbed and descended. Gradually Flight

Lieutenant Newton improved. He became sharper as we went on. Then I ordered them to open fire. I was impressed by the wall of bullets we put up. Next, I had the gunners fire. It was all satisfactory. Finally, I signalled for a barrel roll. It was a tricky manoeuvre but worth a try. To my amazement, they all made it and we were nearly all in formation. I was delighted and I signalled them to land.

Once again Harry Greaves was eager to be the first one to land. Peter Rogers waited until the first Strutter was moved from the flight deck before he landed. He too was cleared away and Bob Newton made his approach. I could see that he would not make it. His wings were not level and he looked too high. When the mechanic waved him off I expected him to gun the motor and make a second pass. He didn't. The mechanic threw himself to the side although the Strutter was too high and he would have been safe. Flight Lieutenant Newton desperately tried to land. He actually got his wheels on the flight deck but he was running out of deck. He was saved by the gallows at the end. I was forced to circle until they could disentangle the Strutter and remove it. Although a disaster it was not a tragedy. I saw the pilot and gunner walk away and the damaged Strutter was pulled to join the other two. It took some time to clear the damaged aeroplane. I had plenty of fuel and I did lazy circles running through the events in my mind.

I climbed out of my Camel after I had landed. I walked towards the pilots. "I am sorry sir...I."

I smiled, "Let's go down to the operations room. I think we could all do with a brew. Well done chaps." I walked over to the air mechanic who had waved off Flight Lieutenant Newton. "Well done Wilson." I turned to the Warrant Officer. "Petty Officer Banks I think Air Mechanic Wilson deserves an extra tot of rum. What do you say?"

He grinned, "Aye, sir. We'll make a sailor of you yet, Squadron Leader."

I went over to Sergeant Hepplewhite and spoke to him. He nodded.

As I headed below decks I was aware that I had treated the incident lightly. It was serious but I did not want either bad feelings or recriminations to ruin the team. I was treating it as an accident. However, I intended to get to the bottom of it.

By the time I reached the operations room Nash had already organized the tea and there was a pot with mugs of steaming tea already poured. A plate of freshly baked shortbread accompanied the tea. "Spot on Sub Lieutenant. Just the job."

Taking my mug of tea and a biscuit I sat. I smiled but I looked at their faces. Greaves looked pleased with himself. Rogers sat next to Newton speaking with him. Hood and Charlton were just happy to have a mug of tea, a biscuit and a cigarette. Hunt had the smug self-satisfied smile he normally wore. It made me want to slap his face just to remove it.

Bert Hepplewhite came in and gave me a piece of paper

"Well that went far better than I might have hoped. The barrel roll was spectacular. How was it all firing at once?"

Harry Greaves said, "If there had been anything in the way of the bullets they would have been destroyed. It was terrific."

I nodded, "And how many bullets did you use, Mr. Greaves?"

"Oh I don't know, probably twenty or so."

I nodded. I looked at the paper Bert had given me, "You used a hundred and ten." His face fell. "Mr. Rogers, forty and Mr. Newton, you did the best, twenty. As for you air gunners. You all used half a drum. I would like you to imagine that you are paying for the bullets you use. That way you will put them to better use."

A seaman knocked on the door. "Message, sir, from the Captain."

"Mr. Nash, would you read it." He took it and I continued. "When we get to take on the Bolsheviks, Mr. Greaves, they will be firing back at you. You need to be patient. Having observed you for the past few days I am guessing that patience is not one of your strong suits."

He had the good grace to accept the criticism with a smile, "You are right, sir. I always haven been eager. I like to be first in everything."

"There is nothing wrong with eagerness but impatience might get you killed. You need to hold your nerve when bullets are coming in the opposite direction. A moving target is always hard to hit so when they are firing at you a slight adjustment in the attitude of your aeroplane can put the enemy gunner off. If you then make sure you are as steady as you can be when you fire, then you have a greater chance of making a kill."

"Sir."

"Yes, Mr. Nash?"

"We cannot fly again today. The weather is deteriorating. The front is coming much faster than we thought. The Captain is heading for Terijoki. The squadron is going there. It is a better anchorage."

"Thank you Mr. Nash. Then that gives us more time to talk about today. I want you all to go to the hangar and speak with your mechanics. Get into the habit. Find out what the flight did to your aeroplane."

Air Observer Hunt snorted, "Wrecked ours would be the assessment I think, sir."

I saw Bob Newton colour. "Hunt would you and Mr. Newton stay behind. I would like a little chat."

Sub Lieutenant Nash was going to stay too but I shook my head. When they had closed the door and left us I took out my pipe and filled it. I needed to be calm. As soon as I had it going I felt calmer. I pointed the stem at Hunt. "I thought that you had heeded my advice but you did not. You and Mr. Newton are a team. You support each other."

"But sir, he nearly got me killed!"

I saw Flight Lieutenant Newton open his mouth to say something and then think better of it. "And when you are in combat it will be Mr. Newton who will save your life. You are his passenger." He looked sullenly at the ground. "Get out of my sight! You annoy the life out of me. I will speak with you later."

"Sir, that is not fair!"

"Son, life is not fair! Get used to it! One more word and you will be on a charge!"

After he had gone I saw the expression on Newton's face. He was terrified. "Another cup of tea, eh Bob? Could you do the honours."

I sat on a chair. I wanted to be on the same level when I spoke to him. He brought the two teas and sat opposite me. He took nervous quick puffs from his cigarette. I held up the pipe. "I never got away with cigarettes, you know Bob. Perhaps it was because my father smoked a pipe, I don't know. There is an art and a ritual to it. You ream and clean the bowl. You pull a cleaner through the stem. You carefully fill it with tobacco; not too tight or it won't draw. Then you use a match." I smiled, "My father always used a spelk from the fire. When it is drawing, you tamp it down with your finger. If you do it right, then a good pipe can last for an hour or more."

He smiled, "I know sir, my grandfather smoked a pipe."

"And it is the same with flying. There is a ritual about it. You check your bus before you take off. You have a set of procedures that you run through and you carry a mental checklist. What went wrong today? Start with the take-off."

"Peter Rogers is a good pilot sir. I saw that Harry rose steeply whereas Peter had a gentle climb. I was trying to copy his take off."

"And that is where you went wrong. You are not Peter Rogers. You know how to take off don't you?"

"Of course, sir."

"Then trust your own ability. Now the landing. What was that all about? You were waved off. You could have killed the Air Mechanic." He was silent. I looked carefully at him. He was the youngest of my pilots and the one who had been at school the most recently. He did not want to speak out of turn. "What did Hunt say?"

His eyes widened like an animal caught in hunter's sights. "How did you know he said anything, sir?"

I smiled. "I have been reading men since 1915. What did he say?"

"As we came in he said I had to make up for the shambles of a take-off."

"And that distracted you."

"Yes sir."

"Why didn't you obey the wave off?"

"He told me to stop being a baby and put the damned aeroplane on the deck!"

"You are an officer."

"Yes sir, but he is clever and knows so much."

I nodded. "I see. Well from now on you are in charge in that aeroplane. He is your observer and he does what you say. Is that clear?"

"Yes sir, but aren't I going to be disciplined? I mean I nearly killed a man and I damaged a valuable aeroplane."

"You made a mistake. They will repair the aeroplane. Now go and have a shower and a walk around the deck. Clear your head. We will have another chat tomorrow."

He looked so grateful. His eyes widened, "Thank you, sir. I won't let you down again."

"Sadly, Bob, when we make mistakes in combat the only person we let down is ourselves because it normally results in our death."

I headed up to the hangar. Peter Rogers was still there speaking with Air Mechanic Jones. I waved him over. "Peter come and take a turn around the deck with me."

"Yes sir."

When we reached the deck, the wind struck us. I wandered over to the turret of the 7.5 and stood in the lee of it so that I could light my pipe. "Hunt and Newton, what is the story?"

"They come from the same town and same school, sir. Hunt was two years above Newton. The captain put them together. He thought it was for the best."

"But you don't?"

"No sir. Hunt is a bully and a damned unpleasant fellow. Sorry sir, but you do want the truth, don't you?"

"Of course, Peter. Always tell me the truth and not what you think I want to hear. Now what kind of pilot is Bob? I saw signs today that he has skills."

"He does sir. He was top of the class at Flight School. It was only when he was put with Hunt that he began to make mistakes."

I nodded and puffed on my pipe. The Baltic was an empty cold sea. The waves were flecked with white and the sea looked almost black. It matched my mood. "I am going to ask you to do something. It is not an order, it is a request and I will not be upset if you refuse."

"Sir."

"What is your gunner like?"

"Jack? Salt of the earth and as reliable as hell. Sorry sir. You could not ask for a better gunner."

"Would you swap him with Hunt?"

He laughed, "You are joking sir?" He saw my face, "Oh, I see sir. Right. I understand now." He smiled, "I can see that leadership is never easy. If I want to be a leader like you someday then I have to learn to make difficult decisions. Of course, sir. Jack is perfect for Bob and I can whip Hunt into shape. I met enough bullies at my school to know how to deal with them."

"Thank you, Peter. I think the disasters of today will prove to be the making of our little flight."

The next day I gathered my crew together and told them of the new arrangement. Hunt look appalled and Newton looked relieved. As a reward and as we had docked in Finland, I gave them leave for the day. There was little we could do anyway. There would be no flying for a few days and the Strutter was still being repaired. I went to see the captain. As he had made the initial pairing I felt obliged to tell him what I had done.

"Of course, you did the right thing. I feel such a fool now. When I put them together your young pilot did not look happy. Now I see why. That explains the crash."

He poured us both a pink gin. "When does the 1st Light Cruiser Squadron arrive, sir?"

"They rounded the Skagerrak this morning. Tomorrow afternoon at the earliest."

"I feel sorry for the Rear Admiral."

"Don't be. He is glad to be going. This is a war which can't be won. You know that. None of us will come out of this with anything worth remembering."

"I think, sir, that was us on the Western Front."

"Quite. Me and my size nines. Putting them in my mouth again!"

"And the Count?"

He smiled, "The Count and Mr. Rees are still in Reval, I am afraid. I suspect that is why we are here so that Rear Admiral Cowans can reap the full benefit of the Rear Admiral's information! Besides it is somewhat safer here than in Reval. The Finns do not like the Bolsheviks, nor the Russians."

"As soon as the weather clears, sir, I would like to practise the take offs."

"Of course, Squadron Leader. Oh, by the by you do know that we are just fifty or so miles from Peterhof here? I daresay you could pop over and have a look see yourself. You seem to me the sort of chap who would do just that."

"You have me right there, sir. I may well just do that."

I went to my cabin and read the reports again. I studied the maps and saw that Captain Parr had given me accurate information. It was just over thirty-eight miles to Peterhof but that would have necessitated flying over the Bolshevik fleet. If I could discover what the airfield looked like, then I could plan better. I then cleaned my weapons. I had had a holster made for my German pistol. I decided to go on deck before dinner and have a practice with my service revolver and my Walther. I warned the deck crew what I was doing. I had one of the sentries drop empty cans in the water and I fired at them as they passed. When I had done that, I went back to my cabin, retrieved the Lee Enfield and took it to the Sopwith. I liked to have it in the cockpit with me. It had saved me before now.

My men took advantage of their leave and did not return for dinner. I ate with Mr. Nash. He was keen to learn more about aeroplanes. "This is the future, sir. Your aeroplanes can fly further than the largest guns can fire. You are right. You could drop bombs and destroy battleships. As far as I know no one else is doing what I do. Captain Parr appointed an officer from the ship. The rest of the carriers, like the Ark Royal, use a pilot or mechanic to do it."

"It might be useful if you could fly Mr. Nash. Then you would appreciate the problems a pilot might face."

"Isn't it awfully hard sir?"

"Actually, if you can drive a car then you can fly. Air combat? Totally different. I know some chaps who are the most marvellous pilots but would not last two minutes in an aerial battle. Next time you are in England have a few lessons eh?"

He beamed, "Thank you, sir. That is splendid advice."

I left the mess and, after fetching my flying coat, took a turn around the flight deck. The wind had dropped and now came the snow. It was a blizzard. It was what they called a white out. At least that was what Mr. Rees told me and I could see why. You could not see your hand in front of your face. One lap was more than enough and I descended to the hangar. I went down the companionway. Slipping silently through the door I discovered that the hangar was empty. I went to the Strutter which had been damaged. It was on the port side of the hangar; the opposite side to my Camel. The repairs were coming on well. They had replaced the propeller and the undercarriage was almost fixed. They were good mechanics. I could not see much because it was dark but it now had the shape of an aeroplane. When it had been brought below decks it had not.

It was as I was walking across to my Camel that I heard the noise. It was the sound of a liquid dripping on to the wooden deck. I paused to identify where it came from. Then I heard a whispered grunt as though someone had hurt themselves. There were no lights. This was not a mechanic working late. I drew my service revolver. The Webley had six bullets and was a handy weapon. It was not, however, as fast as the Walther. It just had a bigger bullet. That might be dangerous in the hangar. If I fired it, I could do some damage to the aeroplanes. I would have to be cautious.

I used the Strutters for cover. I walked stealthily. One of those I was seeking spoke. It was a foreign language and sounded like Russian. An angry voice snapped back. There were two of them. I realised that the smell was that of aeroplane fuel. I had a dilemma. Did I shout to frighten them and risk them throwing a match down or did I try to shoot them? I moved closer; I desperately peered into the dark to try to see them. The movement of one of them gave them away. I saw them. They were close to the engine of my Camel. I saw one of them lay down something that looked like a fuel can. They had soaked my engine and were ready to set fire to it.

They were just twenty feet from me but they were close to the aeroplane. When one turned and seemed to stare at me I could delay no longer. I dropped to one knee and held the gun in a two-handed stance. I would try to wound. I fired two bullets at the one who was not holding the can and then another two at the other. As soon as I had fired I ran up to them. They had both squatted after I had fired. One had a bullet in his knee and a hole in his chest. The other had been hit in the chest by both bullets. They were both dying. The Webley bullet makes a large hole and at that short range they were too easy a target. I saw that the first one I had shot had a lighter. Even dying he was trying to reach for it. I kicked it from his grasp. Although it was dark there was something familiar about him. I took the pistols and knives they had in their belts. The knives were sticky with blood. They had been used recently.

Behind me I heard men running and suddenly the hangar was illuminated as the lights were turned on. Two Marines stood there with rifles at the ready and Petty Officer Banks held his service revolver in his left hand. I looked down at the dying man I had vaguely recognised. He spat at me. It came out as a bloody phlegm. Then he expired. It was then that I knew who he was. He was one of the Count's bodyguards!

"What happened, sir?"

"I am guessing that they were saboteurs. I came down here to have a look at the damaged Strutter and I disturbed them. They have soaked my cowling with petrol."

"Don't you worry sir, we will clean it. The bastards murdered the two sentries. They had their throats cut. You gave these a quick death. I would have made them suffer."

I did not tell them that I recognised one of them. I would save that for Mr. Rees and the Captain.

The Captain and his Master at Arms were heading for the hangar when I emerged. "Did you see anyone else, sir?"

"No. They were trying to sabotage the Camel. I passed the other aeroplanes and I did not see anyone."

The Master at Arms looked relieved, "Sorry about this, sir. It was the snow. The sentries couldn't see that far. I can't speak ill of the dead but their lack of attention has cost them their lives. I will go and check the area again."

Captain Parr shook his head, "He didn't thank you for what you did. I will do. It is lucky you are vigilant."

I lowered my voice, "I know one of them. He was one of Count Fydorervich's bodyguards."

"Are you certain?"

"Yes sir, but it makes no sense. The Count is fighting the Bolsheviks."

"It will be interesting to see his face when we tell him. What is more worrying is how he got here in time to sabotage us. He must have been sent before we knew we were coming here. That means treachery at a higher level than we thought. I think the Rear Admiral will be well out of this. As soon as day breaks I shall go and see him. I had already doubled the guards and ordered a complete embargo on anyone coming aboard. We have raised the gangplank. It does not mean that we cannot be boarded but we cannot be boarded easily and the Master at Arms is mounting a watch on your aeroplanes. Tomorrow we will moor in the bay. My decision to tie up and allow some leave has backfired somewhat and two men have paid with their lives."

My mind was still racing. After returning to my cabin and to calm my thoughts, I added to my letter to Beattie. I would put it aboard the flagship when she sailed.

The snow had stopped by dawn. The flight deck was cleared of snow and the ship got up steam. My officers had bad heads but they still crowded around my table. "You shot them both sir?"

"I did Harry. Had I not done so then the Camel would have been set on fire and the whole of the flight would have been destroyed. I fear this means that their aeroplanes are ready to take to the skies and they are afraid of our four aeroplanes." I smiled, "Take it as a compliment, gentlemen."

"But sir, you shot two men!"

I realised what Harry Greaves was saying, "You will kill men, Mr. Greaves. The only difference will be that you are trying to down their aeroplane and their death is incidental."

Peter Rogers said, quietly, "But you are really saying, sir, that we should think about killing the man behind the yoke."

I nodded, "In many ways it is a kindness. When we first flew, combat took place a couple of hundred feet in the air. If you were hit, then you had a chance to land. If you are hit at ten thousand feet, then you have no chance. And I have seen pilots burned to death. That is not a good way to die. If you are a fighter pilot it is certain that you are going to kill men with your machine guns." I drained my tea. "And if we do knock out the Bolshevik air force then I am certain that the Russians will want us to strafe their troops on the ground."

Flight Lieutenant Newton shook his head, "I am not sure I could do that."

"You would have no choice, Bob. The enemy would be firing at you. You have to get used to the fact that it is kill or be killed."

The attack had a sobering effect on the whole of the flight. It brought their precarious position into perspective. The training was for a purpose. The war they were in was not remote and it had touched them. Even Hunt seemed to change that morning. The Captain went by launch to speak with the Rear Admiral. I gave him my letter to Beattie. He promised me he would put it aboard with the other mail. It was a link to home.

We joined the air mechanics to ensure that nothing on the aeroplanes had been sabotaged. The puddles of blood were being scrubbed by Jones even as we were checking the rigging on the biplanes. The bodies had been taken away but the evidence remained. Each time they came to the hangar they superstitiously avoided stepping on the spot where the two men had died. Even when the mark was eradicated its position was marked in their minds.

The Baltic January 1919

Chapter 5

I did not see the Rear Admiral before he left but I was summoned, two days later, to the new flagship, H.M.S. Caledon. I was taken directly to meet my new commander. Rear Admiral Cowan was not a tall man but he had one of the sharpest minds I ever encountered. His nickname was Tich and he was like a terrier. He almost pounced upon me when I was brought to his quarters, "You are the fellow who shot the saboteurs eh?"

"Yes sir. They were trying to destroy my kite!"

"Good man. Now Mr. Churchill had a long chat with me before I left. Came north especially to see me. He spoke highly of you. He made it quite clear to me that we have to destroy this Bolshevik aerial threat as soon as possible. That means operating in winter."

He stared up at me to watch my reaction, "I know sir. It can be done. Do you mind?" I gestured towards the map on the wall.

"Go ahead."

"We do not need to put the fleet in danger." I pointed to a fort which lay to the north of Kronstadt. "This is Fort Totleben. If you could take the fleet to the north of it, outside the range of its guns, then we could fly to Peterhof and destroy the aeroplanes. We would have to fly over their forts but their guns are designed to stop ships and not aeroplanes. We could use the forts as guidance to get back to the fleet."

"That seems a damned good idea. Why didn't Rear Admiral Alexander-Sinclair use it?"

"I think sir, without speaking out of turn, that the Count's attitude annoyed him. Have you met the Count yet, sir?"

"Not yet but Captain Parr seems to find him annoying too."

"Yes sir, and one of those saboteurs I shot was one of his bodyguards."

"Was he now? I shall allow you to tell him that news when we see him. His reaction will be interesting. You think it can be done?"

"Yes sir."

"So, we wait for a hole in the weather?"

"Yes sir. I intend to fly the route alone first to scout it out."

"Risky, what?"

"Riskier to take the whole flight in. Don't worry, sir, I will risk neither the aeroplane nor my life. I will keep high. We now know they know about the Camel. If they see just one aeroplane, then they won't be worried."

"You know your own business best. It seems damned risky to me in these icy seas. I shall see my captains and tell them what we intend and I will sail east to be ready when the weather breaks."

Four days later and the navigator assured us that the conditions for the next twenty-four hours would be good. We were already on station some twenty miles north of Fort Totleben. Petty Officer Banks and Sergeant Hepplewhite had gone over my bus to ensure that she was perfect. They had rigged a cover for the Vickers. I would just have to undo two buckles and flip it to the side when I wished to use it. Having had to change a Lewis magazine while flying before, this was no trouble. It would mean that we could reuse it. I made sure the camera was secure and then nodded for the propeller to be spun. The clouds were high as I took off and banked to begin my climb to ten thousand feet.

I saw Setrorestsk in Bolshevik Russia to the east. I headed directly over Fort Totleben. They had no weapons which could fire at me. I then headed due south. My plan was to fly over the middle fort of the seven which protected Petrograd from attack. By heading south from there I would reach the coast and Peterhof. I was glad that I had my flying coat, helmet, flying boots and fur lined gloves for it was freezing. I kept rubbing my nose and my cheeks. When I could I put my two hands to my mouth and blew. The warm air helped. I had a Dewar Flask with soup and I took that at regular intervals.

The weather did not play ball. My intention had been to take a photograph or two from ten thousand feet and then head home. The cloud cover began to drop as I passed a mile or two to the east of Kronstadt. I was forced to descend with the clouds. It meant I would be flying over the airfield at five thousand feet. The photographs would be better but they had guns which could reach me.

When I reached the coast, I dropped into the clouds. I was, by my reckoning, ten miles west of the town and the airfield. After five minutes, I dropped from the clouds and headed east. After a few minutes on that course, I saw the town. I readied the camera. I did not intend to take a lot of photographs. A couple would have to do. The airfield would be outside the town in an open area. I peered through the tiny windscreen. I saw the windsock. It was to the south of the town. I corrected my course and readied the camera. I saw that they had some of the aeroplanes covered with canvas but they had cleared part of the field and there were aeroplanes lined up. They looked ready to take off. I clicked the camera twice and circled. I took one more and then I saw three aeroplanes taking off. They were trying to take me. I climbed and banked.

The Bolshevik pilots did not know the capabilities of the Sopwith Camel. I had a good rate of climb and a superior ceiling than all but one of the German aeroplanes. I began a slow ascent to eighteen thousand. There I would be hidden by the clouds. I would be flying on compass bearings but I would drop again after thirty minutes and take a bearing from the forts. To a new pilot flying in clouds was a frightening experience. I was confident that I would not run into any other aeroplanes and so I was safe for I was hidden. I checked my mirror and saw just clouds.

After thirty minutes, I descended. I was above the line of forts. I counted one to my right and five to my left with one below me, hidden by my fuselage. I was too far east and so I adjusted my bearing. I dropped lower to pass over Fort Totleben. By the time I had passed, I was at five hundred feet, and I saw the smoke from the flotilla. I had enough fuel left to circle a couple of times if I wished. I saw Vindictive as she turned to take me. My landing was a good one. I had been advised by Peter Rogers to trim the engine to just above stalling. It worked.

I stepped out and then retrieved the camera. I handed it to Sub Lieutenant Nash who would be responsible for developing the photographs. My pilots crowded around me too. I waved them off. "Go to the operations room and I will join you there. Get a brew on eh? It is as cold as up there."

As much as they wanted to speak with me I knew that my mechanics wanted my attention too. "Well sir?"

"Handled beautifully, Sergeant. I didn't get a chance to try out the guns but I am guessing the blanket worked."

Bert nodded, happy that he not been found at fault. "You look fairly cold, sir."

"I am. The forecast was not a hundred percent right. Cloud cover dropped to five thousand feet. When you top up the fuel let me know how much I had left. Next time we go we will be fighting and that burns up fuel at a greater rate. I need to know when we have to break off."

"Right sir."

As I passed Petty Officer Banks I said, "We will need bombs for the Strutters, Petty Officer Banks. They have hangars and workshops. We might as well do some serious damage. I only intend one flight if I can help it."

"I will sort it sir. Go and get a warm. You look fair nithered!"

"I am Chief, I am!"

The three pilots and their gunners were waiting for me in the operations room. I took off my flying jacket and gloves and grasped the hot tea Rogers had poured for me. "Thanks Peter." After I had finished the tea I held my cup out for another. I began to speak as he poured it. "The forts the Bolsheviks are using make fantastic way points. We use them to navigate. The airfield is to the south of Peterhof. I will wait until I get the photographs from Mr. Nash to confirm but it looked to me as though they had more aeroplanes than we thought. They were also damned quick to get them in the air."

"When do we go, sir?"

I smiled at Harry Greaves' enthusiasm and impatience. "Basically, Harry, as soon as there is an eight-hour window, we go. You will be carrying bombs. That will slow you down but we will drop them as soon as we arrive."

"Sir, we haven't practised much with them."

"It doesn't matter Bob. You have all dropped bombs before. It is a very big target and I don't think they have defences set up to repel aeroplanes. So long as we spread them out then we should hurt them. Of course, my visit may have made them review their defence. In my experience, it takes practice to become skilful enough to bring down an aeroplane. Certainly, the soldiers we had defending our airfields took months to become proficient. If you are low and fast, then you will be gone before they have you in their sights."

77

"You make it sound easy, sir."

"Anything but, Charlton, anything but. You gunners might want to take a couple of Mills Bombs with you. Even an air burst can cause damage."

The door opened and Sub Lieutenant Nash appeared with the photographs, still dripping. "I have them sir!" They were still wet.

"Put them on the board and we can all see them."

I was the one who had studied aerial photographs the most and I sympathised with the other seven who struggled to make out what they were seeing. I helped them by using the stem of my pipe to point them out. "This is a Fokker Triplane and this is an Albatros. They were taking off to try to catch me. These two have the best pilots. They were away and rolling as I came in. You can see other machines ready to take off but look here and here." I pointed to canvas covered lumps. "You can just make out the wings. There are eight aeroplanes here... Gentlemen, they have more aeroplanes than we thought."

I allowed that to sink in. "Does that mean it can't be done then, sir?"

"Oh, no, it can be done. It just means that we need to catch them on the ground and destroy as many of them there where they will be sitting ducks."

"And how do we do that, sir?"

"When we are five miles out we drop to four hundred feet and come in low. We make it hard to see us. We fly in line astern. They might think it is just me again. As soon as we begin our attack we adopt our normal foundation. Your bombs should be able to do the maximum damage." Silence filled the room. They were all adjusting to the new plan. "Look chaps, you can do this. If they have acquired more aeroplanes, then that means they are an even bigger threat and the longer we leave the attack then the better their pilots will become. Now go and check your kites. Have a word with your mechanics. Everything needs to be perfect. I am not certain when we will fly but we must be ready. Early nights and lay off the booze, eh? When we return then we will celebrate."

"Yes sir."

They trooped out leaving Sub Lieutenant Nash and myself alone. "Sir, the Captain said that the Admiral wants Kronstadt photographing too. He wants to know where the Bolshevik fleet is."

"But not before the Peterhof raid?"

"Oh no, sir. And he also said that the Count and Mr. Rees are on their way over to the port to meet with us. As soon as the aeroplanes are recovered we are to return there. Some sort of conference I believe, sir."

"Right."

The weather, however, was against us. The navigator told us that a front was moving west and we had been ordered back into port. It was frustrating and disappointing. We had been ready to go and we had been prepared. Now we headed back to port and that meant a meeting with the Count. We had only been in port for a couple of hours when Sub Lieutenant Nash and myself were summoned to the Captain's cabin. "The Rear Admiral wants you two aboard the flagship. The Count and Mr. Rees are aboard."

I nodded, "It was inevitable I suppose. I wonder how the Rear Admiral will handle the saboteur?"

"Our new commander has a sharp mind, Squadron Leader. And, I think, he has more guile than Alexander-Sinclair. He was chosen for this operation."

"How is the war against the Bolsheviks going, sir?"

"Estonia appears to be our only success. I believe that they are thinking of sending more of your chaps, to the Dvina. Murmansk and the north around Archangelsk is frozen solid and no one is moving."

"At least no one is dying, sir."

"They are though, Squadron Leader. The cold is a killer up there. We are lucky that the Baltic is being so kind to us this winter."

Sub Lieutenant Nash asked, "Why am I to go sir? I am flattered but I am a Subbie."

"I told you, the Rear Admiral is a clever man. You keep your ears and eyes open. You are a Sub-Lieutenant and no one will notice you. They will have their eyes on the Squadron Leader and the Rear Admiral. Keep quiet and watch."

"Yes sir!"

Our anchorage meant that the Sub Lieutenant and myself reached the flagship first. We joined the Rear Admiral. "The Count has requested this meeting. I am anxious to discover if the Count had anything to do with the sabotage." He turned to Sub Lieutenant Nash. "I believe you saw the Count's bodyguards too, Mr. Nash."

"Er yes sir."

"Well I would like to engage in a little deception if you are up to it."

"Of course, sir but I am not certain how good I will be."

"Oh, you should be able to pull this off. When the Count arrives, there will be the normal chit chat. I would like you to ask him, politely of course, if he knew his bodyguard had tried to sabotage the Camel."

"Alexei?"

"That's right. I, of course, as your commanding officer will be outraged and I will dismiss you from the room with promises of dire punishments to follow."

I saw then that this sailor had a sharp brain. The young officer nodded and asked, "But why sir? Why not just ask him outright?"

"I will confide in you, Mr. Nash, for your captain says he has high hopes for you. Like my predecessor, your captain and the Squadron Leader here, I do not trust this Count. I do not know what game he is playing but I do not like it. Unfortunately, I am under orders to cooperate. You will learn, Mr. Nash, if you stay in the service, that a good officer always obeys orders no matter how distasteful they may be. I will apologise for your conduct and then ask politely, as you had brought it up, if he knew."

"Yes sir, but I still don't see what would be gained by the Count sabotaging our aircraft. He wants us to destroy the Bolsheviks."

The Admiral lit his pipe, "Does he? I have read the reports and it is General Yudenich who has made all the gains. The Count was many miles from the front and only arrived when Estonia had been liberated. It is General Yudenich who is planning an attack on Petrograd. It is his men who would suffer if the Bolshevik aeroplanes were not destroyed. The Russians are a funny people. They have warlords and princes. They have hidden plots, plans and alliances. I do not want our people to suffer because they are caught up in such a plot." He poured the three of us a gin and said, "So young fellow, play your part and receive a severe tongue lashing. It will do your career no harm whatsoever. The launch will be waiting to take you back to the Vindictive."

"Sir. I shall do my best."

The Rear Admiral looked at his watch. "They are late. I suspect it is part of the Count's plan. He asks for a meeting and then keeps us waiting." He sipped his gin. "When you flew over the Bolsheviks, did you see their fleet?"

"Yes sir. They are protected by forts. If we had bombers, and I mean a lot of bombers, then we might be able to do something but our three Strutters could do nothing."

"Let us assume that you destroy the aeroplanes then the threat to General Yudenich will be the Bolshevik fleet. My little cruisers cannot harm them. We need something else. I have a Lieutenant Agar who is arriving in the next week. He is coming from Captain Cummins, Intelligence. The Captain has a plan. It is some ludicrous idea to use launches to destroy the battleships. Quite preposterous, of course, but you never know. Apparently our Mr. Churchill thinks the plan might work." He chuckled, "Quite the planner and plotter is Mr. Churchill. I wouldn't be surprised if he had some Russian blood in him."

A runner arrived at the door. "Captain's compliments and your guests have arrived sir."

"Thank you, Jenkins." As the runner disappeared the Admiral said, "Let us see what he makes of the fact that I have ordered his bodyguards to be detained at the gangway."

The Count, of course, entered first. I saw that he now had even more medals. Rear Admiral Cowan gave a half bow, "Delighted to meet you, Count Fydorervich. I am Rear Admiral Cowan. I believe you know Squadron Leader Harsker and his aide, Lieutenant Nash?"

"Yes, yes. Why do you have to moor so far from shore? I am frozen and the journey was most unpleasant." I saw Mr. Rees give the slightest of shakes with his head. I saw that Vladimir was still with him.

"Security, Count."

"And my bodyguards were not allowed to accompany me below decks!"

"You are safe on one of His Majesty's ships I can assure you."

He gave the briefest of glances to Sub Lieutenant Nash who said, "Sir, did you know that Alexei, one of your bodyguards, tried to blow up the Squadron Leader's aeroplane?"

The Rear Admiral should have been an actor. He rounded on the young officer and barked at him, "Sub Lieutenant Nash! Do not be impertinent. Count, forgive him. Take yourself back to the Vindictive and tell Captain Parr that you are to be confined to your quarters until I can deal with you!"

"Yes sir. Sorry sir. Sorry Count!" He was flushed and upset as he left. I studied the Count. For the first time since I had known him I saw the mask slip. He looked discomfited. Was that because he knew nothing about it? Or was it something else?

He regained his composure. "Alexei left my service soon after your flotilla left Reval. I have had his family punished. You say he tried to sabotage your aeroplane, Squadron Leader?"

"I am afraid he did. He and another fellow I did not recognise."

"What happened to them? Did they manage to damage your aeroplane?"

"I shot them both. They are dead and, no, my aeroplane is unharmed. In fact, I flew the other day, to Peterhof. So, we are still able to function."

He should have been delighted. If he had been innocent, then he would have immediately reacted. As it was I saw the information sinking in as he processed it. Finally, he broke into a smile, "Well done, Squadron Leader! That is good news! When do you attack?"

The Admiral said, "That is out of the Squadron Leader's hands I am afraid. It depends upon the weather. At this time of year, we are lucky if we get one day of fine weather and we need two."

I caught his eye and he nodded to me. I took my pipe from my mouth, "However, Count, I have scouted the airfield. When we do attack, it should make life easier for General Yudenich."

It was as though I had let all the air from his balloon. He gave us a smile, which was a false one, "That is good news but the General may not be able to attack until the spring. By then it may be I who leads the army. But first you must destroy the aeroplanes." He turned to the Rear Admiral, "And Mr. Rees has assured me that your flotilla will do all that it can to eliminate the threat of the Bolshevik fleet."

I saw that Mr. Rees kept an impassive face as did the Admiral. "At the moment, Count, a strike against the fleet would be disastrous. We would be outgunned and, at the moment, they enjoy the protection of the forts around Kotlin Island."

"Surely, when the Bolshevik air force is destroyed then the Squadron Leader can attack the fleet!"

Mr. Rees and the Admiral both rolled their eyes. I shook my head, "Count, we would be able to drop a total of just three hundred pounds of bombs. That would not even destroy one of the ships. I fear that you must await the arrival of Major Donald and the rest of the aeroplanes."

He scowled, "Is he an ace too?"

He said it with such scorn that the insult was obvious. I ignored it. "Sadly, sir, my expertise is in shooting down aeroplanes. I know of no ace who has sunk a large number of ships."

"I had heard much about the potential of aeroplanes." He glared at Vladimir. "Perhaps I was misinformed."

"I think you will find, Count, that over the next few years they will change the face of modern warfare."

The next hour was spent in plans to support General Yudenich. It was noticeable that the Count said little and Mr. Rees made the largest contribution to the discussion. When the three of them left, the Admiral spoke with me. "It seems obvious to me that the Count has his own plans. He would lead the White Russian army."

"And he was complicit in the attempt to sabotage my aeroplane. Captain Parr now has extra men watching. It will not happen again. And I believe the sooner we take on the Bolsheviks the better. It will be safer for my aeroplanes."

"Major Donald and the rest of the squadron will be ready to leave at the beginning of March."

"That is almost upon us."

"He has a young squadron and the aeroplanes they have are a mixed bag. I think he would appreciate you leaving him in as good a position as possible."

"Of course. He has a sound start. Those three pilots are made of the right stuff."

"Oh, and one more thing, although I would appreciate it if you kept this to yourself."

"Of course."

"This Captain Cummins is head of ... well let us just say he is involved in a lot of planning of what might be termed subversive activities. He is sending out a Lieutenant Agar and some new-fangled coastal motor boats. Apparently, they are faster than anything afloat and it is believed they can sink the battleships. You are a bright chap. Keep your ears open and if you hear a whisper of this then let me know. My captains know and now you. I trust all of you: the rest…"

Ten frustrating days later we had the all clear from the navigator. We had two days when we could fly. I hoped to get the job done in one but a second would ensure that we had the best chance of success. The ten days had been the coldest we had endured. Even though we were close to shore we had to use high pressure steam hoses to clear the ice from the superstructure. All the cruisers suffered the same problem. Our aeroplanes were carefully wrapped up in the hangar.

We spent the ten days going over our plan until I knew that they could do it in their sleep. We had gone over the photographs again and again so that they could identify the targets for their bombs. They had four under each wing. None were huge but aeroplanes, especially on the ground, were vulnerable things. However, the workshops were a priority. While the other three bombed I would try to take out the most important of their aeroplanes. I also had four Mills bombs as well as my pistols and my Lee Enfield. I was going to war and I would be ready for anything.

Knowing that we would be flying we rose before dawn. I wanted every piece of daylight I could get. This time I allowed the other three to take off first. I was faster and could overtake them. Once we were all safely aloft I took the lead. We climbed to five thousand feet. There was good visibility with clear skies. We needed our covers for our guns as it was freezing. That was also a reason to avoid going too high. We flew in line astern and I glanced in the mirror to make sure that they were on station. I had Peter Rogers at the rear with his new gunner. The wait for the window had helped for Peter Rogers had worked hard to bring the sulky gunner into line. The proof of the pudding would be in the air. I hoped I had made the right decision. After Totleben I headed due south. I was more confident this time. As we passed Kronstadt I saw the fleet. I noticed that they had a destroyer guarding the fifty-yard-wide entrance to the harbour. If that was sunk… I had more useful information to take back to the Admiral.

The engine was not running as smoothly as I would have liked. I put it down to the cold. I made a decision as we passed the line of forts in the sea and I held up my hand to signal a descent. I dropped to two thousand feet. If this had been the Western Front such a move would have necessitated a crick in the neck as I searched for the Hun in the sun. The Bolsheviks would not be hunting. The engine began to run smoother. In many ways, it suited as we would be dropping to four hundred feet a few miles from the coast.

I saw more ships this time. Spring was around the corner and there was more movement than a couple of weeks ago. More information for the Rear Admiral. Ahead of me I saw the smudge that was the coast. I began to descend. I was quite happy at four hundred feet but I knew that my young pilots would find it stressful and intimidating. It would be even more so if the enemy had defences prepared to greet us. I hoped that they had not.

I risked taking the canvas cover from my guns and I cocked them. I had the grenades in my pockets and I took two out and laid them in my lap. The sea seemed to fly by at such a low altitude and I saw the coast loom up quickly. I began to bank to port. I knew that the others would fall into their allotted positions. We were only travelling at ninety miles an hour. It conserved fuel and, until we were in combat, we needed go no faster. As I turned on an easterly course I glanced left and right. My men were in position. I held up my thumb and they all responded. There were no problems. I relied on them following my movements. I adjusted my course to steer more south easterly than easterly. They followed me.

Ahead I saw the town to my left and knew that the airfield was directly ahead. I hoped we had caught them napping. I saw the aeroplanes lined up on either side of the airfield. There were now two lines of eleven. The canvas had been removed. I had no time to assess the quality of aeroplane. We had a plan and we had to stick to it. As luck would have it, there were no aeroplanes in my sights. I heard the other three Vickers as they chattered in short bursts. Then I heard the first crump of a bomb. It was followed in rapid succession by another five. The first loads had been dropped. As I passed the end of the field I banked to starboard, as we had planned. We would now fly obliquely across the airfield. I had deemed that would maximise the damage we could cause. As we turned I saw that some of the enemy were already racing down the runway but there were numerous burning aeroplanes and buildings. We had had success but we had not finished the mission.

This time I did have targets. A Fokker Eindecker crossed into my sights. I fired a short burst and then a second. The monoplane skewed around and stopped. I had either hit the pilot or the aeroplane. I took a Mills bomb, pulled the pin and dropped it as I flew over the Fokker. They were firing all the weapons they had at us. They had rifles and machine guns but we were flying at a hundred miles an hour. By the time they had seen us, we were gone. I prepared a second grenade and dropped that a heartbeat later. I had spied drums. They would either contain fuel or oil. Both were good targets. I heard the last of the bombs as they were dropped behind me. In my mirror I saw explosions and flames. We had hit targets. I did not know what we had destroyed but the mission was a success. Even if we were all shot down we had done what we had intended. When we had passed the airfield. I checked my fuel gauge. I had just over half a tank left. It was time to head home. I whirled my hand above my head and then looked to see the response. They had all understood and I began to climb. My orders were clear. If the enemy pursued us they were to head home and I would deal with the Bolsheviks.

I looked in my mirror as I began my climb. I saw Harry Greaves there. He should have been to the side of me. His gunner was firing at the ground. I frowned. He had been ordered to save the Lewis gun in case we were attacked. I also saw, as they took off, an Albatros D V and two Fokker Triplanes. The Albatros D V was faster than the Strutters. The Fokker was faster than mine. I looked to the side and saw both Rogers and Newton. I waved them ahead of me. Newton, in the absence of Greaves would take the lead. I throttled back to allow them to get ahead and Greaves to catch up with me.

As I dropped back I saw that a pair of old Halberstadt fighters had taken off. Although they were not the fastest, they had synchronised guns and it would mean they outnumbered us. As he came abreast of me Greaves was grinning. He gave me the thumbs up. I waved him forward. I saw that Hood, his gunner, was changing his magazine. It was costly. A third Fokker, a D V this time, must have taken off before the others. The first I knew was when the bullets tore into the tail of the Strutter. One hit Hood in the hand.

Air combat is about decisions made in seconds. I side slipped to starboard and I was already looking for my target. I turned to take on this attacker. I increased my speed as I passed before his guns. I was a smaller target and I was travelling faster. The bullets zipped over my head. My turn allowed me to aim at his side. There were no bullets firing at me and he had failed to try to turn fully and take me on. He was still trying to get Harry who was limping up into the sky. With no rear gunner, Harry was a dead man if the enemy caught him. I waited until I was just forty yards from the Bolshevik pilot before I fired. My bullets tore into the side of the cockpit and I saw him slump forward. The aeroplane began its death dive. I took in the fact that they had left the German markings on it. This one had belonged to Jasta 5.

The combat had allowed the other five aeroplanes to close with me. More importantly it meant they would catch an ailing Greaves. The bullets had damaged his tail and he was now slower. I needed to discourage the Bolsheviks. I still had the advantage of height. They were climbing in a loose V. That was dictated by their speed. The Halberstadt had the worst rate of climb and they lagged behind. I could ignore them. I calculated that they were two hundred feet below me. I would try a flank attack. It would present three good targets and the only way they could defend against me was to turn and that would allow my flight to escape.

I banked to port and throttled back. I needed to conserve fuel and the slower speed would enable me to hit more of the enemy. The two Halberstadt turned to try to attack me. As they were even further back I did not worry about them. I had one Vickers with a full magazine and a second which was half empty. I chose to use the one with the full magazine. I lined myself up so that I would attack the two Fokkers and then I could turn to take on the Albatros. I opened fire on the first one. I fired five short bursts. As I approached I kept edging to port. My first bullets hit his fuselage. My second hit his wings and rigging but my last burst struck his engine which began to smoke and the damage to his wings made the whole aeroplane unstable. It began to spiral to earth. The second pilot showed his inexperience. The pilot of the Albatros banked to port to bring his guns to bear on me but the Fokker pilot saw me coming for him and he pulled his aeroplane into a steep climb. It was too steep. I fired and hit the tail but what killed the triplane was the engine stalling. An aeroplane in flight is a beautiful thing to behold but a stricken one is tragic. It dropped like a stone. The weight of the engine pulled its nose around and it followed its consort to a watery and icy death. The impact would kill the pilot.

I heard the sound of the Albatros' machine guns. He had fired early. I continued my loop. My Camel had a wonderfully tight turn and I pirouetted inside him. I knew that when I had my shot he would be very close to me. It would be a case of which one's nerve held. His engine appeared just fifty feet in front of me. I gave one long burst. I hit his propeller, his engine and his upper wing. I suspect I hit him for he did not fire in return. And then I had passed him. I continued my turn to port and climbed. I saw that the two Halberstadt were still below me and gamely climbing. The Albatros was descending with smoke pouring from the engine. If he was lucky he would make land and crash land.

I looked at my fuel gauge. I had less than half a tank of fuel remaining. As much as I wanted to I could not afford any more air combat. I turned north and began a gentle descent to save fuel. I had the legs on the Halberstadt. They would not catch me. The fastest Halberstadt had a top speed of less than one hundred miles an hour. I kept mine at ninety-nine. I would maintain my lead. At five hundred feet, I was almost skimming the waves. I zoomed over the forts. Above me, in the distance I saw the three Strutters. Flight Lieutenant Rogers was keeping them together. They were flying at the speed of the wounded bird. They had learned something from me. But Flight Lieutenant Greaves had shown me they still had much more to learn. I reached Totleben just after they had begun their descent. I would arrive back shortly after they did. I would be flying on fumes.

I saw the smoke of the flotilla as the three Strutters dropped to my height. I saw that Rogers had waved Greaves to the fore to allow him to land. A generous act, it was not necessarily the wisest move. If it crashed on landing, then we would all have a problem. It was a situation I had not covered. That was my fault. I would remedy that when I debriefed them; if we all got down safely. Greaves was a good pilot and he got his kite down in one piece. By the time I was ready to make my approach, only Rogers had to land. My engine gave an alarming cough and then picked up again. As soon as they had pushed the Flight Lieutenant's Strutter to one side I headed for the deck. I doubted that I would need to cut the engine. It would probably run out of fuel as I touched down. I must have had more fuel than I thought for we not only landed, I was able to turn and take the Camel back to the hangar. I patted the cowling as I descended to the deck, "Well done, old girl!"

Chapter 6

Hood had been whisked away to sickbay by the time I reached my aircrew. Petty Officer Banks was shaking his head at the damage to the Strutter. "Mr. Nash, take the air crew down to briefing."

"Sir."

Harry Greaves turned to speak with me. I held up my hand, "Later, Flight Lieutenant." I nodded to the Strutter. "How long, Petty Officer?"

"It is a mess but I can have it fixed in a few days, sir. Mr. Greaves did well to get her back. Some of the controls were shot out."

"That is better than I might have hoped. Have the others checked over and rearmed. If this weather holds we will be back tomorrow to see what damage we have done."

"Sir."

"When you refuel leave it as late as possible and do it on deck where it is colder."

"Why sir?"

"I want the maximum fuel aboard. I nearly ran out this morning."

"Right sir."

"The machine gun jackets worked. There were no problems with the guns."

Sergeant Hepplewhite pointed to my fuselage, "Either you had moths up there, sir or you were a bit close to the enemy."

I saw the line of bullet holes. They were repairable but it was a lesson. I had not even known that I was hit. "Thanks Sergeant. She did well today."

I took off my flying helmet, jacket and gauntlets. I took off my scarf. I knew that my feet would be too hot in my fur lined boots but I needed to speak with my men.

As I headed down the companion way Captain Parr approached me. "Did it go well today, Bill?"

I had wanted to wait until I had debriefed my men but I understood his anxiety. "Yes sir." I gave him the gist of the operation. "When I have spoken with my men I will have a report prepared by Nash."

He smiled and handed me an envelope, "The Rear Admiral was pleased with Nash. Read this when you have a minute."

"Sir."

As I reached the briefing room I detected the smell of bacon. When I entered, I saw a pile of bacon sandwiches and a bottle of HP sauce. Flight Lieutenant Newton was grinning from ear to ear. "See what Mr. Nash organized sir? Just the job, eh, sir?"

"Well done, Mr. Nash! Well done all of you." I turned to Harry Greaves, "And how is Hood?"

"The sick bay attendant said he was lucky. It missed everything vital but he lost a lot of blood. He was unconscious when we landed. Sorry sir."

"What happened, Harry?"

"I thought we could shoot up more of the enemy aeroplanes. I had run out of ammo and…"

"And you forgot my orders."

"Yes sir. My fault. I will accept any punishment that you deem fit."

"I am afraid, Harry, that you have punished yourself. When we go back tomorrow you will be grounded. Neither your bus nor your air gunner will be available. You will have to wait here for us to go over a second time. If we go over a second time." His face looked as though I had just slapped it. He slumped in his seat and the half-eaten bacon sandwich was dropped to his plate.

I drank some of my tea and ate my own sandwich. I wanted the silence to sink in. Harry knew the consequences of his actions and I wanted the other four to reflect on the results too before I spoke. After eating my sandwich and pouring some more tea I filled and lit my pipe. I pulled out the envelope and read it. I was smiling when I replaced it.

"You did well today. Apart from Harry's deviation from standing orders it was text book but tomorrow they will be ready for us. We will go three hours later."

"Why sir?"

I pointed east with the stem of my pipe. "I think they will have their aeroplanes in the air tomorrow waiting for us. Their endurance is three hours. By arriving three hours later we should catch them on the ground. I am trying to be unpredictable and this time we will approach from Petrograd. I intend us to take photographs tomorrow. Hunt and Charlton, you will photograph the Bolshevik fleet and we will then photograph Petrograd. We will be ten miles away but they may help the Admiral. If we have destroyed the enemy, then we photograph the airfield. If not, we finish the job and then photograph it before we leave if we are able. If we are unable to do so then we may have to make a third visit. I hope not."

"Will we have enough fuel, sir?"

"We are going to fly at a thousand feet. That will save fuel. I have seen no evidence of anti-aircraft guns. Now I want you all to tell Lieutenant Nash what you did and the damage you inflicted."

"Sir, I am only a Subbie!"

I handed him the letter, "Not any more, Lieutenant Nash. The Admiral has promoted you. Well done."

Even Harry was pleased by the news. It made everyone have a spring in their step. I read the report before Nash took it to the captain. We had destroyed or damaged seventeen aeroplanes. I estimated that there were eight or ten left. It was hard to be sure and we would need the evidence of photographs to be certain.

That evening the five of us were applauded as we entered the mess. It was partly pleasure at Nash's promotion, he was a very popular officer, but it was also celebrating our success. Rear Admiral Alexander-Sinclair had captured two destroyers but that had been before H.M.S. Vindictive had joined the flotilla. We were a team and all enjoyed our success. I dare say the Air Gunners would have been enjoying a similar celebration in their mess.

Lieutenant Nash sat with my three pilots. I had warned them not to drink too much. I saw that they obeyed me. Hood's wound and the damage to the Strutter had shown the dangers and they heeded my advice.

Captain Parr said, "I can see why you were sent by Mr. Churchill. Your experience is invaluable."

"A bit like yourself sir."

"Not really, Bill, this is the first time I have commanded a carrier. There is much to learn. All of this turning into the wind and the lack of as many guns as I am used to takes some getting used to. Still it has been relatively easy. Had we been under attack then I am not certain how we would have coped."

I retired early having first ensured that my men would soon follow. I wrote a few lines to Beattie. It was a sort of diary. I now had a son who would want to know what I had done. My letters would be a record.

We had the luxury of a late rise. I went to the sick bay after breakfast to speak with Hood. He looked sheepish. "How are you Hood? Are they looking after you?"

"Yes sir and I feel a bit of a fraud. It is just a flesh wound."

"It is more than that. Besides your bus needs some work so don't rush it eh?"

"Sir, it wasn't Mr. Greaves' fault. I just forgot about being economical with my bullets. I got carried away."

"I know. It is easy to do but if you had done as I said then you might have claimed a kill. You could have brought down the Albatros."

"I know, sir. Good luck for today."

"Well we shall bring back the photographs and you can see the results of your handiwork. Although as I told your pilots, we only count kills if the blighters are in the air."

We had the three cameras ready and my two pilots knew what was expected of them. I would lead, once more, and assess the situation. Having done this once my two crews were more confident. As we took off I noticed there was cloud cover. It was not enough to cause us problems but bespoke a new front coming in. I wondered if the delay might cause us problems.

Sergeant Hepplewhite had assured me that I had more fuel this time. He had measured it and told me that he managed to put in another four pints compared with the previous day. We followed the same course for the first part. Guns popped ineffectually at us as we flew to the east of Totleben. Our course was slightly different and I flew between the most eastern fort of the chain and the small town of Lisy Nos. A mile or two beyond Lisy Nos I turned and saw Petrograd to the east. I took a couple of photographs. The two Air Observers behind me would be able to take better ones.

As we approached the coast I saw Peterhof to the west of us. More importantly I did not see any aeroplanes in the air. I dropped us down to five hundred feet. To the south west of us I saw the windsock. We were on course and I placed my two Mills bombs between my legs before removing the jacket from the Vickers and cocking them. Turning south and west I saw that there were two Fokker D V's taking off. They had seen us. We would have to wait for the photographs until we had bombed the field and dealt with the two D.Vs. They were similar to my two Strutters.

I signalled for my two pilots to bomb the field. I saw that there were other aeroplanes on the ground. I dropped to a hundred feet and opened the throttle. It meant that, albeit briefly, I was travelling at more than my maximum speed. I was going much faster than the two aeroplanes which began to rise. I could have risked a long shot as the two aeroplanes made perfect crosses in my sights. But I did not want to waste bullets. The two of them split left and right. I followed the closest one. I was gaining on him so quickly that I knew I would be able to hit him. When he began to bank and he crossed in front of my sights just eighty feet from me, I opened fired. My bullets stitched a line from his engine, through his cockpit and across his upper wing. His wing began to dip as the engine faltered and stopped.

He was as good as destroyed and I banked right, desperately seeking the other Fokker. He had got onto my tail. I heard his bullets as he fired, prematurely, and then I saw him in the mirror. I could climb twice as fast as he could. I pulled back on the yoke. I heard his single gun as he desperately tried to fire at me. I was always going away from him. His bullets made a parabola and fell harmlessly to earth. I heard the crump of the Strutter's bombs. My men were doing what they had been ordered and I could concentrate on this pilot behind me.

As I reached the top of the turn I felt the blood draining from me. I became dizzy. I had done this before and knew what to expect. I suspected the Russian pilot did not. As I began the descent I knew that I would be catching him. His bullets had stopped. He was still trying to catch me but it was a lost cause. He pulled out of the loop to bank left. Had he tried that in the Dr 1, triplane, he would have ripped off the wings. The D V was slower but more robust.

Instead of following his bank left I banked right. He would lose sight of me and allow me to come at him from the west. He would have the sun in his eyes. I kept my eye on him and I saw his head swivel from side to side as he sought me out. I was in his blind spot. An experienced pilot would have used lateral movements to find me. With the sun behind me I banked to port and readied my gun. I felt almost sorry for the Bolshevik. He had almost outwitted me but I had the better aeroplane. He saw me and swung around to fly directly at me. I had no doubt that he would not blink first. Honour was at stake and his comrades on the ground were watching him. I readied the Vickers I had not fired. We were approaching each other at a combined speed of over two hundred miles an hour. I fired first and I gave a long burst. It took him by surprise. He fired back and then his gun stopped. I guessed he had run out of bullets. By then it was too late. Eighty bullets had shredded his propeller and gone through his engine. I pulled up the nose. Had he had any bullets left then I was an easy target. We were still quite low and I heard an enormous explosion as he hit the ground.

I looked in my mirror and saw that my two Strutters had taken station to port and starboard. They were a couple of hundred feet behind me. I saw that their racks were empty. I turned to head down the airfield. I saw burning aeroplanes and burning buildings. I saw tents laid out to one side. There were four marquees and forty or so smaller tents. They were undamaged. My men had gone, as I had instructed, for the buildings. I dropped to fifty feet and zoomed over the field. I pulled a pin from a Mills bomb and dropped it to port and did the same to starboard. I pulled up the nose and heard the crump of the grenades. I held up my right arm and slowed down. The two of them pulled alongside me. I made the sign for photographs and received the thumbs up. They had done so. I whirled my right hand over my head. Time to go home.

I thought the journey home would be uneventful but, as I looked in my mirror I saw black clouds forming. There was a weather front coming in. I was forced to travel back at the speed of the Strutters and the front caught up with us. It was not the rain and the wind which worried me, it was the landing on a pitching deck. I had a back-up plan and that was to pancake in Finland but I would only use that if we could not land at all. We would be in the hands of the Air Mechanic with the paddles.

When I saw the smoke from the flotilla I breathed a sigh of relief. We had found our ship but the rain was now making me not only uncomfortable but also making it hard to see. The Air Mechanic on the pitching deck was our only hope

Bob Newton landed first. It was not the prettiest of landings. He came down hard and I knew that his undercarriage would have suffered damage. Peter Rogers was just plain unlucky. A sudden gust caught him as he touched down and the tip of his upper wing caught the turret of a gun. He spun around. I thought he might tip over the side but Petty Office Banks and his men threw themselves at the undercarriage and lower wing. They held it.

It meant that I was waved off although I had not even contemplated landing. I flew over the carrier and circled the flotilla. I did not want them to think they had to hurry although I was aware that I was running out of fuel. The two dogfights had burned up more fuel than was healthy. I saw the sailors on the cruisers staring up at me. I banked slowly to make my approach again. They had cleared a path on the flight deck and I lined up. It would not be easy for the weather was on the edge of dangerous. I aimed for the carrier and kept my eye on the paddles. If I was waved off I would have to try to make it to Finland. The deck was pitching and I realised that having a mechanic with paddles was the only way to make a safe landing. He kept me straight in relation to the deck. The deck was rising and falling. As I touched down I felt my wheels start to slide for the deck was slick with sleet and snow. In a perfect world, they would have cleared it. We did not have a perfect world and the snow was as deadly an enemy as the Bolshevik bullets. I cut my engine. My tail began to swing around. Luckily, I did not strike anything and after two revolutions I stopped.

I took the camera and held it over the side. George Baker took hold of it. He peered up at me, "Well sir, that was a lucky one."

"They say, Baker, that any landing you can walk away from is a good one. Perhaps it should be a lucky one eh? How are Mr. Rogers and Mr. Newton?"

"Both fine sir. Mr. Nash ordered them below decks. He did not want to have too many people here and if you would get out sir then we can put this one to bed. She is our only whole aeroplane!"

I climbed out and Lieutenant Nash came over. The wind was now blowing so hard that conversation was hard. "The Captain is putting back into port, sir. This storm is here for a while." He smiled, and shouted, "A fantastic landing sir!"

"I think I have much to learn about landing on a carrier Mr. Nash. The other two cameras have the photographs of the airfield. Mine are of the fleet and Petrograd."

"There is no rush, sir. I will do a better job this time. The last lot were a little grainy. I think I rushed it. I was too keen trying to impress. We have a brew on and the cook made scones. There is strawberry jam too!"

"No clotted cream?"

He laughed, "There is a war on, sir!"

"Then when we have tied up we shall all have a run ashore! We need to celebrate, Mr. Nash. Although I await the photographs to confirm it I do not believe there is a Bolshevik Air Force in Peterhof to worry the flotilla."

There was good natured banter as I debriefed them. Lieutenant Nash seemed to relish his role and I had high hopes for him. When Major Donald took over the young lieutenant would be a valuable asset. It took longer to debrief than I had expected and we had anchored before we had finished. However, the weather was so poor that there would be no launch to take us ashore. The men were disappointed but, with no prospect of flying the next day I allowed them to celebrate in the mess.

The storm had abated somewhat the next day and the captain, Lieutenant Nash and myself were taken by launch to the Caledon where we would examine the photographs in the presence of the Rear Admiral. As we went up to the Admiral's quarters we met a young lieutenant coming out.

"Gus Agar! What on earth are you doing here?"

"Captain Parr! This is a surprise. I am here with some torpedo boats. Some captain in London seems to think that we can sink the Bolshevik fleet with them. I shall see you later. I am assigned here with my CML."

"I should hang on here, Gus. We have photographs of the fleet. They may be of some use to you."

"Jolly good show sir. Yes, I shall wait here."

As soon as the Rear Admiral realised what we had he called in the young Lieutenant. We were only needed to explain the position of the fleet in relation to the island. When we looked at the airfield we could see that any aeroplanes which were left were so badly damaged as to render them useless. "Of course, sir, they will get some more. The Germans will be punished in the peace talks at Versailles, I daresay. The French, in particular, are not happy about them. The Bolsheviks will buy more. Next time they will defend them better."

The Rear Admiral clapped and rubbed his hands together, "That may be true, Squadron Leader, but this is all falling into place. If Lieutenant Agar and his new-fangled torpedo boats can destroy or badly damage the Bolshevik fleet, then we can support General Yudenich and he might just take Petrograd. That would be a great victory. You and your pilots are to be commended!"

"Don't forget the ground crew and gunners, sir. Not to mention Mr. Nash here."

"Quite, good show all around! Oh, I forgot to say, your Mr. Rees is still here in port but the Count has toddled back across the Baltic. I believe Mr. Rees would like to see you. At your convenience, of course."

We spent longer analysing the photographs and Lieutenant Agar took away the ones of the fleet. The time of the aeroplane was almost over and soon it would be the time of the torpedo boat. Major Donald and his aeroplanes would be the ones to deal with the next Bolshevik aerial threat.

Once back at the carrier I decided to write my reports before I headed ashore. In truth, I was intrigued. Why had the military attaché stayed and why had the Count left? We were just half a mile off shore and the Captain's own launch took me in. Some officers had been granted shore leave, along with my air crew and so a tender accompanied us.

"Chief, you can take the Captain's launch back. I shall get a ride with the tender when shore leave is over at ten."

"Are you sure sir? I can wait. It is no trouble."

"I will be fine."

He nodded towards my sidearm. "I should keep that handy, sir. There are Bolshevik sympathisers all over and they would love to get their hands on a British officer."

"I will be with the military attaché. I think I should be safe enough."

"Right then, sir. Enjoy your evening."

Mr. Rees strolled up five minutes after the launch had gone. He looked as dapper as ever. "My dear fellow, I understand that congratulations are in order. You have completed your mission."

"Yes sir. I am glad to say that although they had numbers and courage they had no skills whatsoever."

"Come along then we need to talk. There is a pleasant little restaurant around the corner. I have reserved a table."

The snow had stopped but the cold had intensified. I was glad to be in out of the icy, Arctic wind. I saw that Mr. Rees had chosen a corner table with two walls behind us so that we could not be overheard. He seemed to have a gift for languages for he rattled off an order. "I have taken the liberty of choosing. All the food tastes pretty much the same but I have ordered reindeer. It is quite a pleasant taste and they do it with a good cloudberry sauce."

"As I have never had either that seems agreeable. Where is Vladimir? I expected to see him with you."

He leaned over, "Shall we wait until our drinks arrive before we chat. We are less likely to be overheard that way. Our food will take thirty minutes or so." He smiled, "I came last week to time it all. Preparation, preparation!"

I was bemused but Mr. Rees did not seem to do things in an inefficient manner. I would trust him. The drinks arrived. He had ordered us two beers. He smiled again, "They do a wonderful drink here called Marskin ryyppy. It is, however, a little powerful and we shall save that for after we have eaten." He nodded to the waiter and then leaned in to speak to me after he had gone to see to other diners. "Now, Vladimir. He has, I fear, left my service and joined the staff of the Count. It is a mistake but he his headstrong and determined to fight for Russia. I tried to dissuade him."

"I do not trust the Count."

"My dear fellow he is the most untrustworthy man I have ever met. I stayed close to him to try to find out exactly whose side he was on. I did not manage to do so. He could be out for himself and, equally, he could be working for the Bolsheviks."

"The Bolsheviks?"

"Oh, they can be quite pragmatic. They will use anyone to attain their ends. However, it is a moot point as the Count has decided that he has what he wants. He now has the ear of General

Yudenich. He told the General that he arranged for your aeroplanes to destroy the Bolshevik aeroplanes."

"But we only finished the job today! How does he know?"

"I was with him until yesterday evening. We met with the general at the border at Krasnaya Gorka. It is less than twenty miles from Peterhof. The spy he had planted in Peterhof brought the news. I was there to confirm that the Count had ordered the raid and then I was dismissed and Vladimir left me. I took a boat over here immediately. It was a ghastly journey."

"So, the Count could now be working for the Bolsheviks? Equally, he could be working for himself?"

"I suspected something when Alexei left his service so suddenly. That was a damned fine piece of work from you. Alexie and Sergei, the man with him, were assassins of the highest calibre."

"So the Bolsheviks were behind the sabotage attempt. The Count was working for them?"

"No, he is working for himself. He may well be using General Yudenich. If I was there I might be able to discover his motives but, I fear, that will not happen. Vladimir has been seduced and the Count will soon know that I am more than just an Embassy official. This is my last night in the Baltic, I am afraid. I will be heading to Reval where Captain Hesketh will be docking in a week or so."

"I see." I felt deflated and used.

"I came here to meet you in person because I thought I owed it to you to explain the Count's actions. I genuinely thought I might be able to discover what he was up to but he is a clever man and when he suborned Vladimir then he did not need me."

"I don't understand."

"Vladimir took a notebook from me. I thought I had secreted it somewhere safe but Vladimir is a bright youth. That explains why the Count did not take him before. He was tempting him with the promise of serving Russia in return for betraying me."

"Is the notebook…"

"A liability? No. It is in my own code. If they break it then they are cleverer than I thought but it has rendered me useless. I am no longer an asset for His Majesty's Government. I daresay they will send me somewhere else." He shook his head. "I should have known he was up to something." He reached into his pocket and took out a leather bag. "Young Vladimir asked me to give you these."

"What are they?"

In answer, he emptied on to the table ten gold coins. Each bore the image of the dead Tsar. "I cannot accept these."

"I am afraid you will have to as we have no way of giving them back to the headstrong Vladimir. He came to me poor but, with the Count's help, he managed to access his family's bank accounts. He is a rich young man although I fear that the Count now has the funds. Vladimir said that these were to thank you for destroying the enemy aeroplanes." He put the coins back in the bag and slid it over to me. "Take them. They are as nothing to Vladimir. His family was rich. Keep them as remembrance of a fine young man." The way he spoke suggested that Vladimir was already dead.

"I will take them but I will tell my superiors in London when I return."

He nodded, "As you wish." The food arrived. "Splendid. This meal is on me. Enjoy it Squadron Leader. I have enjoyed meeting you. I can see you will have a glittering career."

We spoke at length about the politics of Russia. He was a very intelligent man and I learned much. Many of the names he mentioned became household names but at that time they were unknowns. He also spoke of the politics of the wider world. I saw that although he was stationed in Russia, he had served the Empire in other far flung stations. We wrapped up for the cold and he took his stick. "What time are you being picked up, Squadron Leader?"

"The boat will be back at ten."

"Good then we can walk back to my hotel. This is a pretty little town. Before the war is a was popular as a holiday resort with people like the Count and Vladimir. I daresay they will enjoy prosperity when the war is over."

He was right. It was pretty. However, we also found out it could be dangerous. He had cut through an alley. He wanted to show me a café which only opened in the summer. It seemed it had been popular with one of the younger members of the Tsar's family. It was just around the corner from Mr. Rees' hotel.

He suddenly whispered. "Squadron Leader, we are not alone. There is danger before us and behind us." Even as he spoke three figures emerged before us. They carried wooden staves. "I should take out your revolver. It may cow them."

As I did so I looked behind us. There were two more men and they held knives. "What are these? Robbers? Footpads?"

"I fear these are working for either the Bolsheviks or, perhaps, the Count. They mean to do us deadly harm."

I took out my revolver and cocked it. Surprisingly it did not seem to worry the men behind us. Of course, there were five of them. Then I heard the hiss as Mr. Rees pulled the sword from his stick. He said, calmly, "If you would deal with the three with the staves I will show these gentlemen that my weapon has a greater reach than theirs."

I turned around and levelled my gun at the three men with staves. They were ten feet from me. The Webley was double action. I would get but two shots off before they were upon me. I aimed at the one in the middle and then pulled back the hammer. I had very little Russian but I used what I had. "Move and you die!" I had no doubt that my accent was execrable but I saw that he understood. I was not certain how we would stand with the police if I shot one. Behind me I heard the swish of the sword stick and a cry. That made one of the men in front of me move. I lowered my gun and fired before his feet. The snow which had lain there as now a slushy mush. The bullet struck the cobbles and sent chips flying up. One caught him in the cheek. The report was loud and the three of them turned and ran. I whipped around and saw the other two running away. One held his cheek and the other his hand. Their knives were lying in the slush. Mr. Rees knelt to pick them up. He gave them to me. "A souvenir!"

"Do we wait for the police?"

He laughed as he sheathed his sword in his stick. "The police will not bother until the morning. Then they will come to see if there are bodies. I fear my deviation has put your life in peril, Squadron Leader. I apologise. Come I will escort you back to the dock."

"I am fine. I still have my revolver."

"I am responsible for you. I will walk you back to the dock."

He put his hand in my back and we headed back down the alley. Once at the dock he left me for there was a pair of marines who were acting as provosts. They would deal with any drunks.

He took off his glove as did I and we shook hands. "Farewell, Squadron Leader. You handled yourself well back there. But then I would expect nothing less of a man such as you." He smiled, "You still have the coins?" I nodded. "Good. Use them wisely."

And then he was gone. As I waited at the dock, smoking my pipe and waiting for the rest of the men on shore leave I tried to take in all that I had learned. I had worked out a tiny part of it all but Mr. Rees had been the biggest surprise. He was a spy. He had seemed an ineffective and dapper official but I now saw that was his disguise. He had handled the assassins well. In fact, better than well. He had done this sort of thing before. My hands had been shaking until I had reached the dock and yet he seemed calmness personified. We had spoken while we ate and I had learned much about him. He had steel in him. I think Vladimir was his attempt to do something good. He had hoped to save Vladimir from himself and the Count. That had been the part which had disappointed the enigmatic Mr. Rees the most. I had been close to a mysterious world and not known it.

Over the next two weeks the weather improved but only slightly. Ten days after the raid I was able to fly back to Peterhof to take more photographs. Only Bob Newton's Strutter was available to come with me. The two of us flew over the Bolshevik fleet and then Peterhof. The airfield was deserted. Blackened buildings showed where the workshops had been but there was no other sign that an airfield had ever existed. We headed back to the fleet. It was confirmation that we had been successful and that Lieutenant Agar could carry out his mission. I had even seen the boats. They were flimsier than the first aeroplanes we had flown but he seemed confident that he could carry out his mission.

A week after my flight Major Donald arrived and with him were my orders. I was to return on the freighter which had brought him and his new aeroplanes and return to England. Mr. Churchill had kept his word but he still wished to see me in London before he would allow me to return to my family. It was a small price to pay.

Bert and George would stay with the carrier. They were both sad to see me leave. The aircrews, however, were positively distraught. This had never happened to me before. Normally I was the survivor and it was others who left. Now I was and it was they who felt abandoned. And, of course, I would be leaving behind my

103

Camel. To me she was more than canvas and metal. She was a living thing. When I had flown her, I had felt as one. After the party in the mess I went down to the hangar and bade her farewell. She was a good bus. Then I took my bags and boarded the tender which took me to the freighter. Many of the crew lined the decks to wave me off. I was touched.

England

Chapter 7

We did not dock in London but in Newcastle. I learned, from dour Captain Armstrong, that they were picking up some tanks and taking them to the White Russians on the Dvina. Despite Mr. Rees' view, the British Government was still supporting the White Russians. I think I agreed with him and that we should stay out of it. I had had time, on the voyage south, to reflect on the situation. Napoleon had once tried to conquer Russia and failed for it was a vast country. The internecine war would go on for years and bleed the country dry. Men like the Count proliferated on both sides. I had learned that during my dinner with Mr. Rees who told me of some of the Bolshevik leaders. It struck me that they were as bad as the Count. The British soldiers, sailors and airmen were there for political reasons. None had died during my time but I knew that some would. When the weather improved brave Gus Agar would try to sink the fleet. I could not see how he could avoid losses.

A travel warrant had been waiting for me on the ship and I took a train from Newcastle to London. I was tempted to take a train directly home but I still had a career to think about and it would not do to upset the Secretary of the Air. I settled into the seat for it would be a long journey. The fields through which we passed were green and it felt strange after the white world of Finland and Estonia. As we left Darlington I wondered how Lumpy, my old gunner, fared in Stockton just a few miles east of me. England was now recovering after the war. Soldiers had returned from four years of hell to a different world. Women were more likely to work. There were moves to give them the vote. We had spent most of the countries reserves funding a war and now we had to rebuild.

I saw signs of the rebuilding as we headed south. I saw building work in Doncaster and Peterborough as we passed through. Returning soldiers needed somewhere to live. Roads were being improved. We now had more and better motor cars. I had even heard that someone, an ex-Flying Corps pilot, was trying to find a commercial use for the old Handley Page Bomber. We had left for war in 1914 and come back to a different country. Was I hiding from it by staying in the service? I would speak to Beattie about that. She was my rock.

It was late when I arrived in London and I went to my club. I had a great deal of luggage. I wondered how I would get it home. My car was many miles to the north. I could not expect Beattie to come south with a baby in tow. The next day I walked around to Whitehall. The orders I had received were to report to the ministry as soon as I arrived. It was Mr. Balfour whom I met. I viewed him differently now. Mr. Rees was not what he seemed. I doubted that Mr. Balfour was either. From what I had learned the planning for my operation had been his work.

He was effusive in his praise, "Squadron Leader, what a delight to see you! I have read the reports and you exceeded every demand made of you. Splendid! Splendid! Mr. Churchill is impressed and he is not a man who is easily impressed, let me tell you." He gestured for me to go upstairs. "If you come with me to my office I will have a little chat and then you can have a month's leave. Mr. Churchill said that you will need it."

His words had an ominous ring to them. His office was a little cubby hole, no more. However, it was well organised and I could see Mr. Balfour's fingerprints all over it. He picked up the telephone. "Tea for two, if you please, Mavis." He looked up at me. "Now you may well be wondering why you are not being sent to the Dnieper as Mr. Churchill suggested?"

I smiled, "I hoped it had slipped his mind. The Russian intrigues are a little much for a country boy like myself."

"Do not disparage yourself. Mr. Rees spoke very highly of you. He suggested to Captain Cummins that you would make a valuable agent. Mr. Churchill thought about it but he has decided to keep you for the Royal Air Force"

"That's very good of him."

The official wagged his finger as he admonished me. "Stop feeling sorry for yourself, Squadron Leader. You will do well with Mr. Churchill's patronage. Anyway, as I said, you will not be needed on the Dnieper. Those aeroplanes are being pulled out. After they are refitted they will be sent to the Middle East or India."

The door opened and a homely looking woman appeared laden with a tray. I rose and took it from her. "Thank you, sir."

Mr. Balfour looked bemused, "I am sure Mavis can handle a tray."

I had known people like Mavis on the estate. They were treated well by Lady Mary but I knew they had a hard life. I smiled, "I am sure she can but my mother raised me to be a gentleman."

Mavis beamed at me, "And she did a good job, sir. Thank you." She closed the door as she left.

Shaking his head Mr. Balfour poured the tea. "Down to business, Squadron Leader. Mr. Churchill has come to the conclusion that people like Count Fydorervich are unlikely to be able to defeat the Bolsheviks and neither the cabinet nor the country is in the mood for another war of attrition."

"So the flotilla and ground troops will be pulled out?"

"Probably but that is not your concern. You destroyed a threat and demonstrated quite clearly that a few aeroplanes, judiciously used and piloted by men such as yourself can have an effect far greater than the actual numbers would suggest." He sipped his tea and nodded appreciatively. Taking a biscuit, he stood and munched as he pointed at the map of the Middle East. "Turkey has lost its Ottoman Empire. It will not be given it back again. The land which formerly made up the Empire has been divided up and France and Great Britain will operate Protectorates over Mesopotamia, Syria, Lebanon and the like. We already police Egypt and the Sudan. It will make the lives of the people living there both safer and more productive."

I was not certain that they would see it that way. I said nothing and sipped my tea. Mr. Balfour must have sensed my unspoken criticism.

"The Turks were both cruel and inefficient, Squadron Leader. Colonel Lawrence helped to liberate them and if you wish to know of their methods then I suggest you speak with him." I nodded. "Mr. Churchill intends to use our squadrons to police the huge expanse of desert. You are to be based, eventually, in Mesopotamia. There will be three squadrons there. Two of fighters and fighter bombers and one of bombers. I suspect that the numbers will increase but this will be enough for you to start with. We would like you as senior Squadron Leader. Each of the

Squadrons will have their own squadron leader but you will have overall control."

"But I have never commanded more than one squadron sir!"

"No one has Squadron Leader. You are part of the experiment." He took a large folder and placed it in a leather satchel. "Here is the information you will need. After your experiences in Russia I have no need to tell you that you need to be security minded. Although you have a month off we will be in touch with you regularly. The Secretary of State is arranging for you to have a telephone put in at your home."

"I am afraid that the house I have is rented. I have some savings and I was going to see what we could buy."

"You will have an increased salary and I am certain arrangements could be made."

I shook my head. Then I remembered the coins. "Before I forget sir." I took out the purse and poured the coins on the table. "Mr. Rees' translator gave me these. I cannot accept them."

He laughed, "Of course you can. Mr. Rees told me about them. They are the spoils of war. If I were to take them what would I do with them? They would disappear into the treasury and no one would thank you for that. Accountants! It seems to me that this is serendipitous. These, with your savings should buy you a good home. I would suggest somewhere close to London. We don't want you in the back of beyond up at Burscough. And as for the paucity of your accommodation... we will put the telephone in and when you move to a better home then we will move it. It is the least we can do. Now, at the moment, the three squadrons are paper only. We know who we want but they have yet to be approached." He tapped a folder. "I have your address and we will be in touch. Enjoy your leave. When you go to Mesopotamia do not expect to be back soon. Your family can, of course, go with you." He shrugged, "I personally would not risk a white woman in that part of the world but then I never married. It is your decision."

I nodded and stood. The meeting was obviously over. I pocketed the coins. I would ask Beattie about them. "Very well, sir."

I went directly to my club. I packed just an overnight bag. I arranged to have my luggage sent on to me and I headed for the station. I would be home by tea time. I had a compartment to myself and so I began to read up on the task I had been set.

Suddenly Gordy and Ted seemed to have made better decisions about their future.

I indulged myself with a taxi from the station. At one time that would have seemed a ridiculous expense but after studying the papers I discovered that my new salary would enable us to live a little better. Money had never bothered me. I had fought for my country and my brothers in arms. Now it was a career and I had a family to consider. I realised that I had now accepted the coins. I would still mention them to Beattie but the coins did not now seem like ill-gotten gains.

The taxi pulled up and I paid him off. I had no key. I had thought, when I left with Bates all those months ago, that I would be back the next day. I knocked on the door, feeling foolish. There was no answer and so I knocked again, harder. I heard Beattie shouting, "Hold on! I'll be there when I can!"

I heard footsteps coming down the stairs of the house which now seemed tiny and then the door opened and there was Beattie holding a giggling Tom in a towel. He was dripping wet. He had been in the bath. Beattie just burst into tears. I hurried in for it was a chilly evening. After shutting the door, I said, somewhat lamely, "I had no key. Sorry!" She had her hands full and so I put my arms around the two of them and hugged them. My face was next to Tom's and I saw that he had more hair and was making deliberate noises. When had that happened? Where was the tiny baby I had left?

Beattie had composed herself, "Why didn't you tell me you were coming home? I had a letter last week and you said nothing then. Oh, look, I must dry Tom. Go into the lounge and make yourself a drink. I am all of a flutter!"

I kissed her on the cheek and said, "Sorry."

For some reason that made her burst into tears again and she hurried back upstairs. I put my bag down and took off my flying coat. I went to the drinks' cabinet. There was a half empty bottle of whisky and I poured myself one. The fire looked welcoming and I sat down. The furniture was not ours it was rented and, as I sat in the armchair I thought about Mr. Balfour's words. Would I want to take Beattie and Tom with me to the Middle East? Would that be fair? Was this fair? It might be better to buy a nice house and then, at least, my family would be comfortable and safe.

"Bill, do you want to come upstairs and say goodnight to your son?"

I put down my whisky and my pipe and headed up the stairs. She held Tom in her arms. He looked scrubbed, clean and rosy. He smiled at me but in a shy way as though he did not know who I was. That was not a surprise. I held my hands out and he buried his head in Beattie's shoulder.

"Thomas, this is your father, give Daddy a cuddle." She nodded for me to hold him.

I did and noticed that he was much heavier than he had been all those months ago. He kept his head turned away from me and so I blew a raspberry behind his ear. He giggled and so I did it again. I put my mouth close to his ear and said, quietly, "Thomas, I am your father. I promise that when you grow I will be there to help you fly and there to catch you when you fall. I will always be thinking of you even though I may not be close."

Beattie nodded, "It is lovely but you know he can't understand that."

"I know but he might recall the words in some dream when he is older."

She nodded and held her arms out for him. "Go down and I will get him to sleep. There is some supper left in the oven. I have eaten already. I was going to have it tomorrow but now that you are home we can go shopping. We can have a feast tomorrow!"

It was shepherd's pie and I wolfed it all down before Beattie made it downstairs. It took some time to get him off. "Was there a problem?"

She kissed me and sat on the arm of my chair. "He was excited." She sipped my whisky.

"I thought he didn't recognise me."

"He is a little shy. We don't get many visitors here. Christmas was lovely but, since then, we have been on our own and it has been a harsh winter. I am glad you are home." She realised she had finished my whisky and she went to get another one. "You are home, aren't you? Your letters told me what a horrible time you were having. Is it over?" She handed me my whisky.

I patted my knee and she sat down. I told her all that had happened since my last letter. By the time I had finished I had finished my whisky.

She looked at me and said, "I need a cup of tea. Another whisky?"

"No. I will have a tea with you."

We went into the kitchen and she filled the kettle and I lit the gas. "So, I have you for a month?" I nodded. "And then what? Off to the desert for God knows how long?"

I sighed. "Mr. Balfour said we could go out as a family or, at least, you could join me when things have been set up."

"But you don't want me there, is that right?"

"Of course I want you there. But it might be dangerous."

"We will come. I had too many nights without you in the Great War. I want to make the most of every moment. You don't want to miss your son growing up do you?"

"No but I don't want you in danger either."

"We will take our chances. But we will need to move house, won't we?"

"What do you mean?"

"We need a bigger house. This one was cosy with two of us but Thomas takes up more space than you would think. Besides we will need you to be able to get into London. Your Mr. Balfour was quite right about that."

"Can we afford it?"

She laughed, "You are a goose! Of course we can. Lady Mary gave us a nice wedding present. It was money! I have not spent much of your salary and I saved during the war. We have enough." She poured the boiling water on the tea. "What about those gold coins? Can't we use them?"

"It doesn't feel right, somehow."

"From what you have told me they were a present. You impressed the young Russian and he was rewarding you. There is nothing dishonest about that! Bill, this is a chance for us. Neither of our families had very much. Don't look this gift horse in the mouth. The only expensive thing we have is your car. We have been frugal. I want Thomas to have a home with a garden. This has a yard. It is a nice house and it is cheap but I want something better."

"Very well. I suppose we need to decide where and then look."

She poured the tea. "This is exciting and I have you all to myself for a whole month!"

She was the bubbly young girl who had first nursed me back to health and we spent the evening talking and planning. Our son cooperated and did not wake until one a.m. I knew nothing about it for I slept the sleep of the dead but Beattie told me the next morning.

"Does he do this often?"

"Often enough."

I could see that I much to relearn about being a father. I smiled as I watched Beattie eating one handed while she fed Tom. She also rattled on to me about what she wanted from a house.

I took it all in and said, "First I need to deposit this gold. I will pop into town and see the bank manager."

She shook her head, "And if you think you are leaving the two of us alone you have another think coming. You are going to find you have two shadows from now on. Isn't that right, Thomas?"

He giggled and showed me an open mouth full of the porridge she had just given him. I had much to adjust to. The next few days were spent in organising and getting used to each other. Beattie and Tom had a routine and I had to fit in with it. I was introduced to the joy of washing nappies; our son got through them at a prodigious rate. I had been in the cavalry and it reminded me of mucking out the stables.

Three days into my new life a lorry arrived from the GPO. They were there to install the telephone. We had both used them as part of our jobs but the only person I knew with one was Lady Mary. Even the engineers were impressed, "You must have some pull, sir. There is a waiting list as long as your arm for one of these. We were told to drop everything and get it installed."

I nodded feeling a little guilty that it would soon have to be moved. As the engineers worked, however, I learned that they were all ex-soldiers. After the Great War, every day felt like a gift as they did not have to face German bullets and a life of hell. When it had been tested and they had gone we looked at each other. Beattie laughed, "Unless we are going to call Lady Mary then I think I will be dusting it more than using it."

It was later that afternoon when it rang. The sound terrified Tom who began wailing. Beattie took him from the room and I picked it up and answered it, "Hello?"

"Ah Squadron Leader. This is Mr. Balfour here. I was just making sure it worked. I hope you are enjoying your leave."

"Er yes Mr. Balfour."

"Good, well I shall ring you when I have news. For the moment enjoy your leave."

As I put the telephone down I realised what it was, it was a shackle. They had me at their beck and call; quite literally. Beattie brought Tom back. She had given him his favourite teddy bear and he was soothed.

"Who was it?"

"The Ministry. Tomorrow we shall pack up the car and go and look at the places you said you would like to visit. I only have a month's leave and I would like to have everything in place for the purchase before we go."

We had identified some very pleasant little places which were close to London. By close I meant that there was a direct railway line and a train would have us in the centre in under an hour. The London underground came quite a long way out too and it was gradually reaching more remote areas. Finally, I was looking for one with an R.A.F airfield close by. I had one advantage over most other people. I could fly home.

After a week of travelling around we found what proved to be an ideal spot. It was a little village close to the River Crouch. North Fambridge was a huddle of houses but the railway station was within walking distance. The seaside was not too far away and Royal Air Force Rocheford was less than fifteen miles away. It was perfect. Although there were only a few houses I saw the telephone pole. The telephone could be connected. I had realised, as we had been driving around, that although it shackled me to the Ministry, it was also a lifeline for Beattie. When I was away, I could, hopefully, telephone her. I doubted that I would be able to do so from Mesopotamia but, nonetheless, there were benefits.

The price of the cottage was well within our budget for it needed work. However, my sister Alice, who was a designer, had promised us that she would help Beattie as the two of them were close. They were more like sisters. By the last week of my leave I had signed all the papers and made all of the arrangements. The move would not take place for some time but I had done all that I could. I had also begun to teach Beattie how to drive. I did not see the point in having my car sitting under a piece of canvas when Beattie could be using it. I was confident enough that, when I left her she would be able to manage my huge beast. When I returned from the Middle East I would think about a car which was better suited to my wife.

Mr. Balfour had been increasingly busy with his telephone calls and I now had the names of all of the squadron leaders and the make-up of the aeroplanes. His last call, the night before I was to leave for Southampton was to tell me that he would meet me in Southampton with my orders. It seemed final. As was the wont of the service my orders had been changed. There were insurgents in Egypt who were now causing more trouble than the army could handle. It was decided to send my three squadrons there to calm the situation. I neglected to tell Beattie that. She would only worry. However, it meant I could not bring my family with me in the autumn as we had hoped.

Beattie helped me to pack while I held Thomas. I would miss him. When I had left for Russia he had been tiny. He had slept, eaten, cried and filled his nappy. Now he had animation. He could smile and scowl. He could make peculiar noises and giggle for the sheer pleasure of it. He could be mischievous. I knew that, when I returned, I would have missed so much of his growing up.

I now had sturdy luggage which we had bought on a trip to London. I also had the uniforms I would need in the heat of the desert. We still packed my flying jacket and fur lined boots. It was comfort more than anything. Beattie looked up, "When you come back we shall be in our new home."

I nodded, "I feel guilty leaving all of that to you."

She reached up and rubbed my son's head, "I will have Tom Tom to help me, won't I?" He giggled obligingly. "And your sister has promised to take a week from work. It will be fine. But you must promise me to think about your responsibilities. You are not a single man any more. There are others who can take risks. You don't need to."

"I suspect this will be slightly more boring than what I am used to. From what Mr. Balfour has told me I shall be an aerial policeman."

"Well I hope that is true."

The journey down would be Beattie's first test as a driver. She would help me drive down and then drive back herself. She was looking forward to it. She saw it as an adventure.

When she left me on the quayside with the others who were travelling on the requisitioned ship, it was a hard goodbye. I was aware that there were three squadron leaders and Mr. Balfour waiting to speak with me before we boarded but I wanted every second I could with my wife and my son.

"And when you are out there I want you to look for a house for us! I intend to join you. I had enough goodbyes in the Great War."

"I will I promise. I want to see my son grow up. Anyway, you will have enough on your plate with the cottage. The GPO said they will be waiting for you to let them know when they can move it."

"How did you get them to be so accommodating?"

I smiled, "Captain Moncrieff, Roger, who served with me in France, is now high up in the telephone section of the GPO."

"Well something good came out of that war."

"A great deal of good came out of it. Think of all the friends I have. They might not be in the service any longer but we are still brothers in arms." I pointed to the huddle of officers waiting for me. "Soon they will be too."

Part Two
Egypt

Chapter 8

June 1919

The weather had become much hotter as soon as we had cleared the Bay of Biscay. Some of the men had put on their shorts. I had been warned by Mr. Balfour that where we were going, it would be much hotter. He had been a mine of information. He had packs of documents for all of us. As he had said to me privately, "Communication is going to be a little difficult. Your adjutant, Captain Connor will make his way over land from Bagdad. He has local knowledge and, more importantly, can speak the language. I have tried to anticipate every possible problem. You have everything that your officers need and a little more." He had seen my quizzical look. "Mr. Churchill is holding a conference. He hopes to increase the number of squadrons. The situation may change, Squadron Leader." I nodded. Mr. Churchill appeared to be an active man. "One more thing. There is a great deal of unrest in Egypt. Some agitators wish to end the protectorate enjoyed by Great Britain. The King of Egypt wishes us to stay. You will not have the luxury of being able to acclimatise to the country. You will be called upon to police the land as soon as you arrive. The change of orders is vital. You will, eventually be sent to Persia but not until Egypt is stable. We must guard our Suez Canal." And with that he had departed leaving me with my three squadron leaders.

I knew that I was lucky with my squadrons. The three squadron leaders had all fought in France. There was another ace amongst them. Henry Woollett had destroyed eleven balloons and shot down nineteen aeroplanes. More than that he had a D.S.O, M.C. and Bar as well as the Legion d'Honneur. Of course, he was remarkably modest and rarely spoke of his medals. Jack Thomson had also shot down eight German aeroplanes. He commanded the DH 9 bombers. He was envious of Henry and I because we had such fame. He was a very skilful pilot. Ben Mannock commanded the squadron of Vickers Vernons. These were a workhorse. They had been developed from the Vimy and were a large twin engined biplane. They could be used for transport and bombing. I did not know it at the time but the big lumbering beasts would be invaluable. He and his pilots had been dropped in France for their aeroplanes were too large to be carried aboard the freighters and they would fly to the Middle East using French and Greek airfields to refuel. He would be the first of us on the ground. The three nights we had with him allowed me to ensure that we all knew our objectives. He and his Vernons would transport some of the air mechanics and all of the spares. He had the task of preparing the new air field which was being built for us by the Engineers at a place called Heliopolis.

Our Snipes and DH 9 aeroplanes were in two freighters which accompanied us. The liner on which we travelled was spacious and had been used in the Mediterranean before the war. The S.S. Roman Star had seen better days and I doubted that she would attract the same clientele now. It explained why the company had been so keen to be awarded the contract to ferry soldiers and airmen to and from the Middle East. The crew were a mixed bag. There were many older crew members who had served before the war and had been too old for military service. They were mainly English and French. There were others who were younger. They represented the nationalities which had not fought in the Great War. We were well served.

It was strange to be the senior officer. Until the last days of the war, when Archie had been killed, I had been junior to someone. It was, perhaps, something about the nature of our service that many died young and that allowed for the rapid promotion. Henry was older than I was but all the rest of the officers were younger. The crew varied in age. Some had served since before the days of the Corps. Some had been like me, and transferred from another arm. There were some air gunners I recognised and one or two of the pilots were familiar.

Our voyage would take us via Gibraltar, Sicily and Cyprus before landing in Alexandria where the aeroplanes would be offloaded and we would fly the rest of the way. As I sat on what had been the upper observation deck with Henry and Jack I realised that we would face some interesting challenges in the desert.

Henry pointed up to the perfectly blue sky, "You know Bill, we have the breeze from the sea here and we are in the Atlantic yet it is still hot enough that two chaps have been taken to sick bay because of the sun. I fear we will have a problem in the desert."

"You are right. We will be living in tents too. Mr. Balfour packed spare mosquito nets but even so I think that we will have to find solutions to problems we have yet to uncover."

"What do you mean Bill?"

"The three of us fought our war in France and Belgium. Mud, rain, snow: all of them caused a problem and we overcame them because we understood the nature of the problem. How will the canvas on the wings react to the heat? Are there insects and animals which might cause problems with the aeroplanes? Will sand damage the engines? Will there be enough water? Fuel? We are going to a place large enough to have France, Britain and Belgium within its frontiers. It will be a vast country. There will not be towns for landmarks."

"You must have experienced strange problems in the Baltic."

"I did Henry but there we were lucky. We had our airfield with us; it was a carrier. Our airfield is in the middle of nowhere. It has to be so that we can cover a large area of desert."

"And that begs the question of how we do that."

"Bombs and bullets, Jack."

"Against civilians, Bill?"

I held up the paper they had both been given by Mr. Balfour. "Insurgents. I am afraid that, as Mr. Balfour said, our enemies will not wear a uniform. We are there to protect the innocent and punish the guilty."

Jack leaned forward and tapped his pipe out on the ashtray. "God but that is a lot of responsibility."

Henry laughed, "I think you have hit the nail on the head Jack. God. That is what we will be doing. Playing God."

"I trust you gentlemen. I rely on you to make sure that our men are all of the same mind. Ultimately, I will be judged for your actions and those of our men. I will fly with you whenever I can. I am not going to be shackled to a table. They have given me one of the Dolphins. That means I can keep up with the Snipes."

Henry laughed again, "The Snipe is a snail compared with the Dolphin."

"I think that as soon as they can the Ministry will send out replacement aeroplanes. We are using what is left from the war. The exception are the Vernons. Ben has the first six off the production line. I think that four of them were built as prototypes. It is a measure of the importance Mr. Churchill places on our work."

There was a loud altercation from the deck below us. I leaned over and saw fisticuffs from two junior officers. "What I think we need to do, gentlemen, is to keep the minds of our officers occupied. A couple of the waiters are Arabs from Iraq. I have asked the captain if we can borrow them for a couple of hours each day. Lessons in Arabic might be handy."

"Really, Bill?"

"Afraid so, Jack. In my experience being able to speak the language can often defuse a dangerous situation. We will have all of the pilots attend."

"And the ground crews?"

"They have less time on their hands. The Sergeant Majors are giving them PT as well as testing them on their knowledge of all types of aeroplanes. We have too great an area to patrol to allow a broken aeroplane to hold us back."

"Very well, Bill."

"Jack your men will have their lesson in the morning from 1000 to 1200 hours. Henry, yours will be from 1400-1600. I will attend both sessions."

"Both sir?"

"I am pretty certain that as senior officer I will have to meet some of our enemies and it will help if I can speak their language. Besides, it will stop me being bored too."

By the time we reached Gibraltar we had a routine. The officers had complained at first but once they realised that we three were in attendance they accepted it. I was not certain what progress was being made but that was not the point for they were being kept occupied. We took on coal in Gibraltar and I received an update from the military attaché at the consulate.

"You will be based in Egypt for longer than was anticipated. The troubles there are escalating. As soon as we have quashed this insurrection there will be other tasks for you. Later you will move to Palestine and Transjordan. The French are not sending aeroplanes and so you will be needed to cover their protectorate too."

"They are asking a lot, sir."

"I know but there are troops who need to be relieved. Many signed up for the duration. The armistice was signed in November and some are still serving now. Until we can get either more aeroplanes or more regiments here then you will be on the spot so to speak."

Thank you, sir."

He smiled. I could tell that he had served in the war. He had that look. "Well it should be a bit easier than in France. I don't think these chaps have a Red Baron to bother you, what?"

"Not yet, sir, not yet!"

If we thought it was hot in the Atlantic, then the summer heat of the southern Mediterranean was almost unbearable. Had we not had the freighters with us then the captain could have increased speed and we would have reached our destination a day or two earlier but we were forced to plod along at a pedestrian pace. One evening at dinner, the three of us were invited to dine with the Captain and his senior officers. We wore our Number 1s. The lighter and cooler uniform helped.

After dinner, the captain passed around cigars but I stuck with my pipe. "We got these in Cuba." The Captain shook his head, "Damned expensive. They cost us a couple of ships torpedoed by the Hun. We were carrying Americans. It would have been unfortunate to lose them eh? Some people say they saved our bacon, coming in when they did. This is much more pleasant. No zig zagging and listening for the sound of a ship exploding in the night."

I nodded, "I wonder if the people at home are aware of the sacrifices made by the merchant navy, sir."

"Probably not. You are the chaps they all knew about. The pilots, the glory boys."

Jack shook his head, "A little unfair, sir."

"I am just talking about the perception of people at home, that is all. I know you have a hard job."

Henry nodded, sadly, "And dangerous sir. I have seen too many of my friends crashing in a burning pile of fuel. Sometimes there was nothing left to bury."

"You are right. Let's toast those who never came back."

"To those who never came back!"

The mood lightened and I sat with the Captain while the others enjoyed the brandy. "You will have to watch out for the locals in Egypt you know, Squadron Leader. I did a few Nile cruises before I was given this palace. There are many light-fingered brigands who live along the river. They hide in the desert when danger threatens and use the night very well indeed. There are many who wish to overthrow the King."

"I know about the insurgents. I fought the Bolsheviks."

He nodded, "They are growing. When we were in Gibraltar I spoke with some captains heading west. They said that there is military law in the major towns. In the countryside, soldiers have been murdered and military bases attacked."

"Thank you, sir. That is useful intelligence."

The next morning, I sought out Captain Fox. He was in command of the Royal Air Force detachment responsible for our security. "Ralph, I have just heard from the captain that British bases are being attacked. It will make your job much harder. It is not just attacks which can hurt us but sabotage too. What plans have you?"

"I have some good lads, sir. I have been passing on what I have learned at the language lessons. What I need to know sir, is how much force can I use?"

"If we have to, then use deadly force." I told him of the problems we had encountered in the Baltic. "A couple of sailors had their throats cut because of a lack of vigilance. We cannot afford that. We are even more vulnerable than a carrier in the middle of the Baltic."

"Quite sir. Of course, until we get there then we have no idea of the size of the problem."

"And another headache for you is that when we land we will be assembling our aeroplanes and then flying them to our airfield. Security could well be a problem there too."

"Forewarned is forearmed, sir. We will cope."

The closer we came to Alexandria the more alarming became the reports we were getting. British soldiers had been murdered in Cairo's streets and martial law had been imposed. I feared for Squadron Leader Mannock. He had the most vulnerable of our aeroplanes; they were the biggest. I hoped that the army had provided security for them. The big Vernons would be invaluable in ferrying troops around. The attacking arm of our strike force was aboard our ships.

After Cyprus, I sought out the Sergeant Major who would be in charge of the ground crews. "Sergeant Major Robson, I am not going to offload all of the aeroplanes at once. They are too tempting a target. How many aeroplanes can you ready at any one time?"

"Two Snipes and one DH 9, sir. It is the rigging which takes time."

I nodded. "Then that is what we will do. We will have the three aeroplanes armed and fuelled and they can fly to the field. I will go with the first ones. So, make it a Dolphin, Snipe and DH 9a. We will take two Snipes and a DH 9a on each flight after that."

"Sir."

"And I want every one of your men with a side arm. I don't care where you get them from but I want our people to be safe. Captain Fox and his men will have a perimeter while you are assembling them."

"Right sir." He smiled, "And I thought life would be easier once we left Belgium, sir."

"Didn't we all."

I had the captain inform the freighters' captains of my instructions. From the look on his face I could see that neither of them was happy but I had to sign off on the cargo. They would not be able to leave if I did not sign. Finally, I saw Jack and Henry.

"I will take the first three to the field. It is north of Cairo. We have less than eighty miles to fly. Jack I want you to come with the last three. They will be just two DH 9a and a Snipe. Henry come in the middle. I want us all out of the port area as soon as possible."

"What about the mechanics and Captain Fox's men?"

"I intend to refuel at the field and fly back with three of your Snipes. We will keep an over watch on the road. I have looked at the maps. There is just one main road. I will speak with Captain Fox. I want you to arrange the order your aeroplanes fly. It goes without saying, Henry, that I need three Snipe pilots who are the most reliable you have. I need cool heads up there with me."

"Not a problem. I have three who will be perfect."

Once I had spoken with Captain Fox I was ready. I knew that Mr. Balfour had arranged for lorries to be waiting for us. Sergeant Major Robson would check them for sabotage before the lorries left. With armed men in the cabs and at the rear, I hoped I had taken every precaution.

We docked at 0300 hours. It was perfect. It was as cool as it was going to get and there were few people around. I went ashore first with Captain Fox and his men and they made a perimeter. An army Lieutenant awaited us. He had two Rolls Royce armoured cars. He looked harassed, "I will go and wake Major Pickwick, sir. He is in command of this detachment of the 17th Hussars. We are to escort your men to your new field."

"Good. How are things here, Lieutenant?"

"Tense sir. The whole place is like a powder keg. This chap, Saad Zaghlul Pasha has the locals stirred up. The King of Egypt and those close to him are all happy for us to be here but there is unrest everywhere. The majority of people want us out, sir."

"That should come as no surprise to you, Lieutenant. Our colonies have always been unhappy about the way they are ruled. Every Empire has had these problems. Just do your duty and trust your men. Is there anywhere near here which is flat enough for us to use to take off?"

"Take off sir?"

"Yes Lieutenant. We have aeroplanes."

"I am not sure, sir."

All we need is a piece of reasonably flat road which is straight."

He brightened, "Oh yes, sir. There is a road which runs parallel to the docks. It is four hundred yards of straight and then there is a curve."

"Good I would like you to block it off for us and keep it clear. Once dawn breaks we shall fly off."

I had been given a small staff to help me run the three squadrons. Sergeant Major Hale was a quiet and thoughtful man. He had a sergeant and two corporals under him. In addition, he had taken it upon himself to assign one of the R.A.F. regiment's privates, Williams, to be my servant and bodyguard. The first I knew of this was as I was organising my luggage. "Don't you worry about that, sir. Williams here will look after that for you." Sergeant Major Hale waved to the private.

"Williams?"

The Private snapped to attention and saluted, "Yes sir. I shall be your gentleman's gentleman, sir. I have never done it before but I will give it a go. Captain Fox and Sergeant Major Hale seem to think I can do it."

"We will talk about this when we get to the airfield. Thank you, Sergeant Major, but next time speak to me first."

He was not put out by my reprimand. He smiled. "You had a lot on your plate, sir. This will be fine sir. I believe you had a servant in France."

"Yes, Sergeant Major, how did you know?"

"Mr. Balfour told me and suggested we get someone for you. A clever man that, sir."

Balfour again. I joined my mechanics as they began to assemble the aeroplanes. Sergeant Major Robson himself was working on the Dolphin. The ships' captains had rigged up lights to enable them to work.

"Nice little bus this sir. Do you know much about them?"

"No Sergeant Major."

"An excellent aeroplane. As fast as they come but the early ones had French engines and they were a bit, well iffy, sir. That is why there aren't a lot of them. This is post war sir. It has a proper engine and we have one spare. But be careful with it eh, sir?"

The mechanics worked as fast as they could but they were careful. Robson saw to that. When he was satisfied, he had the guns loaded and then fuelled.

I waved over the two pilots and the gunner. I pointed to the armoured car which marked the beginning of our impromptu runway. "We are going to taxi down there, turn around and take off. Lieutenant Martinside you are in the DH 9a. You are tail end Charlie. You have a rear gunner. Lieutenant Broome, you will follow me. I have a mirror and I will keep my speed down. If you have a problem, then waggle your wings. When we land, Broome, then you and I will be going back up when Johnson and Wingate arrive. We will keep the road clear. I will brief you at the airfield."

"Right sir."

I turned to Squadron Leader Woollett. "Good luck Squadron Leader."

"And you." He pointed east. The sun was just rising. "You should have the coolest part of the day. I fear that I shall be taking off at noon."

"I will have a cold beer waiting for you, how's that?"

"You, sir, are a gentleman."

The Dolphin was similar to the Camel but I had never flown one. There was no pressure with three ships, two squadrons and a troop of Hussars watching me! However, I had managed to fly off the deck of a pitching carrier. At least this road would not move. I used the taxi to acclimatise myself to the pedals and the yoke. I reached the far armoured car and turned. The DH 9a, the Nanak, seemed to dwarf me. The Snipe, in contrast looked to be of a similar size. I waited until they were past me and then I opened the throttle. It was a powerful beastie and soon had me in the air. I had to throttle back for I did not want to lose my consorts. I banked and turned to head south. The Snipe also climbed well but the DH 9a lumbered. I waited until they were on station and then headed south, using the road to guide me.

The new airfield was at Heliopolis and was to the north east of Cairo. The Pyramids, on the southern outskirts of Cairo, would be a visual marker for us. Even though it was the cool of the day I felt hot already. I was wearing my flying coat. That would be a problem. We would need them when we were high but if we were strafing or bombing then we would not. I mentally stored that problem. I stored that question for a later time.

The DH 9a could not match our speed and so it took us an hour to see the Pyramids. I knew that the field would be to the east of us. I looked for the six huge Vernons. I saw the limp windsock first and then three Vernons. Half were missing. I banked and headed for the field. It was literally that, a field. There were two wooden buildings and tents, including two marquees. It was a flock of tents in a sea of sand. There were more tents than we would need and I saw the lorries and vehicles of the Engineers who had built the base. Even as I lined up for my landing I realised I could not bring my wife and son here. Mr. Balfour had known that.

After I had landed and was taxiing towards the Vernons and the huge tank, which I assumed was the fuel, I saw that there was no perimeter fence. That would have to change. When the Dolphin's propeller stopped turning I forced myself to think of positives. The Dolphin was a good aeroplane and the equal of the Camel.

I climbed out and was struck by a wall of heat. I took off my coat and hung it on the wing. Squadron Leader Mannock strode towards me with an Army Captain. A couple of mechanics hurried behind. They stopped and saluted. I said to the mechanics. "I want the Dolphin and the Snipe topping up with fuel. There will be a couple more Snipes arriving soon. I want then refuelled as well."

"Sir!" They raced back to fetch the bowser.

I looked at Ben and he shook his head, "Sorry about the Vernons, sir. One is still back in France and two of them broke down. They will be here but they are waiting for spares. One is in Cyprus and the other is on Corfu."

"Captain Cooper, sir. Engineers. We are sharing the field with you."

I pointed my hand at the perimeter, "Why is there no fence?"

"We are waiting for the wire to arrive, sir. Everything has to be brought by boat from Alexandria. Since the insurgents began their disruption we have to convoy the boats down here."

I waved a hand above my head. "Well, we have air cover now. When my aeroplanes have all landed we will work something out. We have to have better security than this. From what I learned in Alexandria the situation is worsening by the day."

Ben nodded. "I have been here for a few days and I can testify to that, sir. The men have been sleeping in the Vernons to stop sabotage and thieving."

"Well we can't sleep in Snipes." A Corporal hurried over with a tray. He had four mugs of tea.

"Here y'are sir. A nice drop of Rosy!"

"Thank you Corporal." The first mouthful made me feel better. I could now see why we had been sent. Small in numbers we could have an effect far beyond those numbers. I turned as I heard the sound of engines. The two Snipes and the Nanak were making their approach. I saw the mechanics watching. They had finished. "You two refuel these Snipes as soon as you can. Corporal, another brew for these pilots. They are taking off straightaway." The two lieutenants had joined us and were sipping their tea.

"Sir!"

Ben asked, "What is the plan, sir?"

"The rest of the personnel will be coming in lorries. I want us to keep the road clear and safe. There will be two armoured cars escorting them but I was warned that the insurgents might attack us."

The three aeroplanes landed and I felt better. Their pilots climbed down and walked over to us. "God, it is hot sir!"

"It is Lieutenant Dixon. I shall be leaving my flying coat here. I don't think I shall need it." I put the cup back on the tray and took out my pipe. I had just got it going when I heard the sound of engines. The next three aeroplanes were coming.

Lieutenant Broome said, "They must be getting faster sir."

I nodded, "The Sergeant Major probably has a system. Squadron Leader have the buses parked close to your Vernons. They will be the priority for Captain Fox's men."

"Sir."

"And, Captain Cooper, if you let me have a schedule for the boats I will arrange a patrol to watch them."

"Sir."

The next flight was just approaching as we climbed aboard our aeroplanes. I allowed them to land and then the four of us roared into the air. As we banked to head north I saw the next three aeroplanes in the distance as they headed south. I reckoned we were half way through. We had a three-hour range. I looked at my watch. We would fly back to the docks and stooge around for an hour and then head south above the lorries. I had worked out how they were working faster. The Sergeant Major was working on more than three aeroplanes at a time. That was confirmed when we saw another three aeroplanes heading south.

As we headed north I looked to the land below us. There were mud huts dotted along the road. We were flying at four hundred feet and I could see figures working in the fields. There were other knots of men who pointed up to us. The road looked to be largely empty. I saw no vehicles travelling down it. This was the land of the donkey and the camel. Vehicles belonged to the rich and the British. Vehicles would be the targets for attack.

The outskirts of Alexandria teemed. As we zoomed over the people looked like worker ants. The sheer numbers showed me the problem we faced. I took a loop around the city. I spied the Union Flag and saw that the British buildings were protected by sandbags, machine guns and more armoured cars. The sentries on the roof waved. I headed back to the port. I saw that there were five aeroplanes being assembled. I checked my fuel gauge. We had enough to reach the field and some to spare. I had not used maximum speed. As I had been flying I had realised that fuel might be an issue. We would receive all of our fuel down the river. If that was interrupted then we were in trouble. I now appreciated that I would need an adjutant. I remembered how useful Randolph had been in France. Not a pilot himself he had understood the needs of pilots. I hoped that Captain Connor was of the same calibre.

Two Nanaks and a Snipe took off leaving just Henry and one DH 9a. I saw the lorries being loaded as I watched the three aeroplanes head south. The last two were ready before the three aeroplanes had disappeared from view. The Sergeant Major and his men had worked wonders. Instead of heading south Henry and the DH 9a tagged on to the end of my looping flight. He was disobeying orders but I guessed he had his reasons. Below me the khaki ants were scurrying around and clambering aboard their vehicles. We would have to loop above the convoy as it headed south. Even at our lowest speed we would still be almost twice as fast as the lorries we escorted. The sun was now high in the sky and I knew that I was luckier than the other pilots. The Dolphin's upper wing afforded me some shade. The Snipe and the Nanak were more open.

We were half way to the field when I spied potential trouble. I saw a huddle of men by the side of the road. They were a couple of miles away and it was hard to see what they were up to but I had seen no such gathering heading north. I began a slow descent to a hundred feet above the ground. The speed seemed much greater that close to the ground. I saw that they were building a barricade across the road. I cocked the Vickers. When I was a hundred yards from the improvised road block I fired. My .303 bullets tore into the wood. And then I had passed and was banking around. I heard the other aeroplanes as they fired their bullets to clear the road block. I swung around for a second pass. I saw that the Nanak's gunner was spraying bullets over the heads of the insurgents. They were already beginning to disperse.

I saw that the convoy had slowed. The road block was partly destroyed but it would still stop the convoy and so I levelled up for another attack. I fired from further away. I intended to fire one Vickers for I had another and two Lewis guns. My bullets arced towards the undamaged section of the barricade. Suddenly the whole barricade exploded. The Arabs who were forty yards away were thrown to the ground. It had been booby trapped with explosives. As Lieutenant Broome demolished the other side I saw that the convoy could pass. I banked to pass over the Arabs who were fleeing away from the road. They were heading for the scrub. If I had had a grenade or a bomb then the threat would have been ended. I was not certain how we stood when it came to killing civilians. Were these rebels or just malcontents? That was one problem with air support; it was harder to verify who you were fighting.

I banked to starboard to pass along the length of the column. As we did so I saw the waves and the cheering of the air crew. They, better than anyone, understood what we had just done. It was a clear demonstration to the local population that the Royal Air Force had arrived. Their days of unrestricted mischief were gone.

Chapter 9

I was forced to leave the convoy ten miles from the airfield along with the two Snipes which had accompanied me. We were running low on fuel. Squadron Leader Woollett and the DH 9a watched over them for the last few, uneventful miles. As we came into land, I saw that my orders had been obeyed. The aeroplanes were parked closely together. If the insurgents had aeroplanes we would be in trouble as they made a very tempting target for aerial bombers. However, they could be more easily protected against ground forces.

I climbed out of the Dolphin, aware that I was wringing with sweat. What I needed was a shower or a bath. I looked around at the camp and realised that one would not be forthcoming. In our absence, I saw that more tents had been erected. The cheerful Corporal from London marched smartly up to me.

"Sir, Squadron Leader Mannock asked me to meet you and show you to your quarters sir!"

"Thank you. You seem to be an enterprising non-com. And who would you be Corporal?"

"Corporal Swanston sir."

"And what is it that you do around here Corporal?"

"Well sir, until January, I was a Corporal Clerk but they have done away with that rank now sir so I am a Corporal and as for what I do sir." He grinned, "Pretty much anything that I am ordered to."

"Good man. A useful type eh?"

"I try to be, sir."

"Do we have ablutions yet, Corporal?"

"Sort of, sir. The Engineers have dug a cess pit and we have a water bowser but that is all."

"And a shower?"

He grinned, "Not really necessary here sir. The locals stink worse than we do!"

"Right. Then lead on Macduff."

"No sir my… oh right sir, Shakespeare."

"You know Shakespeare then, Corporal?"

"Well there was a turn at the Hackney Empire did a bit of recitation. It was alright." He pointed at a large tent. It looked like the type occupied by four men. Someone had hung a sign saying Commanding Officer. "Here y'are sir. Home sweet home. I put your flying coat on your cot. I am guessing the rest of your stuff will be on the way?"

"Yes. Be a good fellow and find Senior Aircraftman Williams when he arrives. He has my gear. Fetch it here and unpack for me eh? Let me know when you have done so."

"Right sir."

"And where is the mess or do we not have one yet?"

"Oh yes sir. There are two messes, one for officers and warrant officers and the other one for other ranks. They are the two marquees. The officers are there now, sir."

"Thank you Corporal. I can see that you will be a useful chap to know."

I strode off to the two marquees. It was obvious which was which and I entered the officer's mess. They all snapped to attention when I entered. "At ease, as you were."

Ben came over to me, "Any problems?"

I nodded, "The blighters set up a road block and mined it. We had to shoot it up. The column managed to avoid any damage." I looked around. It was a basic mess. There were trestle tables and foldaway chairs. "I suppose we were luckier than we knew in France. We had stone buildings and furniture."

Ben pointed his pipe at the officers who were seated around tables and chatting. "At the moment, we are dry. The supplies are on the lorries!"

"We should be able to get something from Cairo."

"I thought that this was a Muslim country and they didn't drink."

"The last I heard the Crown Prince, Feisal, drinks like a fish! We will have to wait for the adjutant. Apparently, he knows the Arabs quite well. We will be reliant on his knowledge of the customs of these people."

The last two aeroplanes landed and I heard them taxiing. It was followed a few moments later by the sound of the Rolls Royce engines of the armoured cars.

Captain Cooper came in. His face was covered in dirt and he was extremely sweaty. He was an officer who was not afraid to get his hands dirty. "Well, that is the last of the tents up and we have put the posts in for the barbed wire. I am afraid we can't get the fence erected yet but tomorrow eh, Squadron Leader?"

"That will be fine. I will have double sentries posted tonight."

He pointed to the lorries. "I hope they have some beer on board!"

"It won't be cold you know."

The officer of engineers grinned at Ben, "I couldn't care less sir. It will be wet and fizzy and that will do. I will get some sort of cooling system set up tomorrow and the day after we will begin work on the ablutions."

"I wondered about that."

"Putting in showers is not the problem, sir. It is getting the water here. Unfortunately, we are downstream of Cairo. We will need to put in some sort of water purification or we are in trouble."

"Any help we can give then let us know."

"First we have to get the water here. That will take a couple of days."

"And the fuel tanks?"

"They were the first thing we put in. The bowser you see is to fill the aeroplanes. It is easier to fill the bowser and then used that."

"And have we somewhere for the armoury?"

He pointed to one of the wooden buildings. "One of those is the offices and the other is for stores. The rear half is for the ammunition and ordnance."

"That will need to be secure."

"It will be."

Sergeant Major Hale marched up to me, laden with papers. He stood at attention, "Sir, which is the admin block?"

I pointed to the wooden building. "Over there, Sergeant Major."

"Thank you sir. Williams is sorting your gear out with that Cockney! Oh and that was nice shooting, sir. Impressed the lads that did!"

The rest of what was left of the day was spent in frenetic activities. Even the pilots and gunners had to lend a hand to unload all of the supplies we would be needing. It soon became apparent that the stores building would not accommodate all of the supplies and stores we had brought. I made the decision to give over half of the admin hut. I did not envisage me spending days there. The most important part was the radio. We placed that so that it was close to the generator which powered it and then Sergeant Major Hale worked around it. He seemed a very capable man.

The medical officer, Captain Flynn, came to see me. "Sir, we do not appear to have a sick bay. We have medicines which need refrigeration and we should have a sterile environment."

"Good luck with that, Captain. Feel free to put your medicines and their refrigerator in the admin hut but, for the moment you will have to make do with a large tent." He looked crestfallen, "Have you any patients yet?"

"Well, no sir, but it is a matter of time."

I sighed. I had greater worries than a medical wing! "We need running clean water first. When we have that I will get the engineers to build another hut for you. How's that?"

"Yes sir, that will do. Sorry to fuss so."

"Don't worry about it. It has been a long day for all of us."

Lieutenant Fielding, who commanded the two armoured cars, gave me the welcome news that, until our guns arrived, they would be attached to us for defence. It made the end of the day brighter than I had expected. After making sure that the mosquito nets were distributed and being used I went with Captain Fox and Lieutenant Fielding to examine our defences.

"The problem is, sir, that it is as black as the ace of spades around here at night. We need lights or these insurgents could creep up on us and have everything away while we are watching."

"It is one night that we have to wait for the wire. Have double sentries. If you need me to…"

"Oh no sir, we'll cope but even with the fence we are vulnerable."

"Suppose there was a minefield all around the perimeter?"

Captain Fox brightened, "That would do the trick sir. Have we got any?"

"No, we shall make some."

"Mines?"

I smiled, "Something that looks like mines. Have the cook collect all the empty bully beef tins. We have the men fill them with sand and hammer a nail into the top. We bury them around the wire and put a skull and crossbones sign up."

Captain Fox frowned and then smiled, "That might just work and is cheap enough. My chaps could also rig a few trip wires and grenades up too."

By the time I reached my cot I was exhausted. It had been a long day and we had already done so much that I was amazed. I knew that we could only allow ourselves a day or two, at the most, before we had patrols up in the air. While the camp was being set up that would be the task of me and my squadron leaders.

The bugle which woke me was a reminder of France. I was out of bed instantly. I dressed and donned shorts. Now I would reap the benefit of them. Williams came racing to my tent just as I emerged to view the camp, "Sorry, sir. I am a bit new to this servant lark. Sergeant Major Hale will have my bits for this sir. Sorry sir."

"Williams, don't worry. I do not need help in dressing. Just keep my quarters tidy and have my washing done. I will be happy." I pointed to the bag with the guns. "And make sure that they are secure."

"Yes sir." He nodded to the sky, "I think it is going to be a hot one sir."

"I am pretty certain that would apply to any day out here. We had better get used to it." I saw that Mr. Balfour had thought to supply sun helmets. I had always thought them ridiculous but now I saw the benefit. I donned mine. It would encourage the men to wear theirs.

I went first to the admin hut. As I had expected Sergeant Major Hale was already there with Corporal Winspear and Corporal Hutton. "Morning sir. I checked with the sentries and it was a quiet night."

"Good." I explained to him my ploy. He grinned and nodded his approval. "I think I have just the fellow to implement it too."

Sergeant Major Hale said, "The Cockney, Swanston, sir?"

"That is the chap. Have him come to me after breakfast. I will sort the paperwork out then. Is the radio working?"

"Yes sir. Hutton here got in touch with the army in Cairo and told them we were here. A Colonel Fisher will be coming out to chat this morning, sir."

"And any news of the adjutant, Captain Connor?"

"Last we heard, and that was when we landed was that he left Bagdad a week ago and he was driving himself across the desert."

I wondered why he had not used an aeroplane. It seemed strange but I did not want to judge him. He would be the only one of us with local knowledge. I went to the mess tent. Breakfast was basic fare. It might already be hotter than the hottest day in England but we still had porridge, tea and toast. Some things never changed. When my squadron leaders arrived, they joined me.

"Today we make sure that everything works. See that we are ready to fly at a moment's notice."

"Will we be called upon today then, Bill?"

"I have a Colonel Fisher coming to see me this morning and I daresay we will find out. I don't want any idle hands. The engineers will have their hands full. If our lads can do anything to help then let them do so. We are one team out here. I don't want people being precious about titles."

"Right."

The cook came over. "Sir, Captain Fox said we were to save all the bully beef tins. You want them. Is that right, sir?"

"It certainly is. How many have you?"

"Twenty now and there will be another twenty by this afternoon. We get through a lot of bully beef sir!"

"Excellent." After he had gone I explained to my bemused squadron leaders what I had in mind. They approved.

Sergeant Major Hale gave me a wry smile when I sat at my desk. There was a mountain of paperwork. "This is for one day?"

"The adjutant will normally deal with it all sir but he isn't here."

I was beginning to have a poor opinion of the adjutant and he had not even arrived.

"Sir, you sent for me?"

Relieved to be away from paperwork I looked up at Corporal Swanston. "Yes Corporal, I have a little job for you. I want you to get a team of men together. Six should be enough. Go to the cook. He had twenty bully beef tins. Find Captain Fox and get a bag of nails. Find somewhere that no one can see you from the road. I want you to half fill the tins with sand and fold back the lids. Put a nail so that the head sticks out. Then take them outside the perimeter and bury them."

He grinned, "You want to make the rag heads think that there is a minefield eh sir?"

"We call them Arabs or insurgents but yes, you are right. Make a couple of signs. Skull and crossbones; the usual thing. After dark Captain Fox will go and put a couple of trip wires with grenades around the outside to deter anyone from investigating."

"Right sir. Things are looking up here!" He went away whistling.

I smiled, "Would that I could make everyone as happy. I am not certain that anyone will be happy after a few months here."

"You make the best of it don't you sir. Brew?"

"Why not Sarn't Major?"

"Hutton, get the kettle on!"

I took out my pipe and slowly filled it. I had only managed a couple of smokes the previous day. I still had half a tin of Captain Hesketh's tobacco. I would have to go into Cairo to augment it.

"That's a nice smelling baccy sir."

"I got it from a captain when I was in the Baltic. Flavoured with rum. Do you smoke a pipe Mr. Hale?"

"I do indeed."

I threw him the tin. "Have a fill."

"Are you certain, sir?"

"I put a piece of orange peel in but it is still drying out. Best to use it while it still draws. I'll get some more from Cairo."

By the time the tea arrived we both had them going. "Lovely and smooth, sir and you can just get a faint taste of rum. Where did the sea captain get it?"

"Cuba so I can't see us getting more any time soon."

The pipe, the tea and Sergeant Major Hale's team helped the morning to fly by. I heard a car pull up and Colonel Fisher arrived, "You must be Squadron Leader Harsker,"

"Yes sir."

"Heard a lot about you, all good." He gestured to a young lieutenant, "This is my aide, Lieutenant Simpson-Jones. He will be your liaison. Heard you had a spot of bother on the road yesterday."

I did not ask him how he knew, "Yes sir but it didn't hold us up."

He nodded, "How soon can you begin operations?"

"I could get a flight up this afternoon sir but tomorrow would be better."

He laughed, "Good God man, I thought you would have needed a week! The place looks like a Boy Scout camp. I shall have to reprimand Captain Cooper. He is slacking! I thought better of him."

I shook my head, "On the contrary sir, Captain Cooper has not stopped working since we arrived. His efforts have been exemplary. What do you have in mind for us?"

"There are three areas of concern. The river is vital. We need a patrol there. The road, as you experienced yesterday, is easy to cut and then there are the outposts." He nodded to his aide. "Lieutenant."

The Lieutenant unrolled a map and he pinned it to the wall. He took his swagger stick and used it as a pointer, "Here is Cairo. The red dots represent units of British soldiers. They are guarding crossroads, oases and important installations. Some have been attacked already."

"Right then we know what we have to do. I have twenty-five aeroplanes which are capable of aggressively discouraging the insurgents and I have three large transports which can extract soldiers from difficult positions and, at a pinch, bomb. Your Major Pickwick has loaned me two armoured cars until our machine guns arrive from the Quarter Master's in Cairo."

The colonel shook his head. "I am afraid that our armoury was broken into last week. They took your guns. We will have to wait for the next shipment to arrive up the river."

"The armoured cars are fine. They can do the job until our replacement guns arrive and we can hope that they don't have much ammunition for the guns they stole."

He stood, "Well Squadron Leader it seems you have a well-deserved reputation. You take things in your stride and appear to be a practical chap. I look forward to working with you. The Lieutenant will stay and discuss how he will liaise with you. I shall send the car back for him."

After the Colonel had gone I said, "This is the centre of operations. Until the adjutant arrives you will deal directly with Sergeant Major Hale. I will go and see my squadron leaders. Our work starts on the morrow!"

Even as the Colonel had been telling me of my mission I had been planning. The Vernons had a longer range and endurance. They were not fast. More importantly they all had a radio. Out here, in the desert, they had more chance of working efficiently. I would have one flying each day to over fly the garrisons. The Snipes and Nanaks would work in teams of four; two of each. I would send one section up in the morning to cover the road and on the river and a second one in the afternoon. It would give them all a break and allow for maintenance. I would be the spare. I had no doubt that break downs would occur.

I explained to the three squadron leaders what I wanted. "We need to make sure that we have a flight leader or one of us with each of the patrols. Without radios someone will have to make a decision about the threats that we are presented with."

Ben said, "At least we can call in for help. Bill, do you think I could modify our Vernons?"

"Of course."

"I want to be able to drop bombs and that means fitting bomb racks and devising a sight."

I tapped out my pipe and looked at him, "Go ahead!"

"Really?"

"Of course. You have three Vernons here. Adapt those and when the three which had problems arrive, leave them whole. We will need to use those as transports and air ambulances."

They all suddenly looked pleased. "Do we fit bombs to the Snipes, Bill?"

"We have that option but I would rather use the Snipes and the Dolphin to strafe. The DH 9a has a good bomb load and the mixed flights will help." I put my pipe in my pocket. "I leave it to you to arrange your crews. You know them better than I do. I was pleased with the performance yesterday of Dixon and the other pilots. I shall fly one flight tomorrow with the river patrol and the second with the road patrol. I want to see my pilots in action." I stood. "And now back to the paperwork."

It was the middle of the afternoon and I was ready for a break when I heard a very noisy vehicle drawing up. I went outside, more because I was fed up of sitting down than anything else. I saw a 1912 Siddeley D Easy open topped Grand Tourer draw up. The driver wore goggles, a flying helmet and had a cigar in his mouth. He stepped out and bounded over to me. Pushing the goggles from his head he held out his right hand. Even as I took it, automatically, I noticed that he had a savage scar running down his left cheek and he had a patch where his left eye should have been. He had no left hand, instead he had a sort of metal attachment with what looked like an open ball on it.

"Squadron Leader Harsker." I said it in such a way that he would tell me just who he was.

"Of course, sir. I am your new adjutant, Captain Ted Connor. Sorry I am a little late. I had a spot of bother with some chaps in Palestine. They tried to take the damned car off me. Had to wound a couple of the blighters! Still I am here now and raring to go!"

He was like a whirlwind. For once in my life I had no idea what to say. Sergeant Major Hales, who had been standing behind me, came to my assistance. "What the captain needs is a nice cup of tea. Hutton, tea, Winspear, take the Captain's luggage to his quarters." He stood aside to allow us to re-enter.

I nodded my thanks to the Sergeant Major. "This, Captain, is your domain. I am glad you are here for I hate paperwork!" I gestured to a seat and he sat down.

"To be honest, sir, so do I but since I had my little prang then it is all I can do unless I want to leave the Royal Air Force"

For once Sergeant Major Hale was intrigued and he filled his pipe. It seemed a good idea and I filled mine.

The captain took out a lighter and lit the cheroot in his mouth. He smiled as he sucked in the smoke, "Ah that is better. It is always a shame to smoke when you are driving. It burns too quickly but I like the taste of the cheroot in my mouth, what?" He smiled, "From your expression, Squadron Leader, I take it that I am not what you expected?"

I tried but I could not help glancing at his hand and the attachment.

"Ah this." He grabbed hold of the attachment and unscrewed it. "I use this to change gears. There was a mechanic in Bagdad, looked after the R.E.8s there. The man was a genius and he made this. I have all sorts of attachment to help me do things. Marvellous! Changed my life."

Corporal Hutton brought in the tea. I said, "Thank you Corporal. Yes, well, I was not told of your…"

"Disability?" I nodded. He smiled and sipped his tea. "That, Squadron Leader, is because the Royal Air Force doesn't know about this." I thought that Hale was going to choke on his pipe. The Captain leaned forward conspiratorially. "The thing is I don't want to leave the Royal Air Force. I accept I can't fly." He grinned, "That is to say I am able to fly but I know they won't let me. My old boss let me stay on after my little accident and I became adjutant. I know pilots and I know flying. With a face like this and a disability like this what is there for me back in Blighty?"

"How did it happen?"

"Pure bad luck. We did a lot of flying and raiding for Colonel Lawrence, you know the chap who brought the Arabs on side. Funny fellow he is. Never knew how to take him. Anyway, the Turks are piss poor pilots but one got lucky, or at least his gunner did. He hit the Vickers on my Camel. The bullets tore through my hand and pieces of metal went into my eye. Of course, I shot down the bastard. I watched him burn. But that was the end of my career as a pilot. You can't have a one-eyed pilot with just one hand. I was lucky of course. It was my left hand! Good job I am not a Muslim- I couldn't wipe my bum, could I?"

At that point, the rest of us burst out laughing. "Captain, your secret is safe with us. So long as you can deal with the paperwork, I am happy."

"Good show!" He beamed.

"And can you speak the lingo?"

"The dialect will be different here but, yes. I think so."

"Then get yourself cleaned up. We have no showers yet. Sort out your tent and then Sergeant Major Hale will bring you up to speed. I will then meet you in the mess where I shall buy you the biggest drink to show how glad I am that you are here!"

"Good show, old boy! Good show!"

I took a stroll around the camp. I saw that Swanston had almost completed his work. He gave me a cheery wave. The wire fence was almost up. Once again Captain Fox looked like a coal miner from Durham! The two armoured cars were parked at the two entrances to the camp and the mechanics were sitting around the aeroplanes smoking. They had finished and we were as ready to begin work as one might have hoped. I headed for my tent. My uniform was sweaty. I had a spare and so I decided to change it. Williams was already there. He was polishing my spare boots.

"I can't see me needing those to be shiny, Williams."

"I know, sir, but I was brought up to work hard. It doesn't sit right sitting on my arse doing nowt. Sorry sir."

"I know. I was brought up the same." I looked around the tent. "Where are my guns?"

He pulled a locked box from beneath my cot, "I locked them in there, sir. "He handed me a key. "There are only two keys sir, yours and mine."

"Right then open the box. You can strip down and clean my guns. When you have done that go and have a practice with them. I have a feeling that we are going to need them before long."

"Hoped you would say that, sir." He unlocked the box and carefully took the weapons out. He handled them reverently knowing their value. Then he took out his cleaning rags and oil. He whistled as he worked.

He was happy. I reflected that he was typical of so many British soldiers and working men. A job and something to give them purpose was all that they needed. Money was not the issue. It was a case of self-worth. I had seen it on the estate. My dad never worried about money. He wanted to do the best he could for his lordship. He wanted his lordship's horses to be the best that they could be. That was his job. He was always happy when that happened. I suppose I was the same. I realised that I had been lucky. I had been given a team that was as close to perfect as it got. If we did not do what was expected of then there would be only one man to blame. Me.

Chapter 10

Captain Connor might have the one hand but it did not slow him down. He had various attachments he used for different jobs. The open ball arrangement allowed him to drive and he had another which was a fork. A third allowed him to keep objects steady while he held them. How he managed to tie his tie one handed I will never know. He was a godsend. He helped Swanston paint signs in Arabic warning of the mines and he went with Captain Fox to explain to the locals, the ones who lived just a mile or so from the field, who we were. When time allowed, I intended to take him with me to Cairo. There were things the squadron needed. My priority, however, was the patrols and I had my bus checked over before I went to bed.

I slept easier that night. We had fences and I had an adjutant. The daily update I to Beattie was almost cheerful. She had told me, when I was home, that my moods were clearly evident in my letters. When I had thought I had been hiding my sadness or apprehension she had seen through it. I decided to make my letters as cheerful as I could.

Williams woke me with a cup of tea while it was still dark. "Morning sir. A nice time of the day is this. It is cooler. You feel you can breathe. I like a bit of sun but it is a bit too much here, if you know what I mean."

"I do indeed." I pointed to my soiled uniform. "That could do with a wash when Captain Cooper gets the water going. Until then just hang it for the wind to blow through. Mrs. Harsker packed plenty of other things but I only have the two tunics."

"Yes sir. The lads will be happy when we get the water. No one likes to stink do they sir?"

The smell of toasting bread wafted over from the kitchens. Captain Connor had already told the cook that he knew how to make a bread oven. The men got through a lot of bread. The indefatigable and resourceful Captain had promised to get it organised. Williams and Swanston would be his helpers. Both enjoyed challenges.

Henry and Jack sat with me and we discussed the patrols. I would be accompanying their men on the river patrol that morning. Jack would take the road patrol and Henry would have the afternoon river patrol. It meant the three of us could compare notes that evening. I had decided to try flying in shorts. I saw Ben walk in. He too had on shorts. He would be flying the Vernon himself. "A little late, Ben."

"Yes Henry, I was just making sure that the bomb racks were fitted and I took a Lewis and a Lee Enfield from the stores. Leading Aircraftman Newton has volunteered to use them from the door if we get a chance. We have rigged up a harness for him."

I left Ben to his breakfast and went to check over the Dolphin. The four pilots were all waiting for me. "You chaps will be flying together for the foreseeable future. I am just an extra pair of eyes. Carry on as though I am not here."

Lieutenant Dixon would be leading the flight, "Sir. Can I just be clear on what we are looking for and what we are allowed to do."

"Simple. We fly up the river until we see the sea and then turn around and come back. We provide cover for the ships which ply their trade up the river. If we see river pirates or insurgents trying to disrupt their passage we deter them."

"Strafe and bomb them."

"Yes, Lieutenant Murray. If that is what it takes. Such precise action means we will have to fly low and that means we are in danger of ground fire. That is why we have decided to fly with the Snipes behind the Nanaks. They are faster and can zoom in to deal with problems. Anyway, good luck. I shall be up there with you this morning."

I allowed them to take off first. I had more speed at my disposal. I watched them rise into the sky and then saw Jack lead his three aeroplanes up a moment later. I had the runway to myself. I heard the Vernon start up. Today was a new start for us and I felt quite excited. Although the sun had only been up an hour it was already becoming hot and the cool air from my ascent felt good. The goggles we had been issued had sun blocking lenses in them. Here we needed goggles more than in France and the darkened lenses made it easier to see. I began to quickly catch the four aeroplanes which were in the distance. The Dolphin was even more powerful than my old Camel.

When I reached them, I took station on the port side of them. I also flew above the four aircraft. The Nile snaked below us. It was wide here. Almost half a mile at its widest but I knew that it narrowed in places to just four or five hundred yards. In the winter, when the river was in flood then it could spread even wider. I would be on the limit of my aeroplane if I went all the way to the sea with them. I had decided to turn around before they did.

We were thirty minutes into the flight when we saw the first convoy. There was a gunboat leading four steam barges. I saw crates on three of them and men on the fourth. They wore British khaki and naval whites. The convoy looked out of place amongst the elegant white sailed ships which seemed to dart about the water like water boatmen. I was under no illusions. The local ships could turn from things of beauty into creatures of terror if they chose to attack the ships. The men on the barge waved. I saw Lieutenant Dixon waggle his wings. We spied no danger as we headed north. When I had just over half a tank left, I turned and left the patrol to carry on north. I headed south.

I caught up with the convoy at a bend in the river. I had descended to two hundred feet as I approached them. It proved a fortuitous move for, as I did so I saw something I had not seen as I had headed north, a gun. Insurgents had got hold of an old Turkish field piece. They had hidden it in a stand of palm trees next to the river. Had I not been so low I would not have seen it. Even as I cocked my Vickers, a puff of smoke came from the barrel of the field piece followed by a bang. I saw the waterspout just ten yards short of the leading barge. One sailor was knocked to the deck. I opened fire. They had neither seen nor heard me. The Dolphin was a quiet aeroplane. Although I was aiming at the old gun my bullets sprayed left and right. I saw a couple of the gunners fall, clutching wounds.

As I climbed to attack a second time I heard the gunboat open fire. Banking to make a second attack I saw insurgents fleeing. The gun lay at an unnatural angle. Had I had bombs I could have totally destroyed it but I did what I could. I emptied my Vickers into it. I must have been lucky for, as I zoomed low over it the ammunition exploded. In my mirror, I saw the fireball behind me. The gun was gone.

I landed and Sergeant Major Robson came over with his mechanics. "The guns will need reloading."

"Saw a bit of action did you, sir?"

"Yes, Sergeant Major. They had a gun and were firing on the convoy. I will be up again this afternoon."

I went to the office. Captain Connor was smoking his inevitable cheroot. He looked up cheerily, "Good flight, sir?"

I nodded. "We will need to amend standing orders, Captain. Our buses need to fly lower."

"Righto, I shall get on with it. Cairo was on the radio. There is a convoy heading down the river with guns and gunners for us as well as more fuel."

I nodded, "They were the ones the insurgents tried to ambush. I am glad I was in the right place at the right time." Just then I heard the sound of aeroplanes landing. "How is Captain Cooper coming along with the water?"

"I had a chat with him over breakfast, sir. The water can be piped here within three days. I have told him how to filter it. We will use sand and charcoal. I wouldn't drink it without boiling but it will be clean enough to wash. He is making a boiler. I have your chaps Williams and Swanston at work too. They are building the bread oven. Resourceful chaps they are."

"I know."

I walked over to Lieutenant Dixon and the other three pilots. They had just landed. Squadron Leader Woollett was also heading out to them. He had his flying gear on. "We heard firing sir and saw burning by the river."

I nodded, "We will have to fly lower. When we headed north they had already moved a gun by the river to ambush a convoy. I happened to be at two hundred feet. That is how I saw it."

Henry said, "Righto, Bill. I will take that on board."

"I am not certain that there will be anything to protect this afternoon. However, our presence overhead will serve as a warning."

We looked up as, first the Vernon, and then the road flight, prepared to land. The Vernon had a longer range and was back early. I wondered if there had been a problem. Jack looked happy. He lit a cigarette after he and his gunner had clambered out of their DH 9as.

"Quite as the grave. It looks like they salvaged whatever they could from the road block. We saw a couple of lorries heading down the road. I think you frightened them off the other day."

"They had a gun to try to ambush a convoy on the Nile. What altitude did you use?"

"Eight hundred feet."

"Try dropping down to two hundred. I will try that this afternoon when I go up."

Ben was still at his aeroplane and I wandered over. "Problem, Ben?"

"Dust in number one engine. It is what happened to one of the others. We will have to rig some sort of dust filter over the intake."

"Did you see anything?"

"I saw why they need us. They are small garrisons and totally isolated. I am not even certain that they have a radio. I think that we could do with three flights a day. We need an umbrella to watch over them." Just then we heard the rumble of engines and, looking up, we saw two more of the Vernons as they prepared to land. Ben smiled, "Well they are late but they got here. We just need Chalky now and we will be up to full numbers."

"I will go and get a bite to eat. I am up again this afternoon." As I strolled to the mess I lit my pipe. Once I had made the two patrols I would then just have to escort a Vernon and I would understand the problems my men might face. After that I could go into Cairo with Captain Connor.

Before I got to the mess I heard the sound of a car. It was the young Lieutenant. He leapt out and seemed quite animated. "Well done, sir. I don't know if you heard but one of your chaps stopped the morning convoy being ambushed. The Colonel is delighted."

"We aim to please, Lieutenant. The road patrol saw a couple of lorries but no insurgents and the Vernon reported no trouble."

"That may change, sir. We have intelligence that the resistance is becoming more organised. There are daily riots in Cairo and word has come to us that someone is arming the insurgents in the desert. The Colonel believes this could escalate into a full-blown war."

I had my pipe going now and I said, "We will be ready. We have two more Vernons. When I have seen where they operate I will have a better idea if they can be used for evacuation."

"Thank you, sir. Oh, by the by, the convoy had most of your supplies. Captain Cooper requested more materials for another building and they are here along with your guns and some medical gear. They will be brought up as soon as we can get a convoy organised."

"Fuel?"

"That too but tankers are the issue. We only have one. Still it is only a twenty-minute drive. The problem is we have to convoy them."

I pointed to the two armoured cars. "Then use one or both of them while we can. We must have a good supply of fuel or we can do nothing."

"Understood, sir."

My afternoon patrol was uneventful. The lower altitude helped. We flushed out some Arabs who were lurking by the side of the road. I am not certain that they were up to anything but we made them move. I was confident that we would be able to spot any danger.

That night as we ate in the mess I said, "Ben I shall accompany your morning patrol."

He nodded, "That will fluster young Jennings." He laughed, "He is the youngest of my pilots."

"I will try not to terrify him then."

The Vernon was the newest of our three types of aeroplane. We had them because they could carry eleven men or five thousand pounds of supplies. In the desert that could be the difference between survival and death. I sat in the cabin and acted as a passenger. I had my binoculars and I had a map. I intended to locate features close to the garrisons and outposts. I needed to know if we could land. It soon became obvious that there were few roads. The ones that I saw had been built by the British. They looked solid enough to land a Vernon. I was tempted to ask young Jennings to do so but I remembered Ben's words. I did not want a pranged Vernon. I would ask Ben to land. We needed to test the viability. I saw just how vast the desert was as I watched the desert slip below the Vernon. Ben had been correct, the garrisons were tiny specks of khaki and they were all surrounded by potential enemies.

When we landed, I thanked the young pilot who looked relieved to have delivered his commanding officer safely back to earth. I strode to the Admin hut.

Captain Connor looked up as I entered and said, "The river patrol had a run in with insurgents. They found them setting up an ambush. They dispersed them but one of the DH 9as took some bullet holes in the wings."

"But we had no losses?"

"We had no losses sir. I think the riggers were just annoyed that they would have to repair it. They were cursing the Egyptians something rotten, sir."

"Right, well tomorrow we will take your little motor into Cairo. We'll take Williams and Swanston. There are a few things we can buy for the mess. Mr. Balfour made sure that we had funds for such things."

"Oh, and the medical block is under construction, sir. Captain Cooper thinks there might enough wood left to add an extension to the stores. It will be more secure than storing the ammo in the back of this office. The fuel has all arrived and is safely stored. Once we get the water running then everything will be tickety boo!"

I spent the afternoon with the pilots who were not on patrol. I wanted to share my experiences. Ben would be flying the next afternoon and he said that he would try to land at the furthest point of the patrol. Everything seemed to be well. All I needed was a letter from home and life would be perfect.

Williams and Swanston were happy to be given what they viewed as a holiday. However, when I insisted that they wore side arms they realised that it would be anything but. I took my German pistol. It was an automatic. At the end of the war I had managed to acquire a large amount of ammunition. The Webley was a fine gun but I liked the extra bullets and the fact that I did not have to constantly cock it.

I had wondered if being blind in one eye affected Captain Connor's driving and, as we hurtled down the dusty road in excess of fifty miles an hour, it did not seem the time to ask. The noisy engine and the wind whistling over its open top made conversation impossible. He had learned where the headquarters was and we thought it better to park there where our car could be watched by the sentries. Although there were few cars in Cairo, the streets were packed with people, stalls, donkeys and camels. We had to slow to a crawl. We passed a group of men on one corner. They shook their fists at us and then something was thrown against the car.

"Ey up, sir. What was that?"

Captain Connor took the unlit cheroot from his mouth, "I think it was a piece of rotten fruit. No damage, Corporal. Just keep smiling. The fruit we can clean off. If they meant business it would have been a grenade. Much messier! I can see the Union Flag. We are almost there."

"Thank God for that!"

When we reached the building, I saw that they had two Vickers machine guns in sandbagged emplacements guarding the entrance. There was barbed wire and an improvised barrier of barrels. The Duty Sergeant moved the barrels and saluted. He noticed the tomatoes which had been thrown against the blue paintwork. He smiled, "I see the locals gave you the customary welcome, sir."

I nodded, "Yes, Sergeant. I gather that they are less than pleased with our continued presence?"

"Not particularly. If you want to stick it by that wall sir, it will be out of the sun and we can keep an eye on it."

Captain Connor left it in the shade of the wall. "You two wait here while we go and pay our respects."

The interior was cool. My uniform already felt sticky. Lieutenant Simpson-Jones was at his desk. He seemed to be swamped by paper. "The Colonel is out, sir. There was a spot of bother on the road south of here. A lorry was ambushed."

I suddenly felt guilty. "Were we supposed to be patrolling there, lieutenant?"

"No sir. We thought that it was safe. They had two armoured cars with them. The blighters got hold of one of our grenades and rolled it under the lorry."

"Any casualties?"

"A couple of chaps were wounded by shrapnel but the lorry was badly damaged."

"Well we are here for a spot of shopping. We just thought we would call in and say hello."

"Be careful sir. The main shopping areas are relatively safe but do not be tempted to go down any of the side streets or alleys. Two Highlanders had their throats slit last week."

"Thanks for the information. We will be careful."

As we left the front the Duty Sergeant said, "Watch for pickpockets, sir. And every little bugger has a knife too!"

We headed towards the shops. The Lieutenant had drawn us a simple map. I turned to Swanston and Williams. "If you two need to buy anything then ask the captain here. He understands the language."

The captain had lit his cheroot. "They like to haggle. Whatever they ask you can get it dawn by at least half. If you offer to pay in sterling it will be even cheaper. The local money is not worth much."

Despite the warnings, the faces of the shopkeepers we passed were filled with smiles. They wanted our custom. There may have been many who wished the British gone but they were not engaged in the business which brought British money into their hands. I bought a silk scarf for Beattie. I was glad that I had Ted with me. The Captain brought the price down to what would have been coppers. Neither of the corporals wished to buy anything and they were happy just to take in the colour and spectacle not to mention the smells. The spices were a joy to both the eye and the nose.

We found what we were looking for half way down the busy street. It was a tobacconist. Or at least that is what we would have called it in England. Here they sold not only tobacco but other substances to be smoked. Captain Connor shook his head when Williams sniffed them. "They are not for you, Williams. They make their own cigarettes here. They are more expensive than what you pay but they are of a better quality."

"That is all right sir. I'll stick with service issue."

Ted turned to me, "Those are the pipe tobaccos on the right in those jars. Ask to try one if you like."

The owner spoke English, "Effendi, what do you have in mind?"

I took the tin from my tunic pocket. There was still a couple of pipefuls left. "I would like something similar to this please."

He sniffed it and then took a strand and tasted it. "Cuban and it has rum in it." If he was trying to impress me he failed. It was obvious it was rum. That also implied Cuba. He took a jar down from behind him. "This has no rum, Effendi, but it has a fragrance and a taste which is similar. Fill your pipe and try it."

I did so.

Captain Connor said, "While the Squadron Leader is enjoying your tobacco I will have a hundred cheroots."

Rubbing his hand the owner said, "Of course."

It was a pleasant tobacco. It was not too heavy. It was not as good as the Cuban but it would do. The Captain bought his cheroots and I said, "Half a pound please. Have you a humidor?" I did not want it drying out.

"Of course, sir." He took a humidor from the shelf and placed the tobacco inside. He carefully wrapped it up and then smiled at me.

I let Ted haggle. When he had agreed a price he said, "Now we shall be here for a while and this will be a regular purchase so the next time let us see if you can do an even better deal or we may find another shop like yours."

"Mine is the finest not only in Cairo but in Egypt. My tobacco comes from…"

"Never mind the sales talk. Now you can make us keen to come back if you can tell us where we can buy whisky, gin and wine."

He frowned. "Many of our mullahs frown on such things." Then a sly look came into his eyes. "However, for two such fine officers I will see what I can do. My brother can obtain such things but it must be done away from prying eyes. I will ask him to visit you at your airfield."

"He will be searched."

"Of course and if you would like some advice I would not linger around here. I have heard that there are troublemakers. The English soldiers usually come here to sample the food in the restaurants at noon. I think today they will pay a heavy price for their meal."

I looked at my watch. It was eleven thirty. "Thank you for the warning!" I turned to the other three. "I think it is time we headed back to the car."

They nodded and we left the shop. The tobacconists had been cooler than I had expected and the heat of the street hit us as we stepped out. I wished that I had had my goggles with me for the sun blinded me. I put my hand up to shield my eyes from the sun and, in that instant, I saw the blade flash towards Captain Connor. I reacted instinctively. I pushed my two hands, which held the humidor towards the blade. It clanked off the pottery vessel. Captain Connors and my two Corporals showed great reactions. Williams pulled back his arm and punched the assailant on the chin. Even as he was falling Captain Connor had pulled his service pistol and smashed it across the man's head. Swanston pulled his revolver out and shouted, "One more move and you are a bleeding dead man!"

Even I was taken aback by the venom in his voice. The effect was instantaneous. The crowd dispersed. He swung his pistol from left to right as they moved back. Williams and Connor took out their guns and gave us a clear passage back down the street.

"Captain, watch our front, Williams and Swanston, watch the rear."

"Sir!"

"Sorry about the language, sir! Sneaky bastards!"

"Don't apologise. It worked."

The sight of the guns held out before us made a clear passage for us. When we reached the sergeant, I said, "I wouldn't let your chaps out today, sergeant. I think the natives are a little restless."

He nodded, "I saw the guns and wondered. Stand to, you lads!"

I handed the humidor to Williams. "I will go and inform the Lieutenant of our experience. We will leave when I return."

I entered the office and informed the Lieutenant as succinctly as I could of what we had learned. He nodded, "Sergeant Major, call out the guard. No one leaves headquarters." He looked at me, "I think, sir, that things can only get worse."

"As do I."

By the time I reached the car, it was started and there was a mob approaching the barrier. "Right Captain, time for a rapid exit eh?"

"Yes sir!"

Williams handed me the humidor. "Bloody expensive baccy sir!"

"Quite."

Once we hit the main road north then the road became quieter. Ted said, "Thanks for that sir. Your reactions saved me."

"We are all in this together, Ted. I think we learned a lesson there."

"We did indeed." He took his unlit cheroot from his mouth. "This weed may well be the death of me!"

Chapter 11

The next week saw a huge transformation in our base. The engineers gave us running, filtered water. We could shower. The joy of a shower, even though it was often lukewarm, cannot be overestimated. The medical block was completed much to the delight of the Doctor. The patrols had managed to keep down the heads of the insurgents. Cairo was still a hotbed of disruption but we could do little there. The only action I regretted was the return of the two armoured cars to Alexandria. There was unrest there and Colonel Pickwick needed his men. I understood it but I would miss those two vehicles. We had to make do with the wire which surrounded the aeroplanes. We had a large entrance. It was only at night time that the entrance was blocked. During the day, we had two Lewis guns in sandbagged emplacements on either side.

The tobacconist's brother arrived four days after our visit. We did not let him enter. He had an ancient lorry. I was not even certain if it used petrol or coal for it smoked so much. He did, however, supply us with some Black Label whisky, Gordon's gin and some dubious wine. The price, thanks to Captain Connor, was not exorbitant and I paid, knowing that it was money well spent. We were living in primitive conditions and a little alcohol would go a long way to alleviate discomfort.

We heard by radio, that Alexandria and Cairo were almost under siege. The situation was deteriorating. When the convoys, both on the road and on the river, were attacked then we feared the worst. Luckily our aerial patrols prevented any losses. Our pilots had now mastered their techniques. We flew low and we knew what to look for. We tried to avoid causing casualties but I knew that we had killed insurgents. The Colonel was happy. He and the garrison remained well supplied.

It was early August and the sun was as hot as it would get when Lieutenant Jennings sent back a disturbing report. "Sir, the garrison at Barihaya Oasis is under attack. They cannot hold out for long!"

I was in the office, "Ask him how long he can stay over the target."

Corporal Hutton said, after listening on the headphones, "Twenty minutes, sir."

"Tell him to buzz the attackers. We will be there as soon as we can." I stood. "Winspear, go and tell every pilot from tomorrow's flight that I want their buses in the air now! Sergeant Major find Squadron Leader Mannock, I need his Vernons, all of them, in the air."

"Sir!"

Captain Connor said, "That is at the extreme range of your DH 9as and Snipes."

"I know. I am going to send fuel on the Vernons. We can refuel while they are extracting the garrison."

"You are taking a lot on, sir."

I smiled, "No one said this was going to be easy. Radio Cairo and tell them what we are doing,"

"Sir."

As I ran out, Williams appeared with my goggles and flying helmet. "Go and find Sergeant Major Robson. I want fuel putting aboard the Vernons. We are going to have to land and refuel."

There were two Snipes and two DH 9as. The rest were on patrol. The pilots and gunners faced me. Lieutenant Dixon asked, "What is up sir?"

"Barihaya Oasis is under attack. I am going to attack those who are there and then extract the men. We will have to land and refuel. The Vernons will take out fuel. First, we secure the area. I will be the last to land. Lieutenant Dixon once you have refuelled you will relieve me. I want one aeroplane in the air at all times to watch for danger. When we have all refuelled then we fly home. The Nanaks will use their bombs first. We will all than strafe the enemy."

"Right sir."

"I have flown over the area. There is a road and we will use that to land. I know we have not practised this but I have seen you all fly. We can do this."

I ran to Ben who was waiting by his Vernon, "What's up, Bill?"

"Barihaya Oasis is under attack. Jennings is on over watch. I am having fuel loaded onto your buses. We will clear the ground. You land and take off the fuel. Take on board the garrison and head home. We will land and refuel."

"Damned risky, Bill."

"This is the reason we are here and not a troop of armoured cars. We can be there in under two hours and save the lives of some brave men."

He nodded, "We won't let you down, Bill."

"I know."

When I reached the Dolphin, I saw that Williams had put my Lee Enfield and four Mills bombs in the cockpit. He was a good man. The four aeroplanes were already heading west by the time I started my engine and taxied. I soon caught them up. For once I would not need to worry about fuel. I could refuel at Barihaya Oasis. I overtook the others and flew ahead of them. I had the greatest firepower of the four of us. When I had used my Vickers, I had two Lewis guns too. The oasis was a hundred and eighty miles away. It was the most exposed of the garrisons we were designated to protect. As I flew south and west I tried to remember the numbers in the garrison. As I recalled it was thirty-five. They would be overcrowded on the Vernons but we were their only chance.

The lack of radios was annoying. Ben could speak with base and they could speak with Jennings. We just had to fly as fast as we could. That would be at one hundred and thirteen miles per hour; the speed of the Nanaks. I knew we were getting close when I saw Lieutenant Jennings heading north. I waved at him. I dropped to two hundred feet and the desert zoomed beneath my wings. Lieutenant Jennings's Vernon did not have bombs but I knew that his crew had a Lewis gun. A couple of magazine could not do much damage but they might have distracted the insurgents.

The noise of the engine hid the sound of gunfire but, as I neared the beleaguered troops I saw the smoke from rifles. I cocked my Vickers. The Union Flag still sagged forlornly from the flagpole which rose above the mud hut and walls. Sandbags filled the gaps. The insurgents were a hundred yards from the troops. They were in the cover of the oasis itself and I would have to be as surgical as possible. The bombers would have to use their bombs carefully to avoid causing casualties amongst those we were there to rescue. I saw a projectile raise and explode on the sandbags. They had a mortar. That would be my first target. I opened fire at a hundred yards' range. Four hundred bullets a minute could do a lot of damage and I watched the mortar crew disappear as my bullets

155

shredded them. I fired for just ten seconds and then I had passed the target and I rose and banked for a second pass.

As I banked right I saw more insurgents out in the desert. They were using the rocks for cover. As I came around and they appeared in my sights I fired three second bursts. Behind me I heard the Snipes' guns and those of the DH 9as. When I heard the crump from the bombs I knew that the Nanaks had targets which were worth a twenty-five-pound bomb. Banking around for another pass I saw the Vernons as they lumbered towards us. Ben would make the decision to land. We just had to clear the ground of the insurgents.

This time I changed my angle of approach and I flew on a north to south axis rather than an east to west. I dropped to under a hundred feet and angled my nose down. I emptied one Vickers and, as the hut hove into view, pulled up my nose and cocked my second machine gun. I was so low that I felt as though I could reach out and touch the flag. Once past the garrison I dipped my nose and, with no trees to worry about, dropped to fifty feet. I fired a five second burst at a machine gun. The bullets from the enemy's gun tore into my wings. When my bullets hit their gun it, and they, disappeared in a mass of metal and blood. I pulled up my nose and banked right. I saw that we had broken their backs. The DH 9as dropped the last of their bombs; one to the north of the post and the other to the south.

I watched the Vernons as they landed on the road and then began to taxi towards the post. I flew low overhead watching for any danger. I saw one of Ben's aircrew with a Lee Enfield. He was standing in the open door at the side. Even as I looked I saw a puff of smoke. An insurgent who had been raising his hand fell and the grenade exploded beneath his body as he fell with the bomb still in his hand. By the time I had completed another circuit, the Snipes and Nanaks had all landed.

Ben had already begun to offload the fuel from the Vernons and I saw stretchers being carried from the post. Lieutenant Dixon did a fast turn around and I saw him climb towards me. I waved and prepared to land. The surface of the road was not smooth but it was smoother than many of the fields I had used in France.

As I reached the Vernons the Union flag was being lowered. The post was being abandoned, albeit temporarily. Sergeant Major

Robson, complete with Sam Browne and service revolver was waiting for me with a barrel of fuel.

"Sergeant Major, why are you here?"

"I thought the Squadron Leader might be short-handed, sir." Without further ado he took a length of hose and began to syphon fuel into my tank.

I clambered down and patted him on the back, "You had no need, Sergeant Major, but I appreciate it." I looked up. Lieutenant Dixon was still flying circuits as an aerial sentry. I hurried over to the post.

A captain with his arm in a sling saluted. "Just in the nick of time, sir! We had no more ammo for the machine guns and the chaps were down to their last five rounds. Had the other aeroplanes not arrived we would have had to make a bayonet charge. Go out in a blaze of glory!"

"We can't have that. Get your chaps into the Vernons and we will keep watch."

"Yes sir."

Sergeant Major Robson was already filling the tank of the DH 9as when I reached my aeroplane. He handed the hose to the air gunner and came to help me start my aeroplane. There was just one aeroplane being refuelled. "As soon as Lieutenant Watson has been refuelled get the hell out of here Sergeant Major."

"Yes sir."

I turned to take off. Lieutenant Green in the second Snipe following me. We rose in the air. Even as I began a leisurely circuit I saw the first of the Vernons followed the Nanaks to lumber into the blue skies. I glanced down to my left and saw, in the rocks, the puff of smoke which told me there were men hidden there and firing at us. I still had almost a full belt of ammunition for my Vickers and so I flew at the knoll of rock. I fired three second bursts as I closed with the hidden men. The .303 bullet can make stone splinters out of solid rock. My burst of twenty bullets was magnified as they tore into the rock. One man tumbled over the side and I saw another fall back. I banked right. When Lieutenant Green did not fire, I knew that the hidden gunmen had been silenced.

The last Vernon was taking off as we came around. The outpost was abandoned but the dead were aboard the Vernon. Their bodies would not be desecrated. Their comrades would bury them with honour. The five of us zig zagged across the slower transports as we headed back to base. I did not fear an attack but if they had to land for any reason then we would be needed for cover. As we closed with the airfield we rose to allow the Vernons to land. I saw lorries and ambulances waiting for the men.

Once the Vernons had taxied from the runway, we landed. I was the last to touch down. I was almost out of fuel. Climbing out of my cockpit I reflected that I had learned our maximum range. It was knowledge which would come in handy. I examined the holes. Sergeant Major Robson came over to speak with me. He pointed to them. "They will take a day or two to repair, sir."

"Which is your way of grounding me for an extra day eh Sergeant Major?"

He grinned, "Well sir, you are the Commanding Officer. Let some of the younger lads have a chance, eh sir?"

"Sergeant Major this is not France. There is no glory in shooting rebels hiding in rocks. We have become policemen."

"Aye well sir, there's nothing wrong with that. We need policemen. They are the ones who mean we can sleep in our beds at night."

When I entered the office Sergeant Major Hale was smoking his pipe and there was no sign of Captain Connor. "Nice baccy this, sir. Thanks again."

"You are welcome. Where is the captain?"

"He went to see that the men you rescued were being looked after." I nodded. "Colonel Fisher was on the radio. He was pleased with the rescue, sir. He said evacuation was the right decision."

That evening, in the mess, I sat with Ted and my squadron leaders. The whisky and gin were not abused but we all enjoyed a couple of drinks after dinner when the cooler air meant we could enjoy them. The smoke from our cigars, cigarettes and pipes kept the insects at bay and it was almost pleasant.

"We will have to do more of this in the future."

"I know, Ben, and I can't see what else we can do."

"The Nanaks have a longer range, Bill. We could accompany the Vernon patrol. We only need one bomber on each of the river and road patrols."

Henry was the most thoughtful of us. Often he said little but when he did speak then he was worth listening to. "We could fit bomb racks to the Snipes. I know they affect the aerodynamics and slow us down a little but we are not fighting the Hun in the air, are we?"

"Good idea. So, we use just three aeroplanes on each patrol and send a Nanak with the Vernon."

Henry tapped out his pipe, "Actually sir, I was thinking of just using two aeroplanes on each patrol. It will limit the wear and tear. This might not be France where they are getting shot up but this sand gets everywhere. And, of course, if we had had fewer aeroplanes on patrol then, today, you would have had more aeroplanes at your disposal."

"Right, Ted change the rota. Add a reserve of four buses in case we have to do what we did today."

"Right sir," he lit another cheroot, "They lost four men today, at the outpost."

"I am not even certain why they were there."

Captain Connor looked at Jack, "Keeping the road open and guarded."

Ben shook his head, "We can do that and more effectively too. I am having the other Vernons all adapted to be bombers. I am not having this again. Poor Jennings has taken the loss of those squaddies to heart. If he had had bombs then he might have been able to do something."

"Now that you are at full strength it makes sense. Just do it."

Sergeant Major Robson was much happier with the new system. It meant his fitters and mechanics had more time to work on the aeroplanes and the fewer hours they flew they did not suffer as much wear and tear. I went up on one patrol in every five. Captain Connor and Sergeant Major Hale assured me that I did not need to but it kept me close to the pilots.

I was on the road patrol with Lieutenant Sanderson in a DH 9a and Lieutenant Green in a Snipe. We had had three days without incident. I was not complacent and I kept my eyes peeled. Vigilance was all. I was at the rear. Forty miles short of Alexandria I saw that two lorries had stopped. One of them had a Lewis gun mounted and the gunner was scanning the horizon for danger. He waved to us as we approached.

Immediately suspicious I signalled for the other two to circle close to the lorries while I went further out. I saw that something had been used to puncture the front tyres of the leading lorry. Only carrying one spare meant they had to repair one of the tyres. That took time. I realised that it had only just happened. I ran through the possible outcomes. The insurgents had laid the trap and stopped the lorries. It begged the question why. If they wanted to attack the two lorries then they had the perfect opportunity when they were stopped. I was half a mile from the lorries when it hit me; they were after the aeroplanes. A machine gun suddenly opened up and I saw Lieutenant Sanderson's aeroplane hit. The gunner slumped to the side and I saw smoke from the engine. Even as Lieutenant Green turned to deal with the threat, a second Lewis gun opened fire. The bullets tore into the fuselage and the Snipe showed that something had been hit.

The gunner on the lorry opened fire but he was firing blind. I banked and dropped to twenty-five feet. It was flat and I wanted to be able to see the insurgents. They were camouflaged from the road; they had dug a pit but I could see them. They began to turn the two Lewis guns around to fire at me. I did not give them the chance. I fired most of the belt from one Vickers. By moving the aeroplane slightly from side to side, I was able to spray the ground. As I flew over them I saw that there were still another five who were unhurt. I banked, aware that my wingtip was just ten feet above the ground. If a young pilot had done this then I would have put him on a charge. I flew along the line of the insurgents and gave them the rest of the magazine. I then climbed and rolled. When I was straight and level, I took a Mills bomb from my tunic and pulled the pin. I dived down and, at fifty feet pulled up as I dropped the grenade into the insurgents. Even as I climbed I heard the crump.

When I flew over them I saw that they were dead. Two of the soldiers from the lorry approached with rifles at the ready. I saw that my two wounded birds were limping home. I would make sure that the lorries were safe before I followed them. By the time I had completed a wide loop to look for any others they had repaired their tyres and were heading for Cairo. I waggled my wings as I headed south.

The body draped with a flying coat told me all that I needed to know. We had suffered our first fatality. Poor Lieutenant Sanderson looked distraught. The doctor was tending to his arm. Lieutenant Green was also being seen to. I would not bother either of them yet.

Sergeant Major Robson shook his head, "The Snipe will be in the air within a day or two, sir. He did well to land it. He had damage to his controls. The Nanak though… a week, maybe more."

"Do your best eh, Sergeant Major."

"Of course sir. Did you get them?"

"I did indeed."

Henry came over to me, he was stroking his chin. "Bill, I have an idea for the damaged DH 9a."

"Go ahead. I am all ears."

"You know I trained as a doctor before the war." I nodded, "Well I have had this idea for a while. The DH 9a could be converted to an ambulance." Sergeant Major Robson was listening. Henry went to the fuselage. There was a hole in the side where the bullets had torn through and killed poor Sergeant McIntire. "If we took out the rear gun then we could hinge the fuselage. A stretcher would fit in there nicely. Lieutenant Sanderson has no gunner."

I looked at the Sergeant Major, "Well, can it be done?"

"We are going to have to rebuild it anyway and if we get rid of the rear gunner then the aeroplane will be structurally stronger. But I thought the Vernons were going to be used as air ambulances, sir."

"They are but this adds a string to our bow. Go ahead then. I will explain to Squadron Leader Thomson."

Jack was happy about the arrangement. "I can see how we would benefit, Bill. If Sanderson had had to crash land then we would have had the devil's own job to get McIntire back. After the ambush at the oasis my men have begun to realise that this is a war zone again."

That evening we buried the unfortunate sergeant who had been so tragically killed. Everyone attended and as the bugle sounded last post we all stood at attention and saluted. He had a young wife at home and our thoughts were with her. Lieutenant Sanderson passed the hat around in the mess. It was little enough but we would send money to his wife. It would not make up for her loss but it would show that we thought of her.

"You know the irony of all this, don't you?"

I looked at Ted through a fug of smoke. "Not really."

"The lorries arrived in Cairo. The soldiers had collected the weapons from the ambush. Those Lewis guns and the other weapons were the ones stolen weeks ago. They were intended for us. Our aeroplanes were shot down by our own bloody guns!"

He was right. I determined to do all that we could to make sure that the insurgents received no more of our weapons.

Over the next days we managed to stop two more ambushes. We did so by leaving earlier. I realised that we were becoming predictable. There were Egyptians all around the airfield. I was not foolish enough to believe that all were innocent. Some would be insurgents or spies. Corporal Swanston was all for nipping out one night and bringing a couple back for questioning. We could not do that. We were bound by rules even if they were not. We hurt them for there were ten men in each ambush and more than half their numbers became casualties.

By the time it was autumn we had a system in place which worked. The air ambulance had been used once to bring back a badly injured soldier from a remote outpost. Lieutenant Sanderson even had training as a medic. Henry and the Doc supplied the information he needed.

It was in September that we finally received mail. I had sent letters home regularly but none of us had had any replies. There was only Ted who was unconcerned about mail. He had no one in England. His life was in the Middle East. There were eight letters from Beattie. I smoked three pipefuls as I read them. They were a snapshot of her life with Tom. It broke my heart that he was growing up and I was missing it. His birthday would soon be upon us and I would not be there. I felt frustrated. I knew that Beattie and Tom could not come out to Cairo; it was far too dangerous. I contemplated requesting a leave but I knew I could not do that while others were still serving. The letter in the middle, written in July, gave me the news that Beattie was expecting our second child. My last leave had been memorable for a number of reasons. My second child would be born in January 1920. There was little prospect of me getting home to be with her. My good mood disappeared as I realised that I would not be there again.

It was in November that I received a visit from Colonel Fisher. He looked particularly pleased with himself. I thought it was because we had managed to ensure that convoys still reached Cairo. However, when he produced a letter addressed to me and signed by Winston Churchill I understood the true reason. "Congratulations, Bill, you are now a Wing Commander!" Lieutenant Simpson-Jones appeared with a case of whisky. "I thought we might celebrate eh?"

The Colonel and the lieutenant left after a couple of hours but we continued with the party. Henry and the others kept saluting me and calling me sir. "You can stop that! I am still the same chap I always was. We will save the sirs for those times when the brass is around!"

I knew it was a larger salary. Beattie would be pleased. In her letters, she had described what a lovely house we had and how the garden was a delight. Now she could afford to furnish it well. The promotion still did not make up for my absence.

With the cooler weather came an escalation in violence. Captain Connor woke me one late November morning. "Sir. We have a problem. It seems that the garrison at Beni Suef is under attack. It looks to be a serious attempt to cut off Sudan from Cairo."

"Does the Colonel want us to evacuate them?"

"No sir. The Vernons will take reinforcements and we are ordered to eliminate the threat."

"Right then get the squadron leaders together. We will brief them. Get me maps."

Breakfast was on the hoof. The cooks made corned beef sandwiches which we washed down with mugs of hot sweetened tea. The squadron leaders knew something was up but not what. I told them of our mission and Ted brought me the maps. "It is ninety miles south of here. The Vernons will have to wait for the reinforcements but we will leave as soon as I have finished here. This is a more serious threat than the oasis attack. The outpost guards the road to Sudan and Somaliland. If we lose that then there are even more garrisons which could be cut off. The first thing we need to do is to secure a landing site for the Vernons. I have no idea what the ground is like. I am guessing that the road may be our best option. Ben, you will have to play it by ear."

"At least this time we will be armed."

"Now, looking at the map I can see that the ground to the west of the Nile is very fertile while that to the east is desert. They will be using the fertile land for cover. Jack, I want your Nanaks to go in first and drop a pair of bombs from each aeroplane. We will then strafe them. We use our bombs like a rolling barrage. Once the Nanaks have used their bombs then the Snipes will drop theirs. I want the DH 9as to keep their Vickers to cover the Vernons when they land. We will fly in a formation of four aeroplanes."

Satisfied that they all knew what they were doing we went to our aeroplanes. Williams handed me a couple of Mills bombs. We did not leave them in the aeroplane in case we had saboteurs. It was dawn before we were all ready to leave. It was pleasantly cool. I led the aeroplanes as we took off. The advantage of navigating in Egypt was that the Nile was a perfect marker. Anything of importance lay along it and so we just followed the brown snake south. Once again, I regretted not having a radio but there was little we could do about that. I knew that sometime in the near future every aeroplane would have a two-way radio and then communication would be much easier. We had to rely on hand signals and shared experiences. The four aeroplanes behind me were led by Jack and were the first of the DH 9as. Above us flew the Snipes. The Vernons had not even begun to load and with a top speed, unladen, of only seventy-five miles an hour, they were not going to be following us any time soon.

Captain Connor had told us that the garrison was half a company strong. That meant sixty men. As we had discovered at the oasis it was the lack of ammunition which would cause problems. With so many insurgents and saboteurs it did not make sense to store too much ammunition in case it was stolen or blown up. The garrison would have to husband what they had. As I looked to the eastern sky I saw that it would not be a bright day. There was cloud cover. In this part of the world that rarely meant rain but it would be marginally cooler and I would take that. When we were just under an hour into the flight I began to descend to a hundred feet. I swung east so that we could approach the besieged garrison from the east. I wanted the sun behind us.

As I banked I saw flashes in the distance. There were bigger guns there. Were they the garrison's or the attacker's? Once we had crossed the Nile and flown south east for a few minutes I banked again to bring us around to face west. The Union flag was a good marker. This time the garrison knew that we were coming. They had been told by radio. They would have hope. I saw that the rebels were using the river too. It looked like they had captured a river steamer and were using that to attack the walls of the outpost. I made the signal to the DH 9as behind. I saw Lieutenant Giggs begin his attack. I did not see it but I heard his Vickers and then there was the sound of a double explosion. When we came around for a second pass I would be able to see what effect he had had.

I raised the nose to clear the flag and then cocked my Vickers. The insurgents were hidden. However, you cannot hide a muzzle flash. I fired at the flashes. My bullets tore into the undergrowth revealing a machine gun. The Nanaks were under orders to use their bombs first. The Snipes would follow and mop up any who survived the first bombing run. I pulled up the nose once I had cleared the trees. I saw the road. It looked to be clear. The Vernons could use it but first we would have to drive the rebels from the ground on either side of it. I banked to port to assess the effect of the bombs. Twenty bombs can do a great deal of damage. They tore through the trees and into the men who, until a few moments ago had been hidden.

I continued down the river. I was looking for more enemies. I could not see any but that did not mean that they were not there. The Snipes' machine guns chattered death as they fired into the hidden and camouflaged Egyptians. I continued my turn and headed up the river. The DH 9as just turned to come back on a reciprocal course. Between the Nanak's bombs and the Snipes' machine guns I hoped that there would not be too many enemies left.

I saw the steamer. It was still afloat, just. I dropped as low as I could and then opened fire. The ones who saw me hurled themselves into the river. I saw the deadly shapes of crocodiles. Most would not survive their immersion in the river. I emptied the right-hand Vickers. The bullets tore through the wooden hull. I finished what the bombs had started. Then I climbed and I banked to head for the road. I saw insurgents. They were trying to build a barricade. They must have thought we would send reinforcements by road. I could not allow them to stop the Vernons from landing. They would be just half an hour away.

I swung around to attack along the length of the road. I readied one of the Mills bombs. I dropped as low as I could and fired the left-hand Vickers. The bullets chipped through flesh and wood. I stopped firing when I was twenty yards from the barricade. I pulled the pin out of the grenade with my teeth and, as I raced just forty feet above them, dropped the grenade and then pulled up. I heard the crump and, as I climbed, I saw in the mirror that there was no threat on the road. Just to be certain I climbed and looped. I saw the Snipes chasing away the last of the insurgents. The explosions told me that they were using their bombs on any sign of organized resistance. The road was clear and, in the distance I saw the Vernons as they lumbered along the river. I flew lazy circles to show Ben that it was safe to land.

Neither the Snipes nor myself could afford to stay over the garrison for too long. We did not have the endurance of the other aeroplanes. I watched the troops disgorge from the transports and then the supplies. I waited until they began to load the wounded and then headed north. The last thing I saw was Lieutenant Sanderson as he landed to act as an air ambulance if another was needed.

Once again, I was almost flying on fumes when I landed. Captain Connor strode over to greet me. "Squadron Leader Mannock was on the radio. They managed to take off safely. They have fifteen casualties. Colonel Fisher said well done."

"I am just glad we were able to be of some assistance. Those poor chaps were stuck out on a limb!"

"Oh, and he said he will be coming to see you tomorrow with some new orders. Apparently, he would have come today but the emergency made him postpone it. He sounded ominously serious when he spoke to me."

The three squadrons were in high spirits when we landed. We had inflicted a defeat upon the enemy and we had suffered no losses. The men celebrated. Even Sergeant Major Robson seemed happy for none of the aeroplanes had caused any problems.

Part Three
Somaliland

Chapter 12

When the Colonel arrived, he had with him an officer of Intelligence. He was introduced to me as Major Buchan. He looked to be of an age with me. He had medal ribbons which suggested a more active life than that of an officer of Intelligence. I was going to close the door to give the three of us some privacy when Major Buchan said, "I think Captain Connor should hear the briefing, Wing Commander."

I nodded, "That will not be a problem. Captain Connor would you care to join us."

Ted seemed bemused and he lit a cheroot but his eyes never left the map that Major Buchan unfolded.

"This is Somaliland. Since 1904 we have been fighting Sayyid Mohammed Abdullah Hassan."

Ted sat up, "The Mad Mullah!"

Major Buchan smiled, "Some of the sensational journalists and newspapers have reported him thus however he is a very clever commander. At the battle of Dul Madoba in 1913 he and his Dervishes defeated our troops. Since then he has controlled large parts of British Somaliland, particularly around the Horn of Africa. Mr. Churchill and other members of the British Government are keen to bring him to book. He rules as a warlord. He hides behind Islam and uses it as a weapon against the people. The Christians of the region have been systematically hunted down and slaughtered. It cannot go on. However, there is no appetite in Horse Guards to send large numbers of troops. We lost many troops attacking his numerous hillforts. It is a desolate part of the world at the best of times. This Sayyid Mohammed Abdullah Hassan is a bandit and a warlord. He hides behind Islam but he really just wants to rule Somaliland. The women and children are virtual slaves to his warriors." He shook his head, "They have captured British soldiers and... well I won't go into details but it is barbaric. No one wants to put British soldiers in the front line to face that."

I knew what was coming. As soon as he mentioned Churchill I knew. When I had spoken with the Minister and Mr. Balfour they had intimidated about Somaliland and now I saw why.

"Mr. Churchill persuaded the generals that you and a squadron of DH 9as could defeat them. You are to command Z Force." He took out three sheets of paper. He gave one to me, one to Captain Connor and one to Colonel Fisher. "Here are the forces at your disposal. Apart from your air crew and support troops you will have the Somaliland Camel Corps and a battalion of the King's African Rifles. Both those units are already on their way to Berbera, which is on the coast. They are travelling by ship. The seaplane carrier, Ark Royal, is waiting for you at Suez. You will have your aeroplanes loaded upon her decks. There are vehicles aboard freighters and you will be shipped down to Berbera."

I felt my mouth dropping open. We had only just built a base here at Heliopolis. Now we had to do the same except we had to do it in a land controlled by Dervishes. "With respect Major Buchan, we will be a long way from any sort of help."

"You have a good reputation, Wing Commander. No let me rephrase that. You have an impeccable record. Both Mr. Churchill and Colonel Fisher believe that you can do this. You have shown that no matter what the difficulties you are capable of overcoming them. The Ark Royal will remain on station for as long as you need her and you will be kept supplied through Berbera. Your aeroplanes will be lifted by crane aboard the carrier and offloaded in the same way in Berbera. One of your DH 9as will be fitted with a radio so that you can coordinate with the other two units. That will be done while you are at sea."

I took out my pipe and began to clean it. It was my way of buying time to think.

Captain Connor said, "And I take it I will be there too."

"Yes. You will be the Wing Commander's chief of staff. You will need to take some of your senior warrant officers. The Camel Corps and King's African Rifles have white officers but they are largely native contingents. You, Captain Connor, will be responsible for coordinating them."

Having cleaned out my pipe I began to fill it. All eyes were on me but I waited until I had the pipe going. I saw a smile appear on Captain Connor's face. He knew what I was doing. "I can see how we get the aeroplanes on the seaplane carrier. With judicious handling they can be loaded and unloaded but, once at Berbera, how in God's name do you think we can take off? I doubt that there is a road there let alone an airfield."

Major Buchan nodded, "You are quite right you will need to build an airfield. However, we are providing six trailers. They will transport your aeroplanes to a place suitable to be made into an airfield. I assume you will be taking your Dolphin. That means three trips once you have built your airfield. Your aeroplanes can stay on the Ark Royal until you are ready to offload them."

"Do we have Captain Cooper and his men?"

Colonel Fisher shook his head, "They still have work here and in Cairo. Sorry, Bill."

"So, my chaps have to build our own airfield."

He nodded, "Your people will know the best place to build it. It does not have to be very grand. Just a flat place to take off and land. I believe that, in France, you had quite primitive conditions at times."

"We never had to hew an airfield from desert and rock nor did we have Dervishes attacking us while we did it. Normally our airfields were forty or fifty miles behind our lines.'"

Major Buchan smiled, "You are a resourceful chap and Mr. Churchill has great faith in you."

I glanced at Ted who cocked his head to one side and nodded. I stood and went to the map on the wall. There looked to be nothing, save a solitary road which went through a pass in the highlands. There was rock and desert. We would not have to worry about rain; they had none and sand would make a good surface on which to land if there was rock beneath it. "So, our mission is to defeat this Mullah and then we are done?"

"Yes, once that is achieved then you come back here."

"No, Major, once that is achieved then the men who go to Somaliland get a leave and have some time in Blighty! It is the least you can do!" There was an edge to my voice.

The Major looked at the Colonel. "I am not certain that Whitehall likes such demands but..."

"If Mr. Churchill holds me in such esteem then he can grant me my request, which, after the efforts my men have and will be putting in, does not seem unreasonable. You have been fighting this Mullah for the last fifteen or so years with no success. You now expect us to go and complete it in a couple of months! I would have thought a month's leave was a small price to pay."

A brief silence fell upon the room and I puffed contentedly on my pipe. Colonel Fisher said, "I am certain, Wing Commander, that Mr. Churchill will accede to your request. In my opinion it is merited."

"Then we will deal with this chap and then go home!" They both nodded. There was no handshake but a deal had been made.

"Splendid. Here are the maps and the intelligence we have gathered. It seems Sayyid Mohammed Abdullah Hassan used some forts which control key areas. There are few roads in the area and the forts are the key. Artillery could do the job but the terrain does not allow us to use artillery. We will have to use your aeroplanes as mobile artillery."

"Then keep me supplied with bombs and .303 ammunition and we will reduce his forts to dust."

We spent an hour going over the logistics of maintaining a squadron in the field. As far as I knew it had never been done before.

After we had seen them off I called in my senior warrant officers and my squadron leaders. I told them in plain language what we had been ordered to do. Their faces spoke volumes. "Henry, you will command here in my absence. Needless to say, I intend to take Sergeant Major Hale and Robson with us. Sorry. Swanston and Williams are also vital. As for the rest… you warrant officer can cherry pick. Believe me this will be no picnic. We need the best men we can get. You can request more men for Heliopolis. We will be more than a thousand miles away from any help. What we take is all that we will have. However, I have negotiated leave at the end of it so it is not all bad."

"And when do we leave, sir?"

I smiled, "Tomorrow Warrant Officer Hale, tomorrow!"

I sat with Hale and Captain Connor going through the lists of men. We had to choose carefully. We would not need a doctor. The King's African Rifles had their own. We would not need a Quarter Master that too would come from the Rifles. In the end the men almost picked themselves. In the time we had been in Egypt we had seen which men were adaptable and which ones were still trying to do things the same way as they had in France.

The Vernons would transport the men to Suez and then return for the tents and equipment we would need. We would be under canvas. Major Buchan assured us that there was a large flat area close to Suez where we could land our aeroplanes. We would have to taxi the DH 9as and Dolphin to the port but that was only eight hundred yards. It would take all day for us to load the aeroplanes on to the deck of the Ark Royal and we would leave the following day. That night as I fell exhausted into my cot, I reflected that this would be another Christmas spent away from my family. The way things were going the baby would be born just as we were beginning operations against the Mullah. I wondered if my career choice had been a wise one.

After breakfast, the DH 9as and I took off. We would land first. If there were any problems then we would be able to radio back to Heliopolis. Our goodbyes were perfunctory. Most of us had come through a war where you had not had the luxury of a goodbye. Chaps you knew went out with you in the morning and did not come back. We had brief handshakes and nods which spoke volumes. When you had faced death with brothers in arms then you were bonded for life. We might see each other at future postings or even at the Army and Navy Club but there would be no letters or holiday promises to look one another up. A pilot believed in fate. If we were to meet again then we would. It was as simple as that.

Suez was heavily guarded. The Egyptians might want the British gone but we would never allow the Egyptians to control the Suez Canal. That was our link with India, Australia and New Zealand. It was our umbilical cord to the children of the Empire. I landed first. Major Buchan had arranged for a Petty Officer from the Ark Royal and some ratings to mark the place we were to land and to have smoke for us to see the wind direction. I landed. It was bumpy but I had endured worse.

A rating ran up to me and clambered on to the wing. He clung to the struts. "Able Seaman Ireland, sir. I'll direct you."

"Are you comfortable there?"

The young rating grinned, "Oh aye sir!"

The Petty Officer must have worked out a flat route for it was not straight. It was however, problem free. I saw, in my mirror, Jack and his boys as they followed me. It would take some time to land the Vernons. As we approached the crane lined dock I saw the Ford lorries as they headed towards the field. This was a huge enterprise.

The rating waved to attract my attention as we neared the carrier. "Sir, just pull up close to the crane at the end. The captain wants you loaded from there." I nodded. When we reached the two ratings who waved their arms to stop us I turned off the engine. Able Seaman Ireland leapt off the wing. "Well that is as close to flying as I have got, sir. Thanks!"

"Thank you." He suddenly snapped to attention and I saw an officer walking towards me.

"Lieutenant Commander Wilson, Wing Commander. I am the Number One. If you would like to follow me I'll take you to the captain."

"If you don't mind Lieutenant Commander I would like to see how your boys load the Dolphin."

"Of course, sir, but these are very experienced men. They are used to loading aeroplanes."

Behind me I heard the noise of the DH 9as wheels on the rocks as they arrived. There would be little point in them running their engines. There were enough ratings to push them to the crane. To be fair to the Lieutenant Commander and his men they were efficient. They fitted canvas slings under the engine and fuselage. A Petty Officer checked that there were no problems and then the crane lifted the aeroplane. Mine would be the easiest for it was almost a thousand pounds lighter than the DH 9as. Once it was on board I turned and smiled, "Thank you, Lieutenant Commander. We are a little precious about our babies."

"I understand. We are going to be a little crowded, I am afraid. We normally only carry eight seaplanes."

"How long will it take to steam to Berbera?"

"About a week. It is fifteen hundred miles. We are not a fast ship. Eleven knots is all that we can manage." He smiled. "We will be there before Christmas."

"Last Christmas I had snow. I was in the Baltic."

"So were we! Were you the chap on the Vindictive?"

"Yes, I was."

"You missed those chaps in the torpedo boats. Sank a few battleships. They managed to get themselves a V.C. and D.S.O.s. They lost some boats and some men too but they disabled the Bolshie Fleet."

"I met them. Brave chaps."

We had reached the main deck, "From your medals Wing Commander, so are you. I will take you to the captain."

Captain Mainwaring had a neatly trimmed beard. The grey flecks told me that he was getting towards the end of his career. He shook hands, "Delighted to meet you. Rear Admiral Cowans and Peter Parr spoke highly of you. You are almost a sailor!" He turned to the Lieutenant Commander, "That will be all Number One. Carry on."

"Sir."

"Take a seat." I sank into a leather armchair and when I saw Captain Mainwaring reach for his pipe I did so too. It was his cabin and there were niceties to be observed. "Rum do this." I was drawing on the pipe and so I nodded. "We are going to stay on station in Berbera. Between the two of us I think that is in case this goes wrong and you have to be pulled out."

"I agree sir. In theory, this should be no problem but I have seen maps of the terrain and it looks ghastly. If any of my chaps come down I am guessing that their buses will be a right off and they may well be lost."

"Quite. Your mechanics are more than welcome to use our facilities but you will be on the airfield."

"The airfield which is not yet built. Yes sir."

"It is Dennis and you are Bill, I believe."

"It is. One thing in our favour is that I doubt that neither this Sayyid Mohammed Abdullah Hassan nor his men will ever have seen an aeroplane before. We should have the element of surprise. From what I have read he has managed to defeat our forces by using the terrain and his ferocious Dervishes."

"They have a reputation. I spoke with some of the captains who sail this coast and they steer clear of Somaliland. They are fanatics. Not only that they are pirates. Luckily, we have quick firing twelve pounders and machine guns. If they come close to us then we shall sink the blighters." He laid his pipe in the ashtray. "This will be my last commission. I retire next year. I shall finally get to spend time with my wife. Who knows I may even see my grandchildren before they are grown up. Do you have children, Bill?"

"I have a son I have barely seen. My wife is expecting our second sometime in the next month."

"We are both in the same boat then," he chuckled, "quite literally. We have sacrificed our families for the service of our country."

"So it would appear but I intend to have my family with me when I can."

"But not here."

"No, Dennis, not here."

It took all day to load the aeroplanes. The equipment and the men took almost as long. The result was that we did not leave until late in the evening. The twinkling lights of Suez were left far behind as we headed into the blackness of the Red Sea. Our packed ship was a microcosm of Britain and we were cosily packed within her metal walls. The freighter which accompanied us with our vehicles was so small that there were lorries parked on her deck.

The captain and crew made us feel welcome but we were overcrowded. Ted and Jack spent most of the time with me as we pored over maps and intelligence reports. They were vague. We identified six forts which Sayyid Mohammed Abdullah Hassan used. Although the actual location was a little vague. No one had effectively mapped the area. With few towns and fewer roads it was a nightmare. Our plan was relatively simple. We would begin with the fort closest to us and reduce that one. The King's African Rifles and the Camel Corps could occupy that one and we would move to the next one. I would be able to assist in the attacks on all of them except for Taleh. That would be beyond my range. We had decided to fit the radio in Jack's Nanak. His sergeant was the most senior.

"What do we do if one of our kites crash lands?"

"That, I am afraid, is a difficult one."

Ted pointed at the map with his cheroot. "They are giving us a couple of motorcycles. They can handle rough terrain. We need to make sure every aeroplane has an emergency kit." He used his fingers as he listed what they would need. "Water, matches, blankets, something for shelter, knife and pistol."

"Ted's right. Let us hope that it does not come to this but if it does then they will have to sit tight and rely on someone reporting their position. If they sit tight then the motor bikes might get to them and the Crossley Light Lorry."

It was by no means a perfect solution but it would have to suffice. Egypt seemed as a picnic compared with the prospect which faced us. Ted was the only one who had the remotest idea of what we would be facing. Palestine, Transjordan and Arabia were similar environments.

"You have to remember that as hot as it is in the day it can be equally cold at night. That will be especially true in the highlands of Somaliland. They will need to learn how to make fire. We should give them lessons on conserving water. They can go for quite a few days without food but not water."

Each day took us further south and closer to the equator. Each day began hot and grew hotter. We knew that we were cooler on the water than we would be when we built our airfield. Sergeant Major Robson and I took a daily stroll with Jack to inspect the Nanaks. They were securely tethered to the deck and covered with canvas but we had to make sure that they reached Berbera in one piece.

The captain made us welcome and Jack, Ted and I shared his table each night. The mess was crowded. It was intended for a maximum of twenty officers. We doubled that. I was used to the quirks of the navy for I had been aboard the Vindictive but the others had a lot to learn about the customs and habits. The officers were introduced to Pink Gins and rum. They were bemused by the crew when they were summoned to 'Up Spirits!' We even celebrated Christmas on board the carrier. It was our second night aboard. The crew made it festive and we all enjoyed ourselves but I was sad inside. Beattie and Tom would either be with Alice or my family in Burscough. There would be presents and Christmas dinner. I was on a ship amongst strangers. It was not the same.

One evening, as the sun began to set over the land I stood with Ted on the flight deck. The land had changed little as we had headed south. The next day would see us reach Berbera. I pointed with my pipe. "Apart from the occasional fishing boat I have seen little sign of life hereabouts."

"I know. We are used to Britain where there are thousands of people in our big cities and even our towns are so busy that it is impossible to find an empty street. Here a big town might have just three hundred people and most of the places have just a few dozen families. A lot of the people are nomadic. They follow the little grazing there is."

I shook my head, "Which begs the question why are we hanging on to it?"

"I asked myself the same question in Mesopotamia. I think it is in the nature of Empire builders. The Victorians wanted an Empire because they thought we could civilize the world. We haven't done a bad job. Certainly, we were preferable to the Turks. Occasionally you get someone like Sayyid Mohammed Abdullah Hassan. He is a warlord and he wants to rule his own part of the world. We are doing what we used to do at sea, we are the world's policeman although I am not certain that we will continue to be viewed that way in the future. The Great War changed the way the world thought. If we look back then before August 1914 was a different world. The jinni is out of the bottle. I have a feeling that we will have to adapt."

"You are a philosopher, Ted."

He used his stump to point to his eye. "When I suffered this, I had to revaluate my life and when I did that I looked at the world too. I had time to think while I recovered."

He was right. Lumpy had said the same. What had been important was no longer seen that way. "Well tomorrow our little war begins. I fear that you will have more onerous duties. As Chief of Staff you will have to deal with the Rifles and the Camel Corps."

"That is fine. I enjoy hard work."

Berbera was tiny. I counted but forty huts and the most imposing building was a brick and stone built building by the docks. It was flying a Union Flag. That would be the British resident. We were lucky that the carrier had a crane used for recovering seaplanes as the port had nothing big enough to handle the Nanaks. We would have to use the six trailers to haul the aeroplanes to the site of the airfield. We had heard, on the radio, that the King's African Rifles were there already. We would have to do the work of making it an airfield but we had protection. I had a feeling we might need it.

The British resident was a nutmeg brown gentleman who looked to be as old as my dad. He was small and neat and he coughed a great deal. He was a gentleman and always used a handkerchief. Reginald St. John-Browne was a throwback to the nineteenth century when young Civil Service clerks had left England for warmer climes and never returned. He was a small precisely dressed man. Only his solar helmet looked too large for him and he had the thin look of someone who is close to the end of their life. He was, however, delighted to see us. He positively beamed.

"Wing Commander Harsker, this is a real pleasure! I hear you have come to rid us of these troublesome bandits! They have plagued these people for years."

"We will do our best, sir."

My officers all descended from the carrier to await orders and the poor man took one look at the numbers and said, "Oh dear, I had planned on inviting your officers for dinner at the residence but I fear there are too many of you."

"We will be busy for a while anyway, sir. We have an airfield to build."

He shook his head, "We must make a date! It would be rude not to have you and your senior officers to dine with me. Let us say, next Saturday evening. How does that suit?"

It would have been churlish to refuse. "That will be perfect, sir. Shall we say seven o'clock? There may be five of us. My two companions and the two commanders of our ground troops."

"Excellent! Excellent! The people here are charming but one does miss civilized company eh? I am desperate to hear news from the outside world."

"Quite, sir."

"And I have heard of you, Wing Commander."

"Really sir?"

"Yes. During the war I became fascinated by the exploits of the Flying Corps. I took cuttings about all the aces: Bishop, McCudden, Ball. All of them but especially you. I liked the story of an air gunner who became an ace. And, of course, you survived."

"I am flattered, sir."

"Well now you can see why I am so keen to dine with you and hear your stories."

"Of course. And now, sir, we must see to the unloading of the vehicles and our aeroplanes. We have much to do."

"Quite so. Don't let me stop you. I have a dinner to organize!"

The freighter had unloaded the Ford lorries first. As they were doing that the Nanaks were slowly landed. My Dolphin had been the first on and would be the last off. I did not mind. By the time five of the DH 9as had been unloaded there were three lorries and trailers ready. We loaded three of the aeroplanes and Ted and Sergeant Major Robson went with them. We had directions to the airfield. I was not put out by the fact that the King's African Rifles were not there to greet us. They could not have known of our precise arrival time. I was more concerned that we had a defensible airfield.

Once the lorries and the trailers had all been landed we began to offload the other vehicles and supplies. The three lorries and trailers returned as the next three DH 9as were loaded. I had decided to wait until my bus was landed before I left. Jack went with the trailers. Sergeant Major Hale, Aircraftman Williams and Corporal Swanston took one of the Crossley light trucks and our baggage and tents. It was late afternoon when my Dolphin was offloaded. By then there was just one DH 9a waiting to be transported. The rest of the vehicles had gone.

Captain Mainwaring came down the gangplank to see me off. "We shall be here, Bill. If you need anything then let us know."

"We are invited to dinner with the resident on Saturday. I shall be here then, in any case."

"Good luck."

"Thanks."

I rode in the cab with the driver. "What is the field like, Ganner?"

"A bit rough, sir, but it is flat and the squaddies have managed to get most of the bigger rocks out of the way. I think Sergeant Major Robson was less than happy, sir. He has a bunch of lads clearing it to his satisfaction."

"And tents?"

"Captain Connor has them being erected now, sir."

I wondered how we were going to get on with the two units of ground troops. They were not British regulars. I had no doubt that they would be good at their jobs but they were an unknown.

The field was just five miles away from the port. The road leading to it was reasonable and the airfield was slightly elevated. That would make take-off and landing easier. I saw that the King's African Rifles had established a perimeter with guards. That was good. There was neither sight nor smell of the Camel Corps. Ted had told me that you knew when camels were around from the smell. I saw that they had the aeroplanes parked closely together. "Head for the other aeroplanes."

I climbed from the cab and took out my pipe. This would be our new home. I looked around. It had been chosen well. Nothing overlooked it. There were patches of high ground but they were more than half a mile from the end of the field. The road passed through a narrow gap in the hills. That would be our route in and out of the field. The tents were neatly laid out. There was no mess tent. I saw that each section had their own fire and dixie. That made sense too. I had no doubt that Sergeant Major Hale would organize our own men. Selfishly I watched as my Dolphin was unloaded. That was my priority. Knowing it was the Commanding Officer's the riggers did it with kid gloves and I breathed a sigh of relief as they pushed it to join the others. We would fire them up the next day.

Sergeant Major Hale, Sergeant Major Robson and Captain Connor strode over to see me. "Colonel Pritchard is the commander of the Rifles and he has taken a company out to check on a report that there were Dervishes seen on the ridge yonder, sir. He said he will speak with you on his return."

I nodded, "Reports?"

Sergeant Major Robson said, "All the aeroplanes have been landed safely, sir. We have fuel for tomorrow but we need to find somewhere secure for the rest. I left it on the freighter. I thought it was safer."

I turned to Sergeant Major Hale, "And the ammunition and the food?"

"The same sir. It is just a five-mile journey to pick up fresh supplies and the two ships are safer than here."

Captain Connor, "Where will headquarters be?"

"I have used one of the larger tents. We will have to have squadron briefings outside but we will need shade to work, sir."

"Quite. And we will be having the same arrangement for food as the colonials?"

"Yes sir. The rigger and mechanics will cook their own. The gunners theirs and the officers and warrant officers will share one mess. Williams and Swanston have volunteered to be cooks, sir."

I smiled, "Volunteered?"

"Actually, yes sir. They are good lads. I would like to put them in for promotion. They are what the service needs."

"I agree, Sergeant Major. With Mr. Churchill behind us then I think that the Royal Air Force may become even more important. Don't forget to ginger up the lads. They need their side arms at all times and we all need to be vigilant. These Dervishes are nasty pieces of work and they are religious fanatics."

"Don't worry sir. I told them the stories."

Williams and Swanston cooked a basic meal but we were all so hungry that we wolfed it down as though it came from the Café Royal.

Colonel Pritchard and his men arrived back late. They were in two lorries. They had taken casualties but, thankfully, none had died. He saluted, "Sorry I wasn't here to greet you, sir."

"Don't worry about it. What happened?"

"The usual. The Dervishes are good at letting sentries see them and then fleeing before they can be apprehended. We chase them and they ambush us. We have five men wounded."

The Colonel and his men appeared to be playing into the hands of these Dervishes. "How many of them did you get?"

"We haven't a clue. I am guessing some but they carry off their wounded and dead. All you find is a patch of blood. They have learned how to control the land and to avoid us. They stopped using bases by the coast for our ships were able to blast them. They are the masters of disguise and terror." He shook his head. "It is almost like a game to them."

"Then as from tomorrow we change the rules. We don't chase them. Where are the Camel Corps?"

"They are still on their way. They are good lads and they can cover terrain which our lorries can't but they have a large area to police."

"Then when they get here the three of us will sit down and work out a better way to deal with these Dervishes. I have been promised that I can go home when they are eliminated. I have a real incentive. This Sayyid Mohammed Abdullah Hassan has plagued Somaliland for long enough. We will stop him."

"We have been trying since 1904 to bring him to book. We know where his forts are but they are hard to attack. I admire your determination sir but you have just thirteen aeroplanes."

"Have you seen the Royal Air Force in action Colonel?"

"No sir, I spent the Great War in East Africa.."

"Then I think you are in for a pleasant surprise."

Chapter 13

The first thing I did when I awoke the next day was to get Sergeant Major Robson to have my aeroplane readied. Once I had spoken with Colonel Pritchard, I intended to launch an attack on the nearest Dervish stronghold. I was anxious for the arrival of the Camel Corps. Ted had told me that the camel was the best way to get around the desert. Having been here for less than twenty-four hours I could see why. Once it was eight o'clock it was so hot that it was almost hard to breathe.

I ate with Jack and Ted. "I want us up in the air as soon as we can. If there were Dervishes close enough to draw out the Rifles then they must have a base close by. I want pairs of aeroplanes radiating out from here. I will take three o'clock."

Jack nodded. "The lads are keen to get on with something."

"Ted, when the Camel Corps arrive I need to speak with their Colonel. We have to use every element of Force Z if we are to defeat this Sayyid Mohammed Abdullah Hassan. We must work as a team."

It had been more than a week since I had flown combat. With the help of Aircraftman Williams, I prepared myself as much as possible. I placed four grenades in the pockets I had had fitted to the cockpit. I placed my Lee Enfield in the cockpit. I had a flare gun in case I crash landed and I had the emergency kit I had instructed all of my pilots to carry. I flew with Lieutenant Canning. The runaway still needed work; Sergeant Major Hale and Colonel Pritchard had work parties ready to clear it after we had taken off. Only Lieutenant Sanderson remained behind. He was the air ambulance.

I led the take-off and I headed through the gap between the two ridges. We headed dues west. I had instructed Canning to stay above me. His gunner could act as a spotter. I flew at a hundred feet. It was quite hairy for the ground rose and fell quickly and you needed quick reactions. My aim was for us to search within forty miles of our base. Once we reached forty miles then we would turn south as would the rest of the squadron. We would fly for ten miles and head back to the base. I hoped that, by doing so, we would either find the Dervishes or establish that they were further away than we thought.

We were just fifteen miles south when I saw a line of camels and riders with rifles. I wondered if it could be the Camel Corps and I descended. They did not have khaki nor did they have sun helmets and they fired at us. They were Dervishes. I banked and cocked my Vickers. As they came into my sights I gave them a burst. I hit one of the camels and its rider. Behind me Lieutenant Canning and his gunner joined in. As I banked around and flew over them I saw that we had killed two camels and there were two dead Dervishes. I did not think we had found their base but we had established that they were close to us. I waved my hand around in a circle and we headed back. We had made a start.

There were aeroplanes on the ground when I landed and I saw tethered camels. The Camel Corps had arrived. I climbed out and went over to Lieutenant Canning, "What did you see?"

"Albert here, said there were ten of them. We killed two but another three were hit and they headed for cover."

"Well done, Albert."

He grinned, "They just vanished sir. One minute they were there and the next they had gone."

"It is the terrain. Had there been more, then it might have been an opportunity to drop a bomb." I had a sudden thought, "Next time take some Mills bombs up. Your gunner can drop them if the numbers are too small for a bomb."

I left my goggles and flying helmet in the cockpit and strode to the tent we used as admin. Inside was Jack, Lieutenant Hobson, Colonel Pritchard, Captain Connor and a Colonel I did not recognise.

Jack was excited, "Sir! Hobson here has found them."

"The Dervishes?"

"Yes sir, they are sixty miles to the east of us."

"Sixty miles? I thought I said for you to patrol to forty miles and then turn around."

Hobson looked apologetic, "Sorry sir. We had an engine problem. I sent Lieutenant Hooper to continue the patrol and I descended. I saw an area I thought I could use to land. However, as I descended the problem cleared itself. It was as I was climbing again that I saw the Dervish camp. It is on a high piece of ground here." He pointed to a map.

The Colonel I did not know said, "It is known as Medistie or Koolo depending upon whom you talk to. Little nothing of a place and hard to get to." He smiled, "Colonel Farquhar, Somaliland Camel Corps."

"Pleased to meet you. How many men, Hobson?"

"Hard to say sir. They were camouflaged but they had walls and what looked like ancient artillery pieces."

"Then this is our chance to strike at them. Colonel Pritchard and Colonel Farquhar, could you have your men a mile from Medistie by dawn? Not all of your men, say fifty Camel Corps and fifty Rifles?"

"Yes sir. What do you have in mind?"

"Simple, Colonel Pritchard. If between you the two of you can close the road in and out of Medistie then we will bomb it tomorrow at nine in the morning. We will strafe it. I guarantee that any Dervishes we do not kill will run away. You get as many as you can. Once that is done you enter their base and destroy any ordnance and defences."

Colonel Farquhar said, mildly, "Suppose they are not there? Suppose this officer made a mistake?"

I saw Eric Hobson colour, "My officers do not make mistakes like that, Colonel. If Lieutenant Hobson said there is a base at Medistie then there is one. We attack at nine!"

When the two colonels and Lieutenant Hobson had gone, Ted said, "You came on a little strong there, sir."

"Neither officer knows what we can see from the air. Jack, do you believe Hobson?"

"Of course. He is as reliable as they come."

"And that is my view too. I trust my officers. I do not know these two units. They may be good fellows but, as I recall, it was the Camel Corps which Sayyid Mohammed Abdullah Hassan defeated all those years ago. If the Rifles and the Camel Corps had the ability to defeat the Dervishes then they would have done so long before now. Tomorrow we show them just what we can do!"

We had our engines fired up before dawn. I had Eric Hobson lead the squadron to attack the next day. We headed first out to sea so that we could approach from the east with the sun behind us. One thing I had learned in my time in the Middle East was that every sunrise was bright. I wanted our twelve aircraft to appear from nowhere. They had never seen an aeroplane. I wanted to terrify them.

We had sixty miles to the target but my attack route meant more like a hundred and ten miles. I was not carrying any bombs. My Nanaks had forty-four between them. That would be enough. I knew that Eric Hobson was nervous. Jack had told me so. The Colonel's questions had made him doubt himself. I didn't doubt him for a moment. The men we had fired at had been just twenty odd miles from Medistie when we had shot them up. It made sense. The sun came up as we were heading along the coast. Hobson banked to begin our bombing run. We were ten miles from the camp and flying at four hundred feet. I hoped that the Rifles and Camel Corps were in position.

Hobson waggled his wings when we were just five miles from what passed for a town in these parts. The spirals of smoke ahead told me there were fires and people were cooking. Jack, who was flying alongside Hobson, signalled for us to descend and we dropped to two hundred feet. I cocked my guns. I had the easy job. I would just have to fire my machine gun. The Nanaks had to drop bombs and fire their guns.

Because we were low and coming from the sun the Dervishes heard only the buzz and hum of our motors. Ted said, later, that we would have sounded like a horde of locusts. I could only imagine what these primitive warriors thought as our fiendish machines suddenly appeared through the heat haze. Even before the first bomb had been dropped or the first bullet fired some fled for their lives. It would be a fruitless flight if my two colonels had not done as I had asked. I opened fire. My bullets tore through the branches and bushes they had used to disguise their position. Then the bombs dropped. Jack would make two passes to ensure that the encampment was totally destroyed. I did not waste more bullets. I would wait until the bombs had done their work and attack any other target which was belligerent.

As I made a lazy loop around the hill top refuge I checked my fuel. I had enough to get home. I saw dead camels and donkeys. I saw dead men. What I did not see were women and children. This was a warband of Dervishes. Colonel Pritchard told me that they operated much the way that they had done for hundreds of years. They rode their land taking what they wanted while their families were hidden in safety. When their appetites had been sated and they had enough treasure and glory then they would return, briefly, to their families. I found no targets for my guns. The ancient cannons had been destroyed. When I saw the first of the Camel Corps troopers enter the camp I signalled for us to return.

Flying along the road we saw where some of the Dervishes had been ambushed by the Rifles. The colonial troops waved in greeting as we zoomed overhead. There were knots of prisoners. We had our first victory.

The Nanak pilots were exuberant. I went over to Lieutenant Hobson. "Well done, Lieutenant. You led us there perfectly. I shall mention you in despatches."

"Thank you, sir. If it all goes like this then it will be over before Easter!"

"I hope, Lieutenant, that it is over sooner than that."

The men we had left behind had not been idle. Sergeant Major Robson and Sergeant Major Hale had finished clearing the airfield of rocks. We could now have three Nanaks taking off at once. We might not need to but it was good to know that we could. The two colonels had both opted to take part in the attack. Their adjutants were with Captain Connor. Jack had told them of our success over the radio.

"Well done, sir. A great victory."

I nodded, "Thank you Captain Reed. We caught them napping. We had surprise on our side. I am not certain that we will be so lucky a second time but it is a good start. There will be prisoners. I cannot see them reaching us before dark but you and your men might want to make a pen in which to hold them. I will pop down to the Ark Royal and report our success to Cairo."

Aircraftman Williams appeared with a mug of tea, "Here y'are sir. This will wash away the dust."

I took the mug and swallowed. He was right. It cut through the dust wonderfully well. "Get a motor cycle. We will go back to Berbera and I will visit with the Captain."

"Sir."

It was not a dignified ride as I clung to the back of Williams but it was quick. Aircraftman Williams enjoyed the machine. I was pleased to see that, as I went aboard the carrier, he stood guarding the motor bike with a Webley at the ready.

Captain Mainwaring was waiting to greet me. "We heard your aeroplanes take off this morning. I said to Number One that you would be in action. Well?"

"One camp destroyed and we have prisoners. I do not think we have taken casualties but we will have to await the return of the two detachments I sent."

"Well done. Marley!" His steward appeared, "Two Pink Gins!"

"Sir."

"What now?"

"Well, we found the camp which was closest to us. Now that we know what we are looking for we can spread our search. This is a big country. If this Mullah spreads his men out then it will be a long job."

The steward appeared with the gins, "Cheers. I am not certain he will disperse them, Bill. I had dinner with the Resident last night. He told me that Sayyid Mohammed Abdullah Hassan likes to keep his men close to him. They are like his bodyguard. They swear a blood oath and, of course, he is their religious leader too."

"I know, Captain Connor told me. So, this chap is like a vicar?"

"I know, strange isn't it. Still it is their religion. I take it you want me to report to Cairo?"

"Yes sir. If you let me have pen and paper I will write it as a report. I know that the atmospherics affect the radio. Your chap may have difficulty."

"Of course. Use my desk. I will pop along and have him warm it up."

I spent an hour writing my report. This was the first time that we had operated with two different arms and I wanted to make sure that I omitted no detail. I listened as the radio operator read my report back to me. I wanted no misunderstandings. It was afternoon by the time we reached the aerodrome. A wire enclosure had been built to secure any prisoners which were brought back.

It was after midnight before they did so. I was woken by Corporal Swanston, "Sir, the colonels are back."

"Thanks." The two colonels were weary and dirty. I met them in the admin tent. Williams had lit an oil lamp. "Everything go well?"

Colonel Pritchard nodded, "It did. We took fifteen prisoners."

Colonel Farquhar said, "The trouble is Wing Commander, that the hundred and odd miles we have done has taken it out of the camels. We will need a day or two to rest."

"I can see that. Look, you are both tired. Get a good night's rest. I will take the squadron up in the morning and see if we can find the rest of their strongholds. When I get back we will have a meeting to discuss strategy."

They both nodded, "By the way sir, I see what you meant about aerial power. I watched through glasses. Artillery could not be that accurate."

"I know. It was different in France. We had German aeroplanes and ground fire making life hard for us. So long as they have neither machine guns nor aeroplanes, then we hold all the aces."

I had a briefing with my pilots the next day. "After I visited the Ark Royal yesterday I spoke with the resident. He said that there are a couple of forts. One at Jideli and one at Taleh. It is likely that the Mullah will have gone there. They have now seen our aeroplanes and they will know what we can do. I do not think that they will run so quickly a second time. Today we go for reconnaissance. I want to find this fort at Jideli."

"Do we know where it is sir?"

"South and east of us. It stands on a seven-hundred-foot escarpment and guards the road east and also to the Ogaden."

"Ogaden sir?"

"That is the part of Ethiopia which has even fewer roads and settlements than Somaliland."

Lieutenant Hobson laughed, "Hard to believe that, sir."

"Me too, Hobson. Today we find this fort and then return here. I want us to fly so that every aeroplane is in sight of another. I do not want a repeat of the problem Lieutenant Hobson had. Squadron Leader Thomson will be in the centre. We find the fort and then return. I intend to destroy it but we will need the army to finish the job. This fort has caves beneath it. When we attack, some will hide there where they will be protected from our bombs. The army will be tasked with winkling them out. We leave in thirty minutes."

Jideli was an ancient hill fort. It was just thirty-five miles from us. It was on a solid piece of rock above the road. The guns there could stop us using it. The road ran east to the more inhospitable parts of Somaliland. There were mud huts, stone towers and walls.

They had a ditch and a wooden bridge across it. It was Lieutenant Reed who spotted it. When he waggled his wings and descended Jack and I joined him. We flew over at a thousand feet. Rifles and muskets were fired at us but they had never fired at aeroplanes before and they wasted their bullets. The observers and gunners would see more than I did but I could see that it had a large garrison. There were camels and horses tethered in lines. We had seen enough and we headed home.

The two colonels were waiting for me. They had a shade erected and were sitting in canvas chairs smoking. Williams hurried over with a chair for me. "Well, Wing Commander, how did it go?"

"We found them. They have a larger number of men in the fort."

Colonel Farquhar nodded, "They have half a dozen of these forts dotted all over the highlands. They have caves beneath them. We have tried to take them before but camels are not what is needed."

"My aim is to attack them tomorrow. We will make a dawn raid and then return later in the day."

"We can't be there by dawn even with the lorries."

"That is not what I intend. Leave the men here who went out on patrol yesterday. They will be our reserve. Take supplies for a week in the field. If you leave in the morning then you should be able to reach the fort by the afternoon and we will make our second attack then. Hopefully that will eliminate the defences. When they take to their caves then you can winkle them out. You can stay in their fort. We will then find their other forts and communicate by radio. We have a range of almost two hundred miles. We can cover more ground than you can."

Colonel Pritchard nodded, "Very well sir, you are in command."

I knew that the two colonels were finding it hard to take orders from an officer who was so much younger than they were. "You should know, gentlemen, that as soon as Sayyid Mohammed Abdullah Hassan is no longer a threat then we shall be leaving the area and returning to Egypt. This is only a temporary arrangement."

"Quite." They both seemed mollified and, if I was to be truthful I was not bothered if they resented me. Both had had an easier war than their colleagues on the Western Front.

I left them and joined Ted and Jack along with Sergeant Major Hale at the admin tent. "I want two strikes tomorrow. We leave before dawn. Now that we know where they are we can hit them as the sun rises. We come back, rearm, refuel, have a bite to eat and then hit them again. The army will then take the fort. The days following will see us finding their other forts."

"Are you keeping any troops here to guard the camp sir?"

"Yes, Sergeant Major. There will be two sections left to watch the prisoners and to keep an eye on the tents. However, we need to keep the bulk of the soldiers in the field."

"And what will you do when we attack Taleh sir? That is beyond the range of your Dolphin."

"I have three choices. I can commandeer one of your pilots' buses. I can stay here and listen in on the radio or I can accompany the army. I will make my decision when it is the only target left to us."

"Don't forget, sir, tomorrow is Saturday. You told the resident that the three of us would be dining with him."

I had forgotten. "I suppose it would be rude to cancel."

Captain Connor nodded, "When I went to visit the Ark yesterday I met him. He is really keen to dine with us. He has gone to a great deal of trouble."

I sighed. Beattie would tell me I had a duty to go as would my mother. I had been brought up too well. "Very well. Who will command in our absence, Jack?"

"Why not let the Captain of the King's African Rifles. They will have the more onerous duty, watching over the prisoners."

"Very well. You had better tell him tonight, Ted."

"Right sir."

The two colonels led their men out before dawn. They had plenty of time to reach their destination. I think they left then as it was much cooler. We left not long after them. There was light in the sky but I had fuel burned to mark the runway. This time I led. The bombers flew in lines of three. Two were alongside me. Above us flew Lieutenant Sanderson in the air ambulance. Both army units had a doctor but we could evacuate anyone seriously hurt back to the Ark Royal where they had a clean and sterile sick bay.

We flew directly for the fort this time. They would hear us but, coming from the west we would be in the darker part of the sky. As the sun rose I saw the two towers sticking up from the skyline. When we had flown over the previous day we had been at a thousand feet. We dropped to eight hundred. That would mean we were just a hundred feet above the walls. I cocked my Vickers. While the others bombed, I would strafe. I kept glancing to the two DH 9as on either side of me. We had to hit together for maximum effect.

At a hundred yards I opened fire at the gate. Two hundred and fifty bullets can do a great deal of damage. When the right-hand Vickers clicked on empty I cocked the second one. I fired as soon as we were over the walls. My first bullets threw men from the walls and then my next ones hit the building in the middle. I stopped firing. The first four bombs exploded in my mirror. I saw chunks of the wall and the gate disappear in smoke. Then we were over the wall and we banked to come around for a second pass. As we did so I saw that there was a machine gun on one of the towers. We swept around in a large circle. Overhead Lieutenant Sanderson kept his lazy circles going.

The last bombers had dropped their loads as we came around. I increased my speed. We did not need to keep formation any longer. I aimed my aeroplane at the tower with the machine gun. He saw me and fired at me. It was a Lewis gun and he fired too early. The bullets arced down below me. I waited until I was a hundred yards from him. They were changing the magazine as my Vickers hurled .303 rounds into them. This was a mud covered stone edifice. Even so the bullets tore into it sending pieces of mud and stone to the ground. The blood of the gunners stained the white walls red as they died.

Having emptied my machine guns, I rose to join Lieutenant Sanderson. I wanted to be able to see the damage we were inflicting. The pilots were now choosing the parts of the fort which had, hitherto, escaped damage. The gates had been shredded by me and their remains demolished by a bomb. Terrified horses and camels now fled through the open gate. By the time I reached Lieutenant Sanderson at a thousand feet the DH 9as were strafing the Dervishes who tried to escape. I had no doubt that many took refuge in the caves beneath the fort. I had enough fuel for another hour. When the rest of the squadron had used their ordinance, Jack sent them back to the field and he joined me overhead. He had the radio and he would be communicating with the column. With greater endurance, the Nanaks stayed longer than I could and I left.

The rest of the squadron had landed and were eating by the time I landed. I had just got my pipe going when Captain Connor waved to me from the admin tent.

"Sir, Squadron Leader Thomson has the column in sight. He is on his way back."

"Good. Sergeant Major Robson, have the aeroplanes refuelled and rearmed. We go back after a bite to eat."

"Right sir."

We had bully beef sandwiches. Somehow, Williams had managed to get hold of some Coleman's English mustard. They were delicious! Poor Jack and Lieutenant Sanderson barely had time to turn around. They gobbled down their sandwiches and washed them down with hot tea. Jack reported to me as he ate. "They were trying to repair the gate when we left. The column was about five miles away then."

"I pray that they just surround the fort and wait for us."

"Those were your orders sir."

"I know but they may try to storm it. I hope not. This time concentrate on the gate. Make it untenable."

"We also spotted a smaller redoubt to the side."

"Then have half your bombers take that one out too. You lead the ones attacking the redoubt and I will take in the others. We might just break the enemies' will to fight."

We left at about two in the afternoon. It took just thirty minutes to reach the fort. Smoke was still rising from the fires we had started. We later discovered that some of the bombs had hit the stables and set alight the dung. That would burn and burn. I saw that my orders had been obeyed. The column had encircled the fort. I could see that they had prisoners. The soldiers waved as we zoomed overhead.

The gates had been crudely repaired. We flew in line astern. That way if a target was destroyed then the next aeroplane could take the next target. I cocked my Vickers and looked for a target. They had men on the fighting platform over the gate. Using my rudder, I swung my Dolphin to allow me to clear the whole wall. The parapet was more mud than stone and my bullets tore lumps out of it. Men fell and then I was over. Behind me I saw the first two bombs land just outside the gate. The explosion shattered them.

The second one completely demolished the gatehouse. There was a gap sixty feet wide.

I banked to port and fired at the men standing on the remains of the south wall. Beyond it I saw the redoubt being pounded by bombs. I banked to starboard to allow me to view the perimeter. The walls were now indefensible. As I came around to the front I saw dismounted camel troopers and the Rifles as they raced up the slope. There was no gunfire to greet them. They would have the dangerous task of ferreting out the Dervishes who were hiding in the caves but that could be done by the judicious use of hand grenades.

We headed home.

Chapter 14

When we got back I felt exhausted. It had been a long day and yet I knew that we had to go to dinner with the resident. Corporal Swanston was grinning as we approached the admin tent, "Sir, Captain Connor said as how you were going out to dinner tonight and me and Willy decided that you couldn't go out smelling like the inside of a Turkish camel driver's armpit. No offence, sir. We have rigged up a shower. It is cold water but it is clean, sir and it will cool you down nicely." I saw Aircraftman Williams nodding vigorously.

"That is very thoughtful of you."

"And we will drive you down in the Crossley, sir. We can pick you up after. I dare say you will be having a bevvy or two!"

"I daresay we will. Thank you." The two of them were the salt of the earth and were what had made the British Army what it was. They were resourceful and cheerful. Who could ask for more?

Before I contemplated showering and changing I wrote my reports. I would give them to Captain Mainwaring before the dinner. When I was happy with my account, I stripped down to my shorts and grabbed a towel. "Right gentlemen, lead me to my bath!"

They had rigged a canvas screen up. I saw that they had an old drum suspended above it. I guessed it had water in it and I hoped that it had been cleaned. What I could not work out was how it would work as a shower. Swanston pointed to a piece of rope suspended from the bottom of the drum. When I peered inside I saw that there was a piece of tubing and what looked like a bully beef tin with holes in it. "When you pull the rope sir, it operates a lever. It has a spring so that when you stop pulling the water stops flowing."

Williams handed me a bar of army soap. "Here y'are sir. We will keep watch for you."

Obligingly they turned their backs. I stepped inside and took off my shorts and underwear. Feeling more than a little worried in case the fifty-gallon drum came crashing down on my head I pulled on the rope and was rewarded by deliciously cold water. I almost let too much water flow. I released the rope and the water stopped. I lathered up and then repeated the action. It worked. It was a little primitive and it was cold but it was functional and I felt refreshed. I towelled myself dry and, wrapping the towel around my waist, I picked up my shorts and underwear and headed for my tent. "Thank you, gentlemen. Much obliged."

"There is some hot water in your tent sir and we have stropped your razor for you."

By the time I had shaved and dressed in my best uniform, I felt almost human. I picked up my report and, leaving my tent said, "One of you fetch the Crossley and the other tell the Squadron Leader and the Captain that we are ready to go."

When the other two arrived, I felt guilty. They had had to make do with a basin wash. "I am sorry, chaps. I should have told you that we have a shower now."

Captain Connor shook his head and smiled but Jack glowered at the two airmen. They quickly put the ladder for us to climb in the back of the light truck. It was a twisting five mile drive down the valley to the port. There was a shorter, three-mile route, but that involved walking. Once we reached the port I went aboard the Ark Royal and handed my report to the radio operator. The Captain and his officers were at dinner and I did not bother him. The evening felt pleasant as I walked down the gangway. Perhaps it was the shower or the clean uniform which had put me in such a good mood. As I reached the truck I said, "You don't need to bother picking us up. We will walk back."

"Are you certain, sir? It is no bother!" Corporal Swanston looked nervously at Jack.

"I, for one, would like the walk. We are not flying tomorrow and I daresay we will be celebrating tonight."

Ted nodded, "Splendid idea!"

Jack was forced to nod, "Just so long as you show us the shower tomorrow morning, Corporal!"

"Of course, sir. We will fill it up for you tonight!"

They jumped in the cab and the lorry laboured up the slope. We walked across the road to the residency. We were greeted by a turbaned Indian, "Welcome gentleman, the resident is on the balcony waiting for you. If you give me your hats, swagger sticks and guns I will look after them for you."

We handed over our weapons, hats and sticks. I did not think we would need our guns in the residency, especially as the major domo locked and bolted the door. We ascended a splendid spiral staircase which brought us to a cosy dining room. The major domo held open the door. "If you would care to join the resident I will see to the food."

The dining room looked like it would hold twelve but it was set just for six. The open door led to the balcony and there we saw Reginald St. John Browne. He was smoking a Turkish cigarette. With him was a young man and an older, heavier and rather sweaty man.

"I am so glad you are here." He looked behind us, "Where are the colonels?"

"They are in the field, sir. Sorry."

Nodding he pointed to each of us in turn, "This is Wing Commander William Harsker, V.C., Squadron Leader John Thomson D.S.O and Captain Ted Connor M.C."

We nodded.

"May I introduce Arthur Clarke. He is an American who is here with a view to leasing the mineral rights to Somaliland from the British Government. He has the steamboat which is moored on the other side of the Ark Royal."

"Pleased to meet you fellows. Reggie here has been telling me all about you." From St. John Browne's wince, I gathered he did not like to be addressed in such a familiar manner but he was a diplomat and the smile he faked hid it. I had met Americans before and I put his accent west of the Mississippi. "I hope you can sort out these damned troublemakers! Mineral rights are no good if you have religious fanatics chopping heads from God fearing folk."

The resident shook his head, "Mr. Clarke had two of his engineers kidnapped a month or so back. We found their bodies but not their heads. They had been, er, mutilated."

"Barbaric! I complained to your government! I am glad that they took notice of what I said."

Once again, I saw the resident react. It was obvious to me that it was a coincidence that we had been sent. It would not hurt to give

196

the illusion that HMG listened to businessmen even though they did not.

"And this is my secretary, Peter Hardwicke."

I saw that the secretary could have been a younger version of Reginald St. John Browne. He was small neat, quietly spoken and with precise movements. He looked to be barely twenty. He nodded, "Can I say, that I envy all three of you. Had it not been for a health problem then I would have loved to have served in the Royal Flying Corps."

A second turbaned servant, Gupta, arrived with three sherries. We each took one and I raised my glass, "Thank you, sir. This is a genuine pleasure. Crystal glasses, white linen tablecloths and a cool breeze from the sea. This is as close to perfect as it gets for us fliers, sir."

"Yes, I do like it here. I know many people wondered at my acceptance of this position. I was in Calcutta for many years. You have seen the two servants who followed me here but when I came here in 1916 it was because this will be my last posting and I believe that we owe it to the people of this land to make their lives more bearable. We did it in India and we can do it here."

Mr. Clarke was in bullish mood, "It is a poor country I will say that. If your Government grants me a licence then I will put millions into the economy here!"

I sipped the sherry. It was dry and chilled. It was perfect. I looked at the American, "What minerals are there here, sir?"

"That is what my surveyors will tell me."

"You don't know?"

"It stands to reason that there must be something. The whole country is rock and desert. We found gold and silver in the Black Hills and Nevada. They are similar terrain to this. We will find something believe me. Now that the Turks have gone I intended to have a look at Arabia and Mesopotamia. It stands to reason that you can't grow anything there. The Good Lord must have blessed it with something."

The argument did not follow. I caught the eye of the resident and he subtly raised his eyebrows.

"It is pleasant here is it not, Wing Commander?"

"It is and the view is calming." We could see, for it faced south east, the Indian Ocean stretching before us. It looked almost benign with the sun setting to the west. The Ark Royal bobbed with the tide. It was almost idyllic. Had it not been for Dervishes, that is.

"And the breeze is from the land. Ravi has the windows to the north opened to allow a pleasant breeze. When the wind is from the sea then we could not sit here. However, it is now bringing the smell of your aeroplane fuel wafting from the airfield, Wing Commander. I shall tell Ravi to close the windows for I think we have seen the last of the sun. Shall we go into dinner? We have a rather nice seafood starter."

I was seated next to Reginald St. John Browne with Jack on his other side. The seating arrangement soon became apparent. We quickly realised that the resident knew a great deal about our exploits. "After dinner, I shall show you my scrapbook. I used the London Gazette and the Times to gather information about the air war."

He began to question us both closely about the aeroplanes we had flown and the ones we had fought. It was obvious he had an encyclopaedic knowledge of them. We were just confirming what he knew and giving him a pilot's perspective.

"And you met the Red Baron you say?"

I told him of my meeting, including the fact that I had forced him down, and the story even impressed Mr. Clarke.

The resident lit another Turkish cigarette. He sucked in the smoke. He enjoyed smoking. "I envy you, Wing Commander. I have led an interesting life and I have served the Empire as best I could. But I would dearly have loved to have done as you did and been a pilot. You have a son, I believe."

"Yes, Tom, Thomas."

"And, who knows, he may follow you into the service. That would be wonderful would it not? I am sad that I have no family of my own." He sucked deeply on his Turkish cigarette. He pointed to Mr. Hardwicke, "Do not do as I did, Peter. I was married to the Civil Service. Find a woman and marry her. Have a son of your own."

Peter smiled shyly, "Perhaps sir, perhaps but I think that you have achieved much in your life."

"Yet when I am gone it will be the end of my line. The St. John Brownes will be but a memory."

Mr. Clarke left after the main course. He did not stay for the cheeseboard. I think he was bored with the talk of the war.

When the front door had closed St. John Browne shook his head, "Businessmen! I know the Empire needs them but I do not share their values. At least we can talk more freely now. Come let us go and find more comfortable seats so that we can talk."

We retired to the drawing room for brandy and cigars. I would have preferred my pipe but I was quite fond of the old man already and I followed his lead. He reminded me of many of those who worked on Lady Mary's estate. They had given their lives to the land. St. John Browne had given his to his country and Empire. The cigars were King Edward's and the brandy was Napoleon. We were being feted well. He brought out his scrapbook. It was embarrassing. Most of the cuttings were about me.

When Peter asked Ted about his hand the attention, to my great relief, shifted to my adjutant. He told the story of his wounding with humour. He made light of the potential tragedy which might have cost him his life. He and the resident then shared experiences of living so far from England.

As the night went on the resident began coughing even more. He smoked more than was good for one. I noticed that his handkerchief had specks of blood upon it. That was not good. I would get the doctor from the Ark Royal to have a look at him.

He poured himself another brandy, "You know, I have not been back to England since the Empress died. I was there for her funeral and then back to Calcutta. I didn't even visit my home. It has lain empty since my dear mother died thirty years ago. I think I shall sell it and then, when I retire, I shall buy somewhere in France. I like the wine and I can speak the language." He coughed again. "It is mandatory in my profession to speak French. I would enjoy being St. John Browne and just a villager. That would be pleasant. I have spent my life being someone else. I have played a part for the Empire. I believe that I have done my duty."

I was aware that it was getting late. Ted and Jack had drunk more than I had. I had also noticed that Peter Hardwicke was almost a carer for the old man. He anticipated his moves and needs. When the resident had another coughing fit, Hardwicke rang a bell and the two Indians arrived. "Ravi, take the resident to his bed. I will see the guests out."

St. John Browne tried to speak but he coughed up more blood. He waved an apologetic arm and was helped out.

After he had gone Peter said, "He is dying, you know. I had the doctor from the ship examine him the other day. He has a month at the most. This posting was to extend his life. The drier climate helps him but each day he wakes is a cause for celebration. This evening has been the highlight of the year. As soon as he was told you were coming it was though he had been given a new lease of life. There are many such as he. They are brave in their own way. They do not fight in wars. He would have loved to be a pilot or even a gunner. He just wanted to serve. His is a courage which has little glory. That is why he enjoyed talking to you and why he took the cuttings. He lived vicariously through you. Thank you, Wing Commander. You may not have known it but your exploits made a difference to one man, at least."

"I am sorry that he is ill. I like him. We will call again when time allows. Now we must get back to the airfield."

"Are they sending a car for you?"

"It is only a couple of miles or so. We will enjoy the walk and it will help sober up my officers. It doesn't do for the Erks to see us in our cups."

"Do take care."

Ravi had arrived with our hats and weapons. We strapped on our weapons. "Don't worry, we are armed."

It was a cloudless sky as we set off. The moon shone down and the stars sparkled. The path was clear to see, in the moonlight. It had been used for centuries. Mr. St. John Browne had told us of ancient civilizations which had existed in this part of the world. He mentioned the fabled Queen of Sheba. I daresay the Pharaohs had extended their influence in this part of the world. We set off up the trail which followed the natural contours. Neither Ted nor Jack were drunk although we had all enjoyed the wine. However, we were silent. Each of us was lost in our own thoughts.

I was thinking about the dying diplomat. He could have gone home to die yet he had chosen this to be his final home. It was a desolate spot at the edge of the world. He was a true Englishman who knew how to do his duty to the bitter end. I had been genuinely flattered and more than a little embarrassed by his scrapbook and his interest in my career. The names he had mentioned like Ball and McFadden, they had been the true heroes. To be thought of alongside those greats was humbling.

When I had been growing up on the estate, I had often gone out with Charlie, the gamekeeper. He had taught me how to stalk animals and, when I had been older, poachers. He had shown me that your ears and nose were as important as your eyes. We were less than a mile from the camp. I could hear the sentries as they chattered and I could smell the smoke from their cigarettes. Then I smelled something I should not have. Horses and camels; it was their bodies and their dung which I could smell. The Camel Corps was more than a mile and half away. It was not them. This smell was closer. I could also detect the whiff of unwashed bodies. These were not British bodies, fed on a diet of bully beef, bread and tea. This was the smell of spices, camels and horses. It was not our Camel Corps I could smell. They were camped to the north of the field. This smell was closer. It was Dervishes.

I stopped and raised my hand. I took out my Webley. Jack and Ted looked at me. I made the sign for danger and they took out their guns. I took the lead with the two of them flanking me. Jack was to my right and Ted to my left. Closer to the field I was certain I detected movement. I was about to hurry when a figure suddenly loomed from our left. It was a Dervish. He swung a long two-handed sword at Ted. Even as I fired a bullet at his middle the sword connected. It clanged and sparked off the metal to which Ted fitted his attachments. The Dervish fell back with a puzzled expression on his face.

"Stand to! We are under attack! Stand to!" I used my sergeant voice to shout loudly.

Two more Dervishes rushed at us. Jack shot one and I another. They had swords and rifles. Ted fired at his left. In the flash from his gun I saw another huddle of Dervishes. To run would be to invite death for then they would use their numbers. We stood back to back. The Dervishes ran at us. I emptied my revolver but more came at us. I dropped the revolver and it hung from its lanyard. Kneeling, I picked up the ancient musket which lay at my feet. I had no idea how to fire it and I held it like a staff before me. These ancient warriors liked their edged weapons and one of them swung his sword at my head. Even as it came down towards me I saw that it was not curved but straight. I took the blow on the barrel of the musket. It was a powerful blow and the musket bent. As the warrior raised it to strike again, I rammed the bent barrel into the bridge of his nose and he reeled. I brought my knee up hard and I connect with him, making him fall further. I held the barrel of the musket and brought it over from behind me. The stock connected with his head. It sounded like an axe striking a tree. I saw blood, bone and brains. He was dead.

I looked to my left and saw a warrior kneeling with a musket. It was aimed at me. He was less than twenty feet from me. I was a dead man. A flurry of shots made his body dance as though he was having a fit. Sergeant Major Hale with Swanston and Williams stood there with their Webleys smoking.

"Come along, sirs. Let's get you to safety!"

I heard an English voice shouting, "Number one platoon, skirmish line!"

I dropped the musket and with Jack and Ted in close attendance headed for the airfield. As we ran, we passed the bodies of some of those we had slain. When we reached the camp, I saw that the squadron were all armed and ready. The fitters and the riggers defended the aeroplanes. Sergeant Major Robson held a Lee Enfield. I joined my officers and, with shaking hands, reloaded my Webley. We heard the sound of sporadic firing as the colonial troops used their discipline and superior firepower to clear the rocks of the Dervishes.

Jack said to Ted, "Let's have a look at your arm."

He held out his stump. The metal had a line scored across it. "I think that will need some work, Ted."

My adjutant laughed, "I don't think so, Squadron Leader. I shall dine out on this story. When I pull back my sleeve and show them this I can tell them how a Fuzzy Wuzzy tried to take my head."

An hour later Captain Grenville returned with his King's African Rifles. He looked a little shamefaced. "I am sorry, sir. That should not have happened. I did not set enough sentries on the port side of the field. I thought that would be the safe part."

"These are clever people, Captain. They must have circled around. They came downwind of you so that you would not detect their approach. How many were there?"

"We counted thirty bodies. I have men encircling the field now, sir. Some escaped but I did not think it wise to send men after them."

"Quite right too."

I holstered my Webley. "Well gentlemen, after such an exciting night, I think that I will retire."

The captain looked surprised, "You will retire, sir?"

"Of course. You and your chaps will keep a good watch, I have no doubt and after a fine dinner the exercise has worn me out. Goodnight."

In truth, I would not find it easy to sleep. Had we not walked back then the whole campaign could have ended in disaster. If the Dervishes had attacked then many of my men would have been killed and the irreplaceable aeroplanes destroyed. It showed how desperate the enemy had become. We were winning. I determined to prosecute the campaign to its ultimate conclusion; the destruction of the Dervish threat. After a calming pipe, I turned out the oil lamp and rolled on to my side. I slept.

The next day I sent the Camel Corps detachment out to find any Dervishes who had escaped. Captain Grenville had his men dig a pit and bury the dead warriors. We had suffered minor wounds only.

"I want a flight of aeroplanes to patrol and see if they can see any sign of the Dervishes. Tomorrow we take the squadron up and find the rest of their forts."

Jack nodded, "I will lead them."

While they were in the air we heard from the troops at Jideli. The fort was secured and there were prisoners on their way back. The two colonels were making the fort indefensible. "And, sir, they need Lieutenant Sanderson. They have someone who needs to be evacuated."

"Right send him up with Lieutenant Hobson as minder."

"Right sir."

I went with Williams and Swanston to retrace our steps. I was keen to see where they had lain in wait. I saw that they had used some acacia bushes as cover. I found where they had tethered their animals. I saw the dung they had left. "Good for the roses that, sir."

"I am not certain that they grow roses in this part of the world."

We headed back. "You should have let us come for you last night, sir."

"If you had, Williams, then we would not have stumbled upon them." I stopped for I saw something shiny beneath a bush. I reached in and picked it up. It was a native knife. Crudely handled it was wickedly sharp. "And they would have been amongst us with these." I gave it to him. "A souvenir for you."

I busied myself with the report on the last night's activities. I was not certain if anyone would actually read them or if someone would act upon them but I wrote them anyway. By the time I had finished, Lieutenant Sanderson had landed with his patient. I went to watch as the wounded soldier was taken out of the aeroplane.

"We have to go back, sir. There is a second."

"How is it there?"

"They have done a good job of rendering the fort harmless sir. The lorries with the prisoners are just ten miles up the road. The sergeant who loaded the aeroplane told me that the Camel Corps are off chasing those who escaped. He says they have more forts to the east."

"Thanks. Do you need Lieutenant Hobson with you?"

"No, sir. I will be fine."

Jack landed just before noon with the news that he had found two more forts closer to Taleh. They were a hundred miles away and they were thirty miles apart. "Tomorrow I shall lead half of the bombers and you take the other half. We will attack both forts at once. Ted, get on to Colonel Pritchard. Give him the coordinates of the forts and tell him we will be attacking in the morning."

"Sir."

The prisoners arrived shortly after along with the wounded who had already been treated. The two doctors had an improvised hospital but the two men who had been air lifted out were aboard the Ark Royal. I made the decision to send the Camel Corps contingent to join Colonel Farquhar. He would need all the men he could get. With the walking wounded we now had enough men to guard the prisoners and the camp. The lorries would return to Jideli in the morning.

I briefed my pilots after dinner. I had Lieutenant Hobson as my wing man. "These are small forts. They are at the extreme limit of our range. We do not have long over the target." I smiled, "That is

my fault. I am an old man and my bus and I have small bladders!"
They laughed. The five of you will go in line astern behind
Lieutenant Hobson. He destroys the gate. The next aeroplane will
be one minute behind. If the gates are still there then destroy them
and if not the walls to the left. By the time you have all made your
pass, then we should have destroyed the exterior. We strafe the
interior and when I head home then you all follow. Is that clear?"
"Yes sir."
We left after breakfast. There was no hurry. The army would not
be in place for a while, in any case. This time there would be little
likelihood of surrounding the forts. The survivors would flee to
Taleh. It was what I intended. I wanted every Dervish left on
Somaliland to be in that fort. I would have it surrounded by
infantry and camels. When we bombed it then, I hoped, we would
have destroyed the power of Sayyid Mohammed Abdullah Hassan.

I led and I followed the coordinates given by Jack. He had told
me that both were the size of Jideli but without the exterior
redoubt. I wondered at the wisdom of this Mad Mullah that he
thought his forts would be able to defend against air power. Then it
struck me. He did not know our range. His attack on our camp had
been to eliminate the threat. He knew that neither the Somaliland
Camel Corps nor the King's African Rifles could defeat him on
their own. He had already defeated the Camel Corps. This was a
warlord. He would have absolute faith in himself and his god. He
had men who were true fanatics. Gordon and Kitchener had found
that out at Omdurman when the Dervishes had charged cannons
and machine guns. As I recalled Mr. Churchill had mentioned that
he had been in that battle.

The hill fort occupied a similar position to the others. It was on a
plateau. The steep sides made a direct attack difficult and the road
which wound up to it was enfiladed by the fort's walls. From the
air, however, it had no protection. I rose a hundred feet above the
bombers as we approached. I would watch the fall of bombs. This
time they used their artillery. It was two ancient guns and they had
elevated them to fire like howitzers. It was inventive but unless
they had fused shot then they would be lucky to bring down an
aeroplane.

I watched as Lieutenant Hobson dropped his bombs. The eight of
them demolished the wall and part of the gatehouse. I saw,

however, that the Nanak lurched to the side. As he banked I saw that the gunner was not sitting upright. When he banked to pass me, I signalled for him to head home. His gunner was hit. I came in low from east to west and fired at the Dervishes who were trying to move the gun. I kept firing until there was no one near the gun. My bullets had also damaged the wheel so that it was lying at a strange angle. I rolled up over the wall to make a second pass. I heard the other DH 9as as they strafed the fort. I came in east to west. There was a second gate and men were fleeing through it. I fired at the door. By the time I had emptied the magazine, there were just wounded and dying men left. I waggled my wings and headed home.

Lieutenant Hobson's gunner was our only casualty. Captain Connor was waiting for me. "Hobson is a little upset about his gunner."

"I understand how he feels. Good gunners are hard to come by. Did he say what happened?"

"An enterprising Dervish, apparently. He used a rope to throw a grenade into the air. It exploded just below the Nanak. Hobson saw the man but he was already beyond him. We took Jones to the Ark Royal. He has shrapnel in his legs. It will be some time before he is fit to fly again."

I nodded, "Get Jack to write his report as soon as he comes in and then tell me when you receive the reports from the Rifles and the Camel Corps. I will be in my tent writing my report."

"Sir, do not dwell on this. We have had one casualty. In Palestine, we had two or three every mission."

"But there you were fighting aeroplanes, tanks and troops with modern weapons. We are fighting men who go to war with a spear, a sword and a camel!"

"But you said it yourself, sir, they are fighting men. It is what they were bred to do from the moment they could cling to the back of a camel!"

I nodded, "I know but it does not sit well with me."

I went to my tent and poured myself a whisky. I had husbanded the bottle I had brought from Egypt but I needed it. I lit my pipe and closed my eyes. Gradually my breathing became easier. Ted was right. Jones would walk and fight again. Our enemies would not. We had one fort left to go and then this would all be over but I had had my warning. It would not do to underestimate our enemies. I would speak with my two colonels directly. I had an idea how we would take Taleh. First I would have Jack go with one of his pilots and overfly it. Photographs would have been perfect but we did not have that luxury. Instead I would have them draw what they saw. I would not be rushed into this attack. They were on the back foot and I intended to keep them there.

Chapter 15

I had Swanston take the reports to the Ark Royal by motor cycle. He seemed to enjoy riding it. When the reports came in from the colonels they were positive. Both forts had been taken and more prisoners were on their way back to our camp. I had no idea what we would do with them when this was all over. It seemed a nonsense to me that, having defeated them, we should just let them go. What was there to stop them fighting against us again? I would worry about that when the time came.

That evening we made sure that Hobson was kept occupied. He seemed the type to brood and dwell on such matters. The three of us took him for a walk around the perimeter. It was a way for us to check the security but it also afforded us the chance to chat with the young pilot. It seemed to help. By the time we had got back he saluted, "Thank you, sirs. I appreciate that you took the time to talk to me. I realise that I was being foolish but Jones is a good man. I should have seen that Dervish."

"Hindsight is always perfect, Eric. Ifs and maybes are a luxury we do not have in the Royal Air Force. When we are in the air we make decisions in a split second. If we make the wrong one then we have to live with it. That is the key word, live. Learn from your mistakes but do not let them rule your life."

"I won't sir. Thank you."

As we headed back to our tents I said, "I need you to give me as much information about this fort as you can, Jack. I don't want to chase this fellow all the way to Timbuctoo!"

Ted threw his stump of a cheroot away, "The thing is, that would be a perfectly satisfactory outcome, as it is half a continent away. I do not think that we can guarantee that we will totally end the threat of this Mullah, Sayyid Mohammed Abdullah Hassan. However, so long as we destroy his bases and his men we will have succeeded."

Ted had given me an idea how to kill two birds with one stone. I would sleep on it. I often found that my best ideas came when I did that. When I awoke it had worked. I knew what to do with the prisoners and how to ensure that Sayyid Mohammed Abdullah Hassan was no longer an issue.

After breakfast, I had Sergeant Major Robson give every aeroplane a complete check. Lieutenant Hobson's had holes in the fuselage. It was not being tended to.

"Sergeant Major why is no one working on M for Mother?"

"It didn't seem urgent, sir. He has no gunner."

"But it is a bomber and we need every aeroplane we can get to finish the job. Besides he has a gunner."

"Who, sir?"

"Me!"

Leaving him dumfounded I headed to the admin tent. "I am going to pop to speak with the resident. I shall take a motor cycle. I won't be long."

It had been some time since I had ridden a bike but one never forgot. I donned my goggles and flying helmet and zipped down the hill.

The resident's major domo, Ravi, hid his bemused smile behind his hand as he greeted me, "Wing Commander. Are you expected?"

"Afraid not, is he busy?"

"He will make time to see you, sir." He held out his hand for the goggles and helmet. "If you would like to follow me, sir. He is in the garden with his secretary. He is dictating."

When I appeared the two of them started like guilty schoolboys and then St. John Browne stood and extended his hand. "This is a pleasant surprise, Wing Commander." Then he frowned. "I hear you had a spot of bother after my party."

"Nothing we couldn't handle, sir, and it worked out well. Had we not stumbled upon them then they might have done some damage to our aeroplanes."

Take a seat. Ravi, whisky and water for the Wing Commander and I." Seeing him light a cigarette I took out my pipe. "Now then what can I do for you? I don't think for one moment this is a social visit."

That made me feel guilty. He obviously yearned for company and we were just a few minutes up the road. "In the next few days I intend to bring to an end the threat posed by Sayyid Mohammed

Abdullah Hassan. When I do that the work of Z Force will be finished. Or almost finished. I need to pick your brains."

He leaned forward and grinned, "At last, someone has a use for this dried up old fossil." He looked at his secretary, "We will finish that off when the Wing Commander has finished. Go and ask cook to make us some sandwiches." Ravi appeared with the drinks. The old man toasted me, "Cheers! Your arrival has given me a new lease of life, Wing Commander. I feel I have a purpose once again. Now what do require of me?"

Over the next two hours I picked his brain. Peter Hardwick also helped. I asked the questions and the resident gave me both problems and solutions in equal measure. When I finally rose, I said, "That is an answer to my question, sir."

He stood, a little unsteadily for he had had four whiskies, "You are even more remarkable in the flesh, Wing Commander, than in print. You have hidden depths. You were more than a little modest about the attack the other night. Captain Mainwaring read your report and spoke to Captain Connor. I know what you did. Today you have shown that you are a thinker as well as a man of action. I am pleased to have met you. I have high hopes for the Empire. I thought the best of the best had fallen in Flanders' field. Now I see that there are new blooms. If I had had a son then I would want him to be just like you. Thank you, Wing Commander."

When I arrived back the patrol had returned and there was a delegation waiting for me. I rubbed my hands as Jack handed me the sketch map he had made. "Excellent. So, it is more substantial than the others." I saw that it had three smaller forts or redoubts clustered around it. I looked closely at the drawing. "What are these crosses?"

"They are artillery pieces."

"Like the ones we faced the other day. We need to make our attack a little different when we attack, the day after tomorrow."

"Not tomorrow then?"

"No Jack. Tomorrow I fly up to the forts and meet with the colonels. When we attack, we fly in at five hundred feet and we dive. It need not be a steep angle but I want to minimise the possibility of them using grenades against us."

"Sir, the stresses on the wings."

"The DH 9a is a sturdy aeroplane, Sergeant Major Robson. It can cope." I turned back to the others. "Once the bombs are dropped then we strafe the building and the Dervishes. I want us to support the Camel Corps and the Rifles when they attack. We only leave when we have no more ammunition or we are running short of fuel. I want every air gunner issued with half a dozen grenades. When the bombs are gone, we drop grenades."

I could see that Lieutenant Hobson had been bursting to say something. He looked guiltily at Sergeant Major Robson and burst out, "Sir, is it right that you will be in my bus when we attack?"

"Yes, Mr. Hobson. I will be your gunner."

I had astounded all of them but Ted. He just smiled. "But you are a Wing Commander! You are an ace! You should be piloting the DH 9a."

"Lieutenant, I began life as an air gunner. I shot down many German aeroplanes from the front of a Gunbus! I can assure you that I can do the job!"

"I don't mean that, sir. I mean, well, let me be the gunner and you the pilot."

"Without being rude, Lieutenant, you have never been an air gunner and besides, you know the Nanak far better than I. This will be fine. I need to be in at the kill and you have a spare seat. Argument over."

"Yes sir." I had bemused him. He did not know whether to be happy or sad.

After he and Sergeant Major Hale and Sergeant Major Robson had left us Ted pulled out a bottle of whisky and poured one for each of us, "Sir, I have to say this and I mean no disrespect when I say it but you, sir, are as mad as a bag full of frogs."

"I know, Ted, and the day I change is the day that I hand in my resignation."

"I'll drink to that."

I left after breakfast the next day. The two colonels were expecting me. I had already identified a landing area just five hundred yards from the encampment. Any closer and my landing might have startled the camels. I had asked for a fire to be lit so that I could see the smoke and therefore the wind direction. The two units watched my landing. I had time, as I taxied a little closer, to see that they had managed to bring down most of the walls of the fort. It would still provide shelter but not defence. My orders had been followed.

I chocked the wheels and donned the sun helmet I had brought. It was bakingly hot. I had learned to respect the sun. The colonels had erected a canvas shade and I gratefully stepped beneath it.

Both colonels were effusive in their welcomes.

"Splendid operation thus far, Wing Commander."

"Your chaps know their job and it has been impeccably planned."

"Thank you. It would be a mistake to become careless at this late juncture. We will attack Taleh tomorrow. We will set off at dawn and it will take one and a half hours to be in position to begin our bombing run. I need the fort to be surrounded by then. Once the bombs have been dropped I want you to attack on all sides. My bombers will provide covering fire. I intend to end this war tomorrow. When that is done, we will win the peace."

I explained my plan and they nodded approvingly.

Colonel Farquhar said, "You know that you almost killed Sayyid Mohammed Abdullah Hassan on your first attack?"

"Did we?"

"One of the fellows we captured told us. Apparently, he was standing close to where a bomb exploded. Luckily for him a camel bore the brunt of the explosion. He has been hiding in Taleh ever since. Your aeroplanes have put the wind up him."

"Good, then we have the advantage. When it is over, bring the prisoners back to Berbera. You have been in the field for a long time but if you have time then try to make the fort indefensible. You wouldn't want to take it a second time."

"We could always bomb it again."

"I am afraid that the bombers will be needed in Egypt. Z Force will be disbanded once this police action is over." They both looked genuinely crestfallen. "However, I believe that the Minister of Air will be sending aeroplanes here when the resources are available. I will certainly make that case when I return to England."

"You are not staying in Egypt?"

"When this is over the squadron will be granted a leave and after that... who knows."

As I headed back I wondered at my own words. Perhaps I would be based in Egypt. Who knew what the Royal Air Force had planned for me?

There were looks of relief on everyone's faces as I climbed from the cockpit. I am not certain what they thought I would do in the desert on my own. "We will have a squadron briefing after dinner. Tomorrow will need to go like clockwork. We will be operating further from this base than ever before and timing will be crucial. If all goes well then the men can celebrate tomorrow."

I was left alone and I scribbled a few lines to Beattie.

"Sir, we have the shower ready again if you want it. The water should be a bit warmer today. sir. Not such a shock to the system."

"You know Corporal, that sounds like a wonderful idea."

I made it quite clear, at the briefing, of the difficulties which faced us. "The Dervishes have been learning. As Lieutenant Hobson's gunner found, to his cost, they can now throw hand grenades into the air. They are using artillery to try to bring us down. We fly fragile aeroplanes. They just have to get lucky once and we will be downed. For that reason, we go in higher and dive at an angle of forty-five degrees. There will be two columns and we will fly in line astern. Squadron Leader Thomson will lead one and Lieutenant Hobson the other. I have spoken with the colonels who have watched our other attacks. They agree that the rolling barrage technique seems to work. Our first pass will be to destroy the main fort. Each bomber will drop its bombs forty yards further east so that the last two should take down the last wall. We then peel to port and starboard and take out the three forts in the same way. They are smaller. When we are out of bombs we strafe. The army will be attacking whilst we are bombing. Finally, the air gunners have grenades. They have discretion to use them on any target not destroyed by the bombs. We stay over the site until the army has reached the top or until we need to head back to refuel."

I saw nods. "Gentlemen, if we do not get the job done the first time then we go back... the same day. Let us get it done the first time!"

Even as I wrote a few lines to Beattie I wondered if I would beat my letter home. If all went well, then we would be leaving by the middle of February; perhaps even earlier. Letters had reached us quite quickly in France. Captain Connor had told us that the lack of mail had caused much distress amongst the men in Palestine and Arabia. I could be a father again and not know it. I fell asleep wondering about my unborn child.

As well as my Webley, I took my German pistol. It had been some years since I had been a gunner but I remembered that you had to be prepared for anything. I checked that I had two spare magazines for the Lewis. The Scarff ring which was fitted to the DH 9a made life a lot easier. I was able to traverse the gun through a full circle. While Eric checked the bus, I made sure that it had been greased and worked smoothly. It did. I secured the grenades in the rope nets hanging from the cockpit. It would be cosy. I had my flying coat with me. If it became too hot then I could take it off. I was not the pilot!

"Ready sir?"

"I am indeed, Lieutenant. Forget that I am your Wing Commander. I am your gunner. Do not try to do anything different because you have a different man behind you. Jones will be back."

"Yes sir."

The Nanak was noisier than my Dolphin but we could still communicate by shouting. We needed little conversation anyway. I peered over the side. The land was a true wasteland. Where there was grazing, you would see a few goats or sheep being tended by two or three boys. At the few watercourses I saw girls carrying clay pots filled with water. Life had not changed since the time of the Pharaohs! I saw the other Nanaks in line astern. Their eight bombs looked innocuously harmless hanging from the wings but I knew how deadly they could be. I had seen their effect.

"Forts coming up sir! Descending to five hundred feet, sir."

"Checking my gun!" I cocked the Lewis. The Lewis was a good gun but it was not as reliable as a Vickers. I had never had a Vickers machine gun jam on me. I had with the Lewis gun. I swung the gun around the Scarff ring and aimed it to port and starboard, pointing down. Here the danger would be from the ground and not from the air.

"Prepare for the attack!"

I braced myself with my back pressed against the seat and my feet against the fuselage struts. I looked over the side and saw the lines of soldiers preparing to attack. They were at the bottom of the hill and, as such, seemed like little dots. They had an escarpment to climb. I looked to starboard and saw Jack Thomson in A for Apple. His gunner had the added duty of operating the radio. Jack waved and Hobson shouted, "Diving now sir!"

Even though the angle was just forty-five degrees it was a shock to the system. I was used to this but I normally faced the earth and I was in control. My life was in Hobson's hands. I held on to the Lewis gun. I had no target yet but, when we climbed, then I would. I sensed the movement as the four bombs were released and then I felt the pressure as we began to level out. Hobson began to fire his Vickers at the men on the wall. I stood and aimed my Lewis to the port side. I saw men at a tower. They had an ancient cannon. They were firing it at the ground troops and not at us. They also had machine guns mounted on the walls. I recognised an ancient Maxim as well as a couple of Lewis guns. They would slaughter troops advancing up the hill. I fired a short burst to gauge the effect. It had been some years since I had fired a Lewis as a gunner and it showed. My bullets struck the tower. I raised the barrel as I fired and the bullets made a deadly line up the tower. One of them sent a shower of splinters, making the gunners duck and then the rudder was in the way.

Hobson banked left and began to climb to take us to five hundred feet again. As he did so I found myself losing my balance. Luckily, we now had safety clips to hold us in. I would not be the daring young man on the flying trapeze this time! I fired at the men on the wall. I finally had my eye in and the bullets traced a line along the parapet. The gun clicked empty and I cursed myself for having wasted so many bullets. I changed the magazine but, by then we were past the fort. I could, however, see the damage we had caused. The gate was no longer there. The tower with the gun remained but the other towers were rubble. Men still stood on the walls and we would have to return to them.

As I cocked the gun, Hobson shouted, "Second bombing run."

I was ready for the pull this time as we dived at the smaller fort. Bullets tore holes in the wings as we dived. The Dervishes were learning. "Bombs gone!"

I had the Lewis pointing to starboard as we pulled up. This time there were no targets, at least none left alive. Hobson had placed his bombs in the perfect place and the fort was demolished. It meant that the other DH 9as could switch targets. I saw them peel off to attack the last fort. Below us the Rifles and dismounted troopers were making their way up the slope.

"Hobson, head back to the tower! Go in at a hundred feet."

"Sir!"

I took out two Mills bombs. The artillery piece was still firing and, although ancient, its shells could still hurt infantry. I knew that I would have to be fast. It was an illusion but we seemed to be on a collision course with the tower. I took the pins from the grenades and held them tightly. This was where the safety clips would be a life saver. They were the only things holding me in. The tower would be on our starboard side. I heard Hobson's guns as they sprayed the emplacement. I dropped my grenades a heartbeat apart as we approached. Our movement through the air would naturally arc them and they would explode above the gunners. Hobson's guns had already done much and my grenades cleared the firing platform. I stood and readied the Lewis. I sought targets.

I watched as the last of the forts was demolished by the rest of our flight. Hobson took us in a lazy circle so that I could see the forts. The infantry was already swarming over the first forts. Jack's flight were machine gunning Dervishes fleeing on camels. I scanned the ground below but could see no immediate danger for the troops swarming up the sides. If the machine guns and artillery had not been destroyed then they would have faced canister at short range. It would have been a massacre. I saw why it had taken sixteen years to defeat Sayyid Mohammed Abdullah Hassan.

Hobson shouted, "Fuel is getting low sir."

"Then head on home, Lieutenant. Well done."

"Thank you, sir."

As we flew over the reserves I saw Sanderson as he landed his ambulance. We had taken casualties. Henry's idea had been a splendid one. We had saved lives. I had extolled it in my reports. Hopefully someone at the ministry would take the time to read them and put two and two together.

We were not the first to land. Already the riggers and mechanics were checking for damage on the kites which had already landed. Sergeant Major Robson was rearming and refuelling them in case we needed to go back. I climbed out and when Hobson joined me I shook him by the hand, "Well done, Eric. That was textbook flying. You will go far."

"Thank you, sir. Once I just thought of you as a gunner then it was easy."

Leaving him to check it over I wandered over to the Sergeant Major, "Don't bother rearming and refuelling. We won't need to go back. Taleh is ours."

"Then it is over, sir? We are finished?"

"Pretty much. It is a case of crossing the T's and dotting the I's. When the Mullah is brought here I will feel happier."

I stayed with the Sergeant Major and, with my pipe going, watched the squadron as they landed. Sanderson came back and, after being refuelled took off straight away.

Captain Connor came from the admin tent. "Wing Commander, Taleh and the other forts are taken."

"Excellent!"

"But Sayyid Mohammed Abdullah Hassan has escaped with four others. The Camel Corps tried to stop them but a fanatical group of Dervishes stopped them. They all died but they ensured their leader got away. They are headed for the Ogaden."

Jones and Wintersgill had been the first to land and their kites were refuelled and rearmed. "Wintersgill and Jones. Get up and head for the Ogaden. See if you can see five riders heading into the wasteland. Shoot them."

"Yes sir." Both were eager young pilots and they raced back to their aeroplanes.

Jack and Ted joined me. Ted saw the disappointment on my face, "It is still a great victory, sir. You can't be everywhere at once."

"It should have been over today." I shook my head. I was dwelling on the negatives. "Jack, your squadron performed perfectly today. I shall say so in my report. You can be proud of them."

"The thing is, sir, we have learned things this past month that no one has done before. I can see this being the future. With us as mobile artillery and ground troops ready to mop up then we can deal with any uprisings like this."

"I don't want to pour cold water on you, Jack for you are right, but there will come a time when we have to do this against people who are prepared. They will have weapons which can bring down aeroplanes and, perhaps, have aeroplanes of their own. We first used aeroplanes in war six years ago. They were pushers that flew at sixty miles an hour. Look how far we have come now. What will it be like in ten years' time?"

While I waited for Jones and Wintersgill to return from their four-hour flight I went to my tent and wrote my report. When it was finished, I used Swanston and Williams' patented shower. I felt cleaner. The two aeroplanes landed. Their expressions told me all.

"Sorry sir. We spotted them. They had covered a lot of desert. They disappeared into the warren of ravines and rocks. We fired at them and dropped grenades but I don't think we got them. We might have but..."

"No, Lieutenant, do not apologise and do not make something up which is not true just to placate me. You did not let them escape in the first place. It is almost victory. Just not quite. However, it is enough of a victory to allow us to celebrate tonight! There will be no flying tomorrow!"

The party was a huge success. We had no more losses and the enemy was vanquished. Ted, Jack and I did not overindulge. I felt like a parent at his son's twenty first birthday. There would be thick heads the next day.

I was up early. I had much to do. Colonel Farquhar would remain in the field with the mobile Camel Corps and Colonel Pritchard would bring the prisoners back. When we heard that they were just two hours out I sent Williams and Swanston in the Crossley to pick up the resident, Captain Mainwaring, and Peter Hardwicke. They were all essential to my plan to end this conflict. My reports had been radioed back and I had informed the powers that be of my decision to return to Egypt. That had been confirmed by Colonel Fisher for the insurgents were causing even more trouble in Cairo. Relief pilots were on their way from Malta to take over the Nanaks.

When the resident arrived, he was like a child at Christmas. The Captain and Peter Hardwicke stood to the side. Hardwicke held a bound package in his hands.

The resident pointed to my Dolphin, "Do you think I could have a look around the aeroplanes, Wing Commander?"

"Of course." I showed him the single seater first.

"What a splendid aeroplane. How does it compare with the Camel?"

"Faster and better armed. It has a higher ceiling."

He laughed, "But you prefer the Camel."

"Of course. Every pilot loves the Camel."

His eyes lit up when he saw the DH 9a. "It has a second seat?"

I could see what he was thinking. "Would you like a flight, sir? We have time."

"Do you think I could?"

Over his shoulder, I saw Peter Hardwicke nod vigorously. The man did not have long to live. "Of course. Captain Conner get a flying coat, goggles and helmet for the resident. Sergeant Major Robson, I shall take M for Mother."

"Sir, she is all ready to go; armed and fuelled."

"This is tremendously exciting, Wing Commander."

Williams hurried over with the ladder to help him aboard. Captain Connor helped to dress St. John Browne. He said quietly, "Now if you ask him nicely I am sure the Wing Commander will perform some loops for you!"

"Really?"

"Captain Connor!"

"Sorry sir."

Once he was dressed my men helped him into the cockpit and Williams clipped him in. I said, "When the engine is going it is a little loud. You will have to shout."

"I understand!"

I started the engine and it roared into life. We now had a windsock and soon I was roaring down the runway. I pulled back on the stick and zoomed through the gap. I decided to take a course over the column which was heading back. I flew south first to afford the resident a view of the desert and then swung back to fly over the column. I saw it two miles away snaking along the road. The road followed the contours of a long dried up valley I was just about to say something to the resident to direct his view when I saw the flash of light ahead me of. It was not the column. I dropped the nose. I had intended flying at a thousand feet. Now I dropped to six hundred, just a hundred feet above the ridges and escarpments. The reason for the flash became apparent. There were Dervishes. There were not many of them but they had a machine gun. I took all of that in as I roared towards them. I had learned to make snap decisions. It was exactly what I had told Hobson. I cocked the Vickers.

"Hang on, sir, we are going to attack some Dervishes."

I heard a squawk which I took to be his acknowledgement. The column was just five hundred yards from the ambush. Colonel Pritchard was in his open topped Crossley. There would be no protection from the machine gun. The Dervishes turned when they heard my aeroplane and hurriedly tried to bring the machine gun to bear. That action would save the Colonel but it might put us in jeopardy. I gave a burst at a thousand yards. The range was too far away to be accurate but it told the column that there was danger. I saw the six Dervish warriors as they aligned the machine gun. I was travelling quickly towards them. I fired a long burst with the right-hand Vickers. Stones flew up before them and two fell clutching wounds. I saw flames spurt from the barrel of the machine gun as I used the left-hand Vickers. I dropped the nose which threw their aim off and, as my nose came up, the bullets tore into them. I pulled back on the stick and banked to starboard. They were dead and soldiers were racing up the slope to see what had happened.

I shouted, "Are you all right, sir?"

There was silence. Had the bullets they fired hit us? I had not felt them but the judder of my own guns would disguise the sound. "Mr. St. John Browne?"

There was a long silence then I heard, "Wonderful Wing Commander, simply wonderful!"

I would not risk him any longer and I banked to port. I saw the colonel standing in his Crossley and waving. His men were doing the same. In my mirror, I saw that his men had reached the Dervishes and were holding up the machine gun.

The action had taken place so close to the field that I knew they would have heard and wondered what I was doing firing with the resident aboard. When I landed, Williams was ready with the ladder. Sergeant Major Robson said, as the wheels were chocked, "We heard firing sir. Were you testing the guns?"

"No, Sergeant Major Robson, the Dervish had set up a machine gun to ambush the column. They are dead." I climbed out of the cockpit and slid down the lower wing. The resident was just being helped to the ground, "Sorry about that, Mr. St. John Browne."

He shook me by the hand, his thin fingers feeling like claws, "Do not apologise, Wing Commander. You have fulfilled one of my dreams. I have been in action for His Majesty! It was the most exhilarating experience of my life. You, Wing Commander, are a jinni! You have granted me my most fervent wish."

Captain Connor had a wry look on his face, "Come along, sir, let us get you out of those clothes and into a whisky!"

Captain Mainwaring said, "What would have happened if anything had happened to him?"

"I think it would have been the end of my career but let us not dwell on that." I turned to Sergeant Major Hale, "The column will be here shortly. I would like to get this over with and then the resident can return to his quarters. Have the prisoners brought and place them between the two columns of aeroplanes."

The prisoners we had already incarcerated were fetched from their pen. Their hands and feet were bound and they shuffled rather than walked. They were made to kneel on the runway. There were thirty of them. The ones with wounds had had them tended to. We had parked the aeroplanes on either side of the run way and they were brought there so that they could see the monsters of the air. They looked fearfully at the DH 9as as though they were some kind of mythcial beast. The convoy arrived. Captain Connor brought the resident and his secretary back. The resident had more colour in his cheeks than I remembered.

Colonel Pritchard knew what we had planned and his officers and sergeants took charge of the prisoners as they were brought from the lorries. Colonel Pritchard came up to me and shook my hand, "I want to thank your pilot and his gunner. You saved us back there. That gun would have had us dead to rights."

I smiled, "Actually, colonel, I was the pilot and the resident was the gunner."

His face was a picture and St. John Browne had a look on his face which showed his delight too.

"Captain Connor!"

"Sir."

I walked with the colonel, the resident, Captain Connor and Peter Hardwick towards the prisoners. There were now almost fifty of them. Captain Mainwaring stood at the entrance to the admin tent. The resident spoke. We had no idea if the Dervishes understood his words. It did not really matter as they would be translated by Captain Connor later.

"All of you have broken the peace of Somaliland. You have followed this false leader, Sayyid Mohammed Abdullah Hassan. You have killed British citizens and the soldiers who guard them. For that you could all be executed."

Captain Connor translated. In their faces, I saw resignation. They all expected to die. It was the way of their people. Colonel Farquhar had told me of finding decapitated tribesmen who had fallen foul of the Mullah.

"The Emperor who rules this land is a just man. He is a Christian and he would like you to be forgiven."

Some of the older men looked up, hope in their faces, as Ted translated.

Waving Hardwicke forward he continued, "This is the Quran. It is your holiest of books. Ours is the Bible. When we swear on the Bible then it is binding. I would have you all swear on the Quran that you will never again take up arms against the Emperor or his warriors."

This time they looked at each other.

Captain Connor translated and then added, "Well, who will swear? If you swear then you can go free."

A few of the older ones came up and, one by one swore. There remained a hard core of, perhaps twelve. They were all young warriors; Jihadists. We had thought this might happen and I knew what Ted would be saying. Captain Connor spoke as he pointed to the aeroplanes. "These birds of death can find you wherever you are. They can see you wherever you are. They will hunt down Sayyid Mohammed Abdullah Hassan and he will be brought to justice. However, we have another weapon we have yet to use. We will now show you the power the Emperor has at his command."

He turned and dropped his hand. Captain Mainwaring nodded and went into the tent. After a few moments, the air was filled with the sound of Ark Royal's four twelve pounder quick firing guns sending blank after blank into the air. It seemed to last forever although each gun only fired ten shells. It had the desired effect. The Dervish ran to swear on the Quran.

When they had left the field, we turned to go back to the tent we used as a mess tent. Jack and Sergeant Major Hale had organised drinks. Captain Mainwaring said, "Well that appeared to work. How did you come up with the plan?

"It was the resident really. He knows the people. They are religious but very superstitious. We knew that they feared the DH 9a but when we concocted the plan we realised that your ship had never opened fire. The fact that they could not see her made it even more terrifying."

The resident nodded, "The Wing Commander is being modest. I have learned that about him. This was all his idea. I could never have conceived of such a plan. However, we have all proved to be a good team but I fear that its days are at an end. You are to return to Egypt?"

"I am afraid so, sir. We begin loading tomorrow. There is no hurry. It will take a couple of days. Then back to Egypt."

"And you get to go home and see your son and your new child." I nodded. "You cannot know how much I envy you and your future but you have given me, today, something I can relish and enjoy for the rest of my life. I flew in an aeroplane and I helped defeat the Dervishes. This has been a great day and I would like to thank you all for it."

The Colonel said, "We will be here a little longer but we too will be heading back to East Africa. I can say, however, that I was proud to serve in Z Force under you, Wing Commander. It has been an experience to cherish."

As parties go it was subdued but it seemed a fitting end to the venture.

It took us a good ten days to reach Suez and then we had to make our way back to our field. That took another few days and there was a great deal of paperwork to be done before we could all leave. Captain Connor stayed on in Heliopolis. The DH 9as were to be flown north to Palestine by Jack and his men. They were needed in Mesopotamia. Henry and his Snipes would join them there. My Dolphin would be attached to them. I was flown by a Vickers Vimy. We landed in Palestine first where we picked up more passengers and then made our way back to England. It was not comfortable and it seemed to take forever. I was in the air for what seemed like weeks and not days. We had to stay overnight at some of the airfields to allow the crew to sleep but I did not mind for I was going home.

We landed at Hendon where a Royal Air Force car was waiting to take me home. The driver nodded knowingly to me as I sat in the back. "You must have some pull, sir. This is the Minster of Air's car."

"I have been away for some time."

"Then I had better get you home quick as, eh sir?"

"That would be delightful."

"There is a letter addressed to you in the back, sir. A Mr. Balfour gave it to me. He said would you read it before you got home?"

I opened it, and saw that it was handwritten.

February 1920
Ministry of Air-Intelligence department,
Wing Commander,
Congratulations on three missions successfully completed. Mr. Churchill was not happy about the ultimatum. He does not respond well to threats. Had you asked for the leave then it would have been granted. However, he is pleased with your achievements.

Enjoy your time in England and your new daughter.

You have been granted a month's leave. I will be in contact with you on the telephone. It is already installed in your new house. I hope you enjoy the house. The garden looks promising.

Your next posting will be in Mesopotamia where we hope you will be reunited with Squadron Leader Woollett and Squadron Leader Thomson. You seem to work well as a team.

Yours,
Arthur C Balfour,
Undersecretary

As I folded it up I read between the lines. He had seen my house and knew that I had a daughter. Even I did not know that. Mr. Balfour was more than he seemed. I would have to be careful what I did and said around him.

Epilogue

April 1920

It was the last week of my leave. Mary, my daughter, was a joy but she was still at the gurgling stage and seemed to be forever attached to her mother. Tom, on the other hand could toddle and talk. Beattie had shown him photographs of me and read him the parts of my letters which she could. She had told him stories of me each night so that I did not seem as a stranger to him.

The Undersecretary was correct. The garden did have prospects. While Beattie fed, winded and changed our daughter, Tom and I were in the breezy April garden tidying and planning. There was a lovely old chestnut tree which would make a perfect tree house. I also carried him on my shoulders as I walked down lanes with new growth burgeoning on the trees. After the white of the Arctic and the brown of the desert, the green of England was wonderful. England in April was the antithesis of both of my recent postings. It was good to be home.

I reluctantly traded in my motor for something a little more practical. I bought a smaller Morris shooting brake which suited Beattie. She would be driving it more than I would. I was changing. I was becoming a family man.

Mr. Balfour had rung during the third week to confirm what he had told me in the letter. He reiterated that it would be the same team and that meant Captain Connor, Sergeant Major Hale and Sergeant Major Robson as well as my squadron leaders and, after I asked for them, Swanston and Williams. There was something comfortable about having them with me. They felt more like family.

I had told her of my new posting and she was adamant that she would be coming with me. "There is no war there and in a month's time Mary will be old enough to travel. You have four weeks to find us somewhere to live. You are a Wing Commander now. Surely that must bring some perks!"

That had been a week ago. Mary had just gone down for her sleep as had Tom. Beattie had chided me for keeping him going so long. "He is still a baby, really. He will have to have an afternoon nap."

He had just gone down and we were cuddling on the settee when a car drew up and I heard a knock at the door. I had no idea who might be calling. Beattie had been too busy with the family to make friends and only Balfour knew where I lived. I had yet to tell Lumpy, Gordy, Ted and Randolph. I was being selfish. I wanted my wife to myself.

"Who can that be?"

Beattie rolled her eyes, "I bet it is that nosy woman from the Post Office. Every time I posted a letter to you she asked me about you. She said a Wing Commander raised the status of the village."

"Well I shall smile and say I have malaria or Beri Beri: some such tropical disease. If I cough she will run a mile!"

Beattie laughed, "Bill, you can't!"

I opened the door and looked down at Peter Hardwicke and a serious looking man dressed in formal clothes. "Peter! I would say I am surprised but that would be an understatement. Come in, come in!"

"We are sorry to bother you at home, Wing Commander. I got your address from the Ministry. This is Mr. Collins. He is a solicitor."

"Pleased to meet you, Wing Commander."

"Here, give me your coats."

Beattie had heard the voices and she appeared in the hall, "We have guests? I shall make some tea."

The solicitor said, "Not on my account."

Peter shook his head, "That would be delightful, Mrs. Harsker."

"It's Beattie."

"This is Peter Hardwicke, Beattie. I told you about him and Mr. St. John Browne."

"Of course. I shan't be a moment."

The lounge was a little messy. Tom's toys littered the floor. We were used to just stepping around them. "Let's go into the drawing room eh?"

We sat around the table and Mr. Collins began to take out papers. I had been brought up too well to ask the purpose of their visit. I stayed on safer subjects. "When did you arrive back in England, Peter?"

"I arrived back two days ago. I have been in London." He smiled sadly, "I have no people. My father died in the Great War. Mama followed him a year later. I think it was a broken heart."

It was a familiar story. I saw the solicitor glance at Peter. He had not known of the tragedy. "Shall we get on?"

Peter gave the lawyer a withering look, "Let us wait for Mrs. Harsker. This involves her too, albeit indirectly."

He shrugged.

"Did you serve in the Great War, Mr. Collins? You look to have been of the right age."

"Sadly, I did not. I never seemed to have the time. I think that those of us who stayed at home contributed as much to the war as those who served."

Peter and I exchanged a look. He had been too young and had an ailment. An eloquent silence filled the room and I took the opportunity to light my pipe. When Mr. Collins wrinkled his nose, I saw Peter smile.

Beattie had tidied herself up; not that she needed to. Even casually dressed with baby milk spilled on her blouse she was still stunning. She laid a tray down, "Sorry I took so long. I shall be mother eh?"

Peter said, "I believe you are the only one qualified to do so."

When she had poured the tea and handed around the home-made biscuits Peter said, "Now you may begin, Mr. Collins."

He put a pair of pince nez on the end of his nose. "I am the executor of the will of the Honourable Reginald St. John Brown of Burton Leonard, North Yorkshire."

I looked at Peter, "He is dead?"

He nodded, "A week after you left."

The solicitor looked up, annoyed that he had been interrupted. Peter ignored him. I could see that he was quite emotional. Beattie reached over and put her hand on his. "Bill told me about the two of you. He seemed like quite a character."

"He was. Don't be upset, Wing Commander. He knew he was dying but his last week was joyous. He regaled Ravi and Gupta with the story of his flight and the fight. He finally got to do that which he had wished to for his whole life. He died with a smile on his face. An hour before he died he gave me his will and a letter for Mr. Collins here. He gave Gupta and Ravi a hundred sovereigns each and told them that they should go home and enjoy a life instead of watching over a desiccated old man. His words Wing Commander. Then he lay down, folded his arms and an hour later he was dead."

I nodded, "He spoke with you, of course."

"Of course and that, if you do not mind, Wing Commander, will remain private."

"I would expect nothing less."

"If we might get on, time is wasting!"

Beattie looked at the solicitor and said quietly, "Speaking well of the dead and reflecting on what they have done is never time wasted, Mr. Collins."

He looked abashed, "I apologize. If we may?"

I nodded, "The two of you are his sole beneficiaries. He leaves the family home of Burton Leonard in North Yorkshire to Mr. Hardwicke. It is a fine property and represents the bulk of the estate. He has made other bequests to Mr. Hardwicke."

I smiled, "He thought well of you."

"I believe so."

"To you, Wing Commander, he leaves the sum of twenty thousand pounds and a large number of shares in the Anglo-American Oil Company and the British- American Tobacco Company."

I was astounded. Twenty thousand pounds was a small fortune. I realised how lucky Peter was if he had the bulk of the estate. "But he barely knew me!"

"There you are wrong. Wing Commander. As he told you in Berbera, he had kept a record of your achievements along with other aces. He told me, after you had dined with us, that he had concentrated on you as you represented, to him, the true Englishman. You had humble beginnings and yet you became a classic English gentleman. He also admired this," He waved a hand around Beattie and my house, "and that is why he left me his home. He knew you have a new home and a family. He wanted a family more than anything. He had been engaged when he was a young man but when he left for India she married another and he remained a bachelor."

Mr. Collins pushed papers over for us to sign which we did and then he packed them back in his case. "Well Mr. Hardwicke, shall we head back to town?"

I could see that Peter was torn and I said, after glancing at Beattie, "Peter, stay the night. I will run you back to town in the morning."

"If it is not too much trouble."

Beattie jumped up, "Of course not! You shall be our first guest!"

After dinner and when the children were in bed the three of us shared a bottle of whisky. I learned more about the kind old Englishman who had changed our lives.

"Well, Bill, do you have plans for that money?"

"I do." Beattie looked surprised. "St. John Browne always spoke of owning a house in France. Albert helped me in the war. I would buy something in France to honour them both. It would be a holiday home for us but Tom and Mary could learn French. I could, hopefully, live for two old men. I would want something with purpose so that when I meet them in the hereafter I could say, I left a memorial to you in Northern France."

Peter nodded, "I think that the resident would have liked that. He made a wise choice."

"And you Peter?"

He looked at me sadly, "I was in Berbera for the same reason as St. John Browne. I too, am not in the best of health. I have been told not to exert myself. I have the scrapbooks. I think I shall become a writer and make these stories something which young people read. North Yorkshire sounds the perfect place to do so. I shall write under the pen name of St. John. Perhaps he might approve."

"I think he will. And put him in the stories too. He deserves it."

"I will. They will all be in there, Wing Commander. I shall use my time wisely."

As I cuddled up to Beattie I reflected that was all any man could ask, to use his time wisely. I now knew that I had made the right decision to stay in the service. It would be my career and, hopefully, my son's. Time would tell.

The End

Glossary

Beer Boys-inexperienced fliers (slang)

Bevvy- drink (beverage) (slang)

Blighty- Britain (slang)

Boche- German (slang)

Bowser- refuelling vehicle

Bus- aeroplane (slang)

Corned dog/Bully Beef- corned beef (slang)

Dewar Flask- an early Thermos invented in 1890

Donkey Walloper- Horseman (slang)

Erks- Slang for Other Ranks in RAF

Fizzer- a charge (slang)

Foot Slogger- Infantry (slang)

Fuzzy Wuzzy- Dervish (slang) named because of their hair style.

Gaspers- Cigarettes (slang)

Google eyed booger with the tit- gas mask (slang)

Griffin (Griff) - confidential information (slang)

Hun- German (slang)

Jasta- a German Squadron

Jippo- the shout that food was ready from the cooks (slang)

Killick- Leading seaman (slang-Royal Navy)

Kite- aeroplane (slang)

Lanchester- a prestigious British car with the same status as a Rolls Royce

Loot- a second lieutenant (slang)

Marskin ryyppy – Finnish Schnapps (see text below)

M.C. - Military Cross (for officers only)

M.M. - Military Medal (for other ranks introduced in 1915)

Nanak- Nickname for Airco DH 9

Nelson's Blood- rum (slang- Royal Navy)

Nicked- stolen (slang)

Number ones- Best uniform (slang)

Oppo- workmate/friend (slang)

Outdoor- the place they sold beer in a pub to take away (slang)

Pop your clogs- die (slang)

Pukka- Very good/efficient (slang)

Reval- Tallinn (Estonia)

Rosy – Tea (slang- Rosy Lee- tea)

Rugger- Rugby (slang)
Scousers- Liverpudlians (slang)
Shufti- a quick look (slang)
The smoke- London (slang)
Toff- aristocrat (slang)
V.C. - Victoria Cross, the highest honour in the British Army

Historical Notes

There are a number of real historical figures I have used: Bruce Lockhart was a famous spy as was Captain Crombie who was killed by the Bolsheviks. Rear Admiral Cowan took over from Rear Admiral Alexander-Sinclair in 1919. Lieutenant Augustus Agar and Major Donald were also real. Captain Cummins was the first head of the Intelligence Service and it was he and his spies who came up with the plan to use the torpedo boats to attack the Bolshevik Fleet. It worked.

These were different times. Colonialism was not yet a dirty word and no one had any idea what racism actually was. My characters reflect those views. They are all people of their time. I have not airbrushed history just to suit the sensibilities of modern minds.

The British flotilla consisted of a carrier, H.M.S. Vindictive, as well as two Seaplane tenders, C Class Cruisers and W Class Destroyers. In December 1918, they helped the Estonians under General Yudenich to recapture most of Estonia. It was a short-lived victory for by 1922 the Bolsheviks had recaptured it. The threat posed by the CMB boats and the British Flotilla forced the Bolsheviks to despatch a young Joseph Stalin to help defend Petrograd. I have had H.M.S Vindictive beginning operations in the Baltic just a few months earlier than she actually did. For the purists out there, I apologize; it is in the interests of the story. This is historical fiction

RAF Ranks

RAF other ranks (1 April 1918)			RAF other ranks (1 January 1919)
Technical other ranks	Administrative	Service	
Chief Master Mechanic Major 1st Class	(Chief Master Clerk)	Sergeant Major 1st Class	Sergeant
Master Mechanic Major 2nd Class	(Master Clerk)	Sergeant Major 2nd Class	Sergeant
Chief Mechanic Sergeant	Flight Clerk	Flight Sergeant	Flight
Sergeant Mechanic	Sergeant Clerk	Sergeant	Sergeant
Corporal Mechanic	Corporal Clerk	Corporal	Corporal
Air Mechanic 1st Class Aircraftman	Clerk 1st Class	(Leading Aircraftman)	Leading
Air Mechanic 2nd Class Aircraftman 1st Class	Clerk 2nd Class	Private 1st Class	
Air Mechanic 3rd Class Aircraftman 2nd Class	Clerk 3rd Class	Private 2nd Class	

Aeroplanes referred to in the text

Source: File: RAF Sopwith Camel.jpg – https://en.wikipedia.org

Sopwith Camel

Crew: 1
Length: 18 ft. 9 in (5.72 m)
Wingspan: 28 ft. 0 in (8.53 m)
Height: 8 ft. 6 in (2.59 m)
Wing area: 231 ft2 (21.46 m2)
Empty weight: 930 lb (420 kg)
Loaded weight: 1,453 lb (659 kg)
Zero-lift drag coefficient: 0.0378
Drag area: 8.73 square feet (0.811 m2)
Aspect ratio: 4.11
Power plant: 1 × Clerget 9B 9-cylinder Rotary engine, 130 hp
(97 kW)
Performance
Maximum speed: 113 mph (182 km/h)
Stall speed: 48 mph (77 km/h)
Range: 300 miles ferry (485 km)
Service ceiling: 19,000 ft. (5,791 m)
Rate of climb: 1,085 ft./min (5.5 m/s)
Wing loading: 6.3 lb/ft2 (30.8 kg/m2)
Power/mass: 0.09 hp/lb (150 W/kg)
Lift-to-drag ratio: 7.7
Armament
Guns: 2× 0.303 in (7.7 mm) Vickers machine guns

De Havilland DH 9

Crew: two
Length: 30 ft. 5 in (9.27 m)
Wingspan: 42 ft. 4⅝ in (12.92 m)
Height: 11 ft. 3½ in (3.44 m)
Wing area: 434 ft² (40.3 m²)
Empty weight: 2,360 lb (1,014 kg)
Max. take-off weight: 3,790 lb (1,723 kg)
Power plant: 1 × Armstrong Siddeley Puma piston engine, 230 hp (172 kW)
Performance
Maximum speed: 98 kn (113 mph, 182 km/h)
Endurance: 4½ hours
Service ceiling: 15,500 ft. (4,730 m)
Climb to 10,000 ft.: 18 min 30 sec
Armament
Guns: Forward firing Vickers machine gun and 1 or 2 × Rear Lewis guns on scarff ring
Bombs: Up to 460 lb (209 kg) bombs

Source: File: DH.9 F1258 LeB 05.07R.jpg -
https://en.wikipedia.org

Vickers Vernon

Crew: three
Capacity: 11 passengers
Length: 42 ft. 8 in (13.01 m)
Wingspan: 68 ft. 1 in (20.76 m)
Height: 13 ft. 3 in (4.04 m)
Wing area: 1,330 ft² (124 m²)
Empty weight: 7,981 lb (3,628 kg)
Loaded weight: 12,554 lb (5,706 kg)
Power plant: 2 × Napier Lion, 450 hp (336 kW) each
Performance
Maximum speed: 87 kn (100 mph, 161 km/h)
Cruise speed: 65 knots (75 mph, 121 km/h)
Range: 278 nautical miles (320 mi, 515 km)
Service ceiling: 11,700 ft. (3,600 m)
Wing loading: 9.44 lb/ft² (46.0 kg/m²)
Power/mass: 0.0717 hp/lb (0.118 kW/kg)
Source: File: Vickers Vernon on ground.jpg -
https://en.wikipedia.org

(I have introduced this aeroplane a few months before it actually entered service.)

Albatros D V

Crew: 1
Length: 7.33 m (24 ft. 1 in)
Wingspan: 9.05 m (29 ft. 8 in)
Height: 2.7 m (8 ft. 10 in)
Wing area: 21.2 m2 (228 sq. ft.)
Empty weight: 687 kg (1,515 lb)

Gross weight: 937 kg (2,066 lb)
Power plant: 1 × Mercedes D.III aü piston engine, 150 kW (200 hp)
Propellers: 2-bladed wooden propeller
Performance
Maximum speed: 186 km/h (116 mph)
Endurance: 350 km
Service ceiling: 5,700 m (18,700 ft.)
Rate of climb: 4.17 m/s (821 ft./min)
Time to altitude: 1,000 m (3,281 ft.) in 4 minutes
Armament
Guns: 2 × 7.92 mm (0.312 in) LMG 08/15 machine guns

H.M.S Vindictive 1918

Source: File: HMS Vindictive carrier.jpg -
https://en.wikipedia.org

In 1910, Thornycroft had designed and built a 25 ft (7.6 m) speedboat called Miranda IV. She was a single-step hydroplane powered by a 120 hp (89 kW) Thornycroft petrol engine and could reach 35 knots (65 km/h).

A 40 ft (12 m) boat based on Miranda IV was accepted by the Admiralty for trials. A number of these boats were built and had a distinguished service history, but in hindsight they were considered to be too small to be ideal, particularly in how their payload was limited to a single 18-inch torpedo.

Several companies were approached, but only Thornycroft considered it possible to meet such a requirement. In January 1916, twelve boats were ordered, all of which were completed by August 1916. Further boats were built, to a total of 39.
The restriction on weight meant the torpedo could not be fired from a torpedo tube, but instead was carried in a rear-facing trough. On firing it was pushed backwards by a cordite firing pistol and a long steel ram, entering the water tail-first. A trip-wire between the torpedo and the ram head would start the torpedo motors once pulled taut during release. The CMB would then turn hard over and get out of its path. There is no record of a CMB ever being hit by its own torpedo, but in one instance the firing pistol was triggered prematurely and the crew had a tense 20 minutes close to the enemy whilst reloading it."
Source: Coastal Motor Boat - https://en.wikipedia.org
Marskin ryyppy (lit. The Marshal's drink/shot; Swedish: Marskens snaps) is a strong alcoholic drink of Finnish origin, served as a schnapps. The drink is named after Carl Gustaf Emil Mannerheim, the Marshal of Finland.
Source: Marskin ryyppy - https://en.wikipedia.org
Churchill's use of the Royal Air Force in the Middle East and India
Taken from Pictorial History of the RAF Volume One 1918-1939- John W.R Taylor

"(Winston Churchill) approved the plan for basing seven squadrons in Egypt by 1920-21, to be followed by a training wing and schools of air pilotage and gunnery by 1922-23. Eight squadrons were to be based in India and three in Mesopotamia (now Iraq), with seaplane flights at Malta and Alexandria and afloat in a carrier in the Mediterranean. Thus, of the total of 33 Royal Air Force squadrons, including eight in process of formation, in March 1920, more than half were in the Middle East. At home there were twelve squadrons: five with the Inland Area (including three in process of formation) and five with the Coastal Area (including two in process of formation). Two others were in Ireland and one on the Rhine. No increase was contemplated, the

main emphasis being on building the squadrons to peak strength and efficiency, as specified in Trenchard's 'White Paper'"

Captain Henry Winslow Woollett from Southwold, Suffolk, was a medical student when war broke out. He at once joined the Lincolnshire Regiment, taking part in the Suvla Bay landings in the Dardanelles in 1915. He transferred to the RFC in 1916, joining No 24 Squadron in France in November. He claimed one victory in a D.H.2 during April 1917, and then four more in D.H.5 A9165 during the summer, becoming a flight commander and receiving an MC. He then returned to England as an instructor until March 1918, when he joined No 43 Squadron. During the next five months he claimed 30 more victories, 11 of them balloons - the second highest total of these opponents in the British service. He was awarded a DSO, a Bar to his MC, a Croix de Guerre and the Legion d'Honneur. (Taken from Christopher Shores' book.)

The use of Vernons as bombers

'Harris, typically, was not enamoured of the passive role of the Vernon, so he had bomb-racks fitted and cut a hole in the nose of each aircraft, into which a bomb-sight was installed, complete with a remarkable 'Heath-Robinson' bomb-release gear. Their efficiency was recalled by Air Chief Marshal Sir Basil Embry in his auto- biography (Mission Completed, Methuen). Although serving as second pilot to Saundby, he related: 'When we carried out both training and active bombing, he always used the bombsight and released the bombs while I flew the aeroplane. We worked well together as a team, our average bombing error from 3,000 feet being only ten and a half yards . . . which enabled us to hit the smallest target with all our bombs when we carried out active operations.'

Taken from Pictorial History of the RAF Volume One 1918-1939- John W.R Taylor

Somaliland Campaign

The subjugation of Somaliland took place almost exactly as I described. 'Black Hawk Down' occurred almost a century later but things had not changed much in the intervening years. I find it incredible to think that they had to build an airfield and fly to the absolute limit of their fuel and yet they managed to end the rebellion in four weeks! Group Captain Robert Gordon, and his

Chief of Staff, Wing Commander Frederick Bowhill were the actual officers. I have replaced them with my own characters.

By the January 1920, the following British forces were assembled for the ending of hostilities against the Mullah and his dervishes.

Z Force ('Z Unit' in some sources) provided by the RAF from their forces in Egypt. The force consisted of:

12 Airco DH.9a aircraft. used for bombing. One was converted into an air ambulance. A vehicle fleet made up of ten Ford trucks, two Ford ambulances, six trailers, two motorcycles and two Crossley light trucks.36 officers and 183 men.

The Somaliland Camel Corps which was permanently based in the field as the local gendarmerie regiment. One battalion of the King's African Rifles.

In the actual campaign the DH 9s were loaded at Malta and taken by the Ark Royal through the Suez Canal to Berbera. I have changed the events to suit my story.

The Mullah escaped Taleh but he spent the rest of his life hiding from the Camel Corps in the Ogaden. Z Force did just what they were ordered to.

The Mullah's forts

239

Taleh

Converted DH 9a (Air ambulance)

Eric Hobson was a real pilot who flew the DH 9a in Somaliland. It was he and his gunner who found the forts. He may even be one of the men in the photograph above. He was decorated for his action. He was involved in an air accident over Hendon in 1933 in which a friend died. He was based in Palestine at Ramelah in 1938 and when Arabs broke into the aerodrome he led the defence against them. For his actions, he was awarded the D.S.O. Some months later he shot himself. No explanation was given for he left no note. I have tried to get into the character who appeared to be a gifted flier yet a troubled man.

Griff April 2017

I used the following books to verify information:

- World War 1- Peter Simkins
- The Times Atlas of World History
- The British Army in World War 1 (1)- Mike Chappell
- The British Army in World War 1 (2)- Mike Chappell
- The British Army 1914-18- Fosten and Marrion
- British Air Forces 1914-1918- Cormack
- British and Empire Aces of World War 1- Christopher Shores
- A History of Aerial Warfare- John Taylor
- First World War- Martin Gilbert
- Aircraft of World War 1- Herris and Pearson
- Military History Monthly Issue 79
- Pictorial History of the RAF Vol 1 1918-1939- John W. R. Taylor

I used Wikipedia for the photographs.

Other books
by
Griff Hosker

If you enjoyed reading this book, then why not read another one by the author?
For more information on all of the books then please visit the author's web site http:www.griffhosker.com where there is a link to contact him.

Ancient History
The Sword of Cartimandua Series
(Germania and Britannia 50 A.D. – 130 A.D.)

Ulpius Felix- Roman Warrior (prequel)
Book 1 The Sword of Cartimandua
Book 2 The Horse Warriors
Book 3 Invasion Caledonia
Book 4 Roman Retreat
Book 5 Revolt of the Red Witch
Book 6 Druid's Gold
Book 7 Trajan's Hunters
Book 8 The Last Frontier
Book 9 Hero of Rome
Book 10 Roman Hawk
Book 11 Roman Treachery
Book 12 Roman Wall
Book 13 Roman Courage

The Aelfraed Series
(Britain and Byzantium 1050 - 1085 A.D.)

Book 1 Housecarl
Book 2 Outlaw
Book 3 Varangian

The Wolf Warrior series
(Britain in the late 6th Century)

Book 1 Saxon Dawn
Book 2 Saxon Revenge
Book 3 Saxon England

Book 4 Saxon Blood
Book 5 Saxon Slayer
Book 6 Saxon Slaughter
Book 7 Saxon Bane
Book 8 Saxon Fall: Rise of the Warlord
Book 9 Saxon Throne
Book 10 Saxon Sword

The Dragon Heart Series

Book 1 Viking Slave
Book 2 Viking Warrior
Book 3 Viking Jarl
Book 4 Viking Kingdom
Book 5 Viking Wolf
Book 6 Viking War
Book 7 Viking Sword
Book 8 Viking Wrath
Book 9 Viking Raid
Book 10 Viking Legend
Book 11 Viking Vengeance
Book 12 Viking Dragon
Book 13 Viking Treasure
Book 14 Viking Enemy
Book 15 Viking Witch
Bool 16 Viking Blood
Book 17 Viking Weregeld
Book 18 Viking Storm
Book 19 Viking Warband
Book 20 Viking Shadow
Book 21 Viking Legacy

New World Series
870-1050

Blood on the Blade

The Norman Genesis Series

Hrolf the Viking

Horseman
The Battle for a Home
Revenge of the Franks
The Land of the Northmen
Ragnvald Hrolfsson
Brothers in Blood
Lord of Rouen
Drekar in the Seine
Duke of Normandy

The Anarchy Series England
1120-1180

English Knight
Knight of the Empress
Northern Knight
Baron of the North
Earl
King Henry's Champion
The King is Dead
Warlord of the North
Enemy at the Gate
Fallen Crown
Warlord's War
Kingmaker
Henry II
Crusader
The Welsh Marches
Irish War
Poisonous Plots
The Princes' Revolt
Earl Marshal

Border Knight
1190-1300

Sword for Hire
Return of the Knight
Baron's War
Magna Carta
Welsh War
Henry III

Struggle for a Crown England
1367-1485

Blood on the Crown
To Murder A King

Modern History
The Napoleonic Horseman Series
Book 1 Chasseur a Cheval
Book 2 Napoleon's Guard
Book 3 British Light Dragoon
Book 4 Soldier Spy
Book 5 1808: The Road to Corunna
Waterloo

The Lucky Jack American Civil War series
Rebel Raiders
Confederate Rangers
The Road to Gettysburg

The British Ace Series
1914
1915 Fokker Scourge
1916 Angels over the Somme
1917 Eagles Fall
1918 We will remember them
From Arctic Snow to Desert Sand
Wings over Persia

Combined Operations series
1940-1945

Commando
Raider
Behind Enemy Lines
Dieppe
Toehold in Europe
Sword Beach
Breakout

The Battle for Antwerp
King Tiger
Beyond the Rhine
Korea

Other Books
Carnage at Cannes (a thriller)
Great Granny's Ghost (Aimed at 9-14-year-old young people)
Adventure at 63-Backpacking to Istanbul

Made in the USA
Columbia, SC
20 February 2019